WITH EVERY BREATH

By Alex Alexander

WITH EVERY BREATH

ISBN 1-933113-39-1

THIS TRADE PAPERBACK ORIGINAL IS PUBLISHED BY **INTAGLIO PUBLICATIONS**, GAINESVILLE, FL USA

CREDITS

EXECUTIVE EDITOR: TARA YOUNG

COVER DESIGN BY VALERIE HAYKEN (www.valeriehayken.com)

DEDICATION

To the little bird that sat on my shoulder the day the forklift crashed.

ACKNOWLEDGMENTS

I had an enormous amount of support while working on *With Every Breath*, and I'd like to thank the following people:

Karen To, you read, edited, supported, and believed in me while I wrote this book. That was quite a gift, and I am eternally grateful. Thank you.

Denise Avitabile, each week, you took home the few pages I had hammered out since I saw you the week before. Your desire to know what happened next kept me going. Thank you.

Leslie Heizer, for the poem, the countless hours reading and editing, and the bittersweet lesson, thank you.

More thanks for reading, editing, and encouraging go to Gabrielle S., Kerri S., Letitia C., Megan G., Bridghe, and Laura B. Your feedback was invaluable. And thanks to the amazing Julia Watts for making it exactly as I dreamed it.

To the remarkable Intaglio Publications team: Kathy L. Smith, president and darn nice person; Tara Young, editor extraordinaire; and Valerie Hayken, superlative graphic artist, thanks for making this process fun, exciting, and manageable.

A special thanks to Sheri C. for hanging onto the journal entries I mailed you from Desert Storm, to Illa for being my best friend, to Edie G. for being yourself, to my platoon for letting me think I was in charge, and to Linda B. for holding down the fort.

Finally, to Adrienne, Robbie, Wallis, Chance, and the rest of my family, thanks for loving me.

Chapter One

"Hello," I said in a voice barely audible. The clock was on the nightstand beside the telephone. I could see that it was 4:30 in the morning.

"What are you talking about…who are you?" Waking came suddenly. I sat soundless but rapt as I heard again the harsh words.

"When?" I listened. My eyes were stinging. "Oh, my God, that son of a bitch. Where is he?" I screamed for an explanation. "What do you mean they don't know? Why don't they know?" Shock was taking over.

"Oh, God." I dropped the receiver and fell back onto my bed crying furiously. My housemate Jeff must have heard the screams and dashed to my room because seconds later he was shaking me as if I were dreaming.

"Abby, what's the matter? Abby, are you okay?" He saw the receiver dangling and picked it up, still holding me with one arm. I didn't speak.

"Hello, is anyone there?" he said into the phone. "Who is this?" He listened attentively. "I'm Jeff. I'm Abby's roommate …Yes, I know of her...Oh, no," he said quietly. "Oh, damn." He held me tighter as he listened to the news that had sent me into hysteria.

There was a long silence.

"I'm deeply sorry for your loss." He was shaking. "Can we do anything to help you?" He offered our assistance, even though we were twelve hundred miles away. Is Evelyn there?" he asked. "Oh. When will she return?" He continued, "So she knows already? Is someone meeting her at the airport when she arrives?" Jeff was amazingly calm and levelheaded. He was asking all the questions I would have asked had I been able to think.

"Yes, Abby will be there," he assured. "She'll leave as soon as we can get the arrangements made." There was another long pause. "Oh," Jeff sighed. "You don't need to do this now. We'll get all the information later. This must be hard for you," he said, listening. "Oh, you do? Yes…I'd like to have a look if you don't mind sending it." I had no idea what he was talking about. "Yes, whenever you get a chance. Our fax is always on." He was speaking slowly and softly. I was still sobbing but somewhat less hysterical.

"Yes, it's the same number as our phone except the last digit is zero." As Jeff gave our fax number to the woman on the other end of the line, I left my conscious mind. I felt as though I were watching everything from a safe distance.

"I'm sorry, what is your name again?" He was polite in his confusion. "I don't think I've heard Abby mention you before."

"She doesn't…okay, I get it." His tone was a little less bewildered. "She's right here, but she's still crying pretty hard." He pulled me to his side as we sat on my bed. I buried my head in his shoulder and continued to cry.

"Yes, we're very close friends." He stroked my head as he spoke. "This must be horrible for you," Jeff said tenderly. "Can you have Evelyn call if you hear from her?" he asked. "I know Abby will want to talk to her."

He was right. I wanted to talk to Evvie so she could tell me this was a really bad joke. I wanted to hear her say it was a lie. I didn't want to believe the stranger on the phone who told me my dear friend and former lover had been brutally murdered.

It was six years ago when I left South Carolina bound for Colorado. I was jobless and practically broke, but living in the western mountains had been a childhood dream. There was no better time to make the move than 1991.

I was crazy from the Persian Gulf War. I couldn't stand the confinement the narrow streets of my hometown offered, so I fled. I resigned my commission in the Army National Guard, packed my pickup truck, and headed west. I had no idea what I would do or how I would live.

Six years later, I am living comfortably and working steadily. I share a house with my friend Jeff Hunt, a wonderful thirty-five-year-old man I met the spring after moving here. We were contractors on the same job, but I was new and struggling and he was established and doing well.

Jeff is like a tree. Tall and spindly, his core is solid, yet he moves like rubber in the strong winds of the fast-paced, high-stress environment in which he works. I can almost imagine his roots penetrating the earth and holding him firmly on a foundation that allows for enough give to never break, regardless of the force. His baby-fine, sandy-colored hair complements his tan, smooth face and soft features with a masculine but gentle look. Even his clothes reflect his unregulated spirit by simply hanging freely about his lanky frame, relaxed and laissez-faire.

He walked up to me about two weeks into the job and asked if I'd be interested in teaming up. It was out of the blue but felt completely right. I told him I was interested but had no real masonry experience. I was a skid-steer operator and earth-worker. I built boulder retaining walls, dry-lay stone patios, and moved large amounts of dirt every day, but that hardly qualified as masonry.

He'd been watching me operate my skid loader and said he had a gut feeling we'd be awesome together. He was willing to teach me his trade if I was willing to teach him mine. He did mostly interior jobs, ceramic tile and the like, but wanted to expand to landscape construction. He figured with my resources and work ethic and his knowledge of masonry tools and techniques, we'd be in business in no time.

And we were. In just a year, we became the primary custom stone workers for a wealthy residential area. Booked eighteen months in advance with only the jobs we want, it is the best business I could have lucked into. It's hard work but extremely rewarding, requiring artistic vision and a strong back. No day ever ends without all my senses being tapped to their fullest.

Jeff and I became friends easily. We never had the sexual tensions often found in a friendship between two people of opposite genders. Jeff accepted my sexual orientation without question and fulfilled my requirement for a friend to be respectful and non-judgmental. His gentle manner and kind disposition make him the perfect business partner and housemate.

People often mistakenly assume we are a couple, but that's fine with us. It's too hard to explain, and most people would never understand anyway. I suppose if I were an outsider, I, too, would score it odd, but I'm glad I have Jeff and he has me, regardless of public opinion. He's less than a year older and as much like me as my own twin brother; we both know we're lucky to share our bond.

I was thankful that Jeff was with me to cushion the savage blow of Clara's murder. He hung up the receiver and put both arms around me, holding me as I cried until sunrise.

Chapter Two

I met Clara Stokes in 1988, and we lived contentedly in chaos for the next three years. I never figured out how we could have been so happy while the world around us crumbled into ruins, but we were oblivious for the most part.

During college, I worked part time as an emergency medical technician. I was on the crew that responded to the 911 call Clara made after her husband had beaten her one of many times. She was a mess, bruised and bloody—but in remarkably good spirits. There had been a birthday party for her husband, Charlie, at their apartment earlier in the evening, and Clara said things just got out of hand. She reported that everyone was drinking and dancing without incident until a male friend and co-worker of Charlie's began flirting with her.

"Charlie went a little nuts," Clara said as we dressed her wounds and prepared to transport her to the hospital for possible broken ribs and a broken nose. From the looks of things, he went more than just a little nuts.

The apartment was small—one bedroom, a kitchen and living room joined, and a bath, but there was not an undisturbed piece of furniture or unbroken window. Clara noted that he had not hit her with any of the furniture this time so it might not be as bad as we were thinking.

I was appalled and infuriated. Domestic violence was the worst part of my job. At the hospital, I asked the attending physician if I could stay in the treatment room while they worked with her. The doctor agreed, and I stuck around.

"Don't you have other sick people to pick up?" Clara smiled at me still sitting quietly in the corner after everyone else had momentarily left the curtained room.

"Oh, yeah, I probably do, but I wanted to see if I diagnosed you correctly." I tried to laugh but quickly turned serious. "What makes you stay there?" My question was way out of line.

"Are you going to preach?" she asked, never losing her slight pained grin and wide, shiny eyes. "'Cause if so, I would ask you to save your breath." She stared at me.

"Okay." I knew I was over my boundary. "I'm sorry, I'm just a little shocked by what I saw at your place, and I never get it." I shook my head and started to get up.

"Stay." A sudden flash of desperation overtook her face replaced at once by well-trained calmness. "I mean, I'd love to talk to you," she said softly. "Do you always take your job so personally?" She smiled at me.

"I guess," I admitted. "I've been in trouble for it more than once." I was still shaking my head.

"I could say he doesn't mean to hurt me, but that isn't necessarily true." She wasn't looking in my eyes anymore, and I was relieved. "He was in Vietnam for a couple of tours, and he's not been the same since, or so his people tell me," she sighed. "My mother said I was asking for trouble marrying a man with eyes like his, but I was the only twenty-year-old woman in the county who still lived at home," she explained. "I figured he'd be a good way out."

"So he's a lot older than you?" I was over the border and full speed ahead into the inappropriate conversation we had begun.

"Only eight years," she counted. "That's not a lot, is it?"

"You just don't look your age," I said, smiling and remembering from the report that she was thirty years old. "Even black and blue, you look about twenty-five." I was sincere but had no idea where I was taking the conversation or why. I was drawn in by something beyond her physical beauty. "Does he always beat you up?" I snapped back to reality.

"No, just when he's had too much to drink and gets jealous," she said. "Funny thing is, there was nothing for him to be jealous about this time. He just doesn't think straight after a little whiskey, and he imagines things that aren't happening. I'm all he's got, and I suppose he sees me as his property." She didn't sound as though this was as repulsive to her as it sounded to me.

"So he beat you up because he thought somebody else was hitting on you?" I didn't get it.

"Doesn't make a lick of sense, does it?" She grinned. "He thinks I'll leave him for the first new thing that comes along, so he goes off the deep end at the thought."

I was dumbfounded and staring at her.

"Go ahead and ask," she offered. "Why don't I leave him? I don't leave because if he does this when he thinks I might leave, what the hell would he do if I left?" Her grin was gone, and the desperation in her eyes was clear.

"Come on, Abby, let's ride." My partner Jesse poked his head in the room and summoned me. "I couldn't find you anywhere." He sounded annoyed.

"Does he get jealous of women friends?" I asked Clara as I was leaving the room. I must have lost my mind.

"Never." She focused her solemn stare directly in my now watering eyes.

"I'll see you soon," I promised as I pulled the curtains to the side and hurried out to Jesse and our waiting ambulance.

"Stupid broad's gonna go right back home and fuck him tonight. Mark my words," Jesse commented as I put on my seat belt.

"Probably." I looked at the floor.

It was my brother Alvin who got me interested in becoming an EMT. He took the class a year before I did but only worked nine months on the ambulance crew before he got a really good offer at a local factory. His wife pushed him to take the factory job, and although I never really understood why he let her make the decision for him, he gave up the work he loved. Hearing his stories of helping people and the adrenaline rush of it all sold me. I loved both, and I stuck with the job.

In addition to school, twenty paid hours a week on the ambulance crew and another ten volunteering, I was a member of the South Carolina National Guard. I had enlisted right after high school, and they sent me through the state-run officer candidate program to become a second lieutenant the same year I met Clara. I pinned on those gold bars August 24, 1989, with no way of knowing how heavy a couple little pieces of metal would become.

I was ignorant of the responsibility and commitment being an officer in the United States armed forces entailed.

When I think back on the way Clara and I got together and the constant danger we were in for our secret love, I get a chill. I kept my promise to see her again, but it was not the way I had hoped it would be. Two weeks to the day of the last call we responded to, we were again on the way to her apartment. A neighbor had heard a gunshot and called the police and us. The police were the first to arrive and found that Charlie had fled seconds earlier.

Clara was sitting on the sofa, wet-headed and wearing a bathrobe. It seemed that Charlie had discharged the weapon into the floor while Clara was showering. She had no idea what he was doing with the gun. No one was hurt, but I couldn't help wondering if he was planning to assault her with it as she showered.

"He'd been drinking and came home late from work," she explained to the officers. "We didn't quarrel at all. I just got into the shower, and a few minutes later, the gun went off. I didn't know what to do, so I stayed in the bathroom and listened. When I heard the front door close, I crept out and looked. The gun was on the floor, and he was gone," she recalled. "You all showed up right then."

"Well," one of the officers said, "we'd like to talk to him if he comes home soon."

Clara nodded.

"We'll be outside for a little while." They were about to leave when she asked them if Charlie was in any trouble.

"Depends," the same officer spoke again, "on how cooperative he wants to be." They left the apartment without asking any more questions.

"Are you sure you're okay?" I asked on my way out the door.

"I'm fine." She looked happy to see me. "Look, my nose is much better!" She pointed to her face. "Do I look any different without two black eyes?" I could not understand how she could be so detached from her own pain and suffering, but I agreed she looked better and followed the others.

"I need to talk to you, miss," Clara called after me as we walked down the hall to exit the building. The four of us stopped. I was the only female present.

"Go ahead, you guys, I'll be right out." I turned and walked back toward where she stood in her open apartment door.

"Can we have a drink or something when you get off your shift?" she asked nervously.

"I don't drink, but I could meet you for coffee." I was puzzled. "Won't you get in trouble for going out late?" I did not want to precipitate any further violence.

"He won't be back tonight." She sounded certain. "He's very predictable. What time do you finish?"

"Midnight," I said. "If all goes well." I never really knew.

"I'll meet you at the Shoney's on Broadway," she said. "That's not too far, is it?"

"My name is Abby. I'll be there." I turned and left her standing in the doorway, hair dripping and eyes watering. My heart was pounding so loud I'm sure she could hear it.

Chapter Three

Most serious lesbians know the signs of a straight woman who is either desperate or curious. They are equally dangerous, but while Clara was both, she was neither. Unlike the desperate, she made the choices that molded her life. Unlike the curious, she accepted the choices she had made.

She chose to marry a man against her mother's advice in order to leave home. She chose the lesser sentence of monthly battering and bruising over the possible worse fate terminating the relationship might bring. She chose to abort the fetus she was carrying without Charlie's consent or knowledge and elected for surgical sterilization to prevent any further occurrences. She chose to keep her situation a secret from her family, which led to their estrangement.

In essence, she chose to be miserable alone over dragging other people, even her own child, into her misery. I was determined to be the next choice she made.

The first night we had coffee, Clara told me she wanted to get to know me but that she also wanted me to be safe from her situation. It's funny how we never mentioned that I dated only women and that she was attracted to me or that we both had an unexplainable desire to be intimate that night. Those things just never came up. We continued to meet at the same place, drink our coffee, and go our separate ways for over a month.

I knew everything there was to know about Clara, and she knew more about me than I knew about myself in that short month of coffee and conversation. We discussed Charlie and her family and Evelyn and my recent breakup. I told her about my love of music, and she told me about her love of poetry and writing.

"I write to escape, and I read poetry to heal." She smiled a contented smile. "I keep a diary of my life, and I even write a few of my own poems every now and then." She blushed. "More now than then."

"What do they say...your poems?" I urged her to continue speaking.

"Oh, I could never read them to you." She was beet red. "What if you laughed?"

"Why would I laugh?"

"I don't know...because they're mostly about you?" I suddenly felt the warmth of her legs wrapping around mine under the cover of the booth where we were sitting. I could hardly breathe.

"What time do you think you need to be home?" I asked before I could stop myself.

"Hours yet," she whispered as we hurried out of the restaurant and to my truck.

That night was the beginning of a transformative affair between Clara Stokes and me. She was six years older, but it may as well have been six hundred. I was an infant soul in the presence of one that was old and wise. I never knew strength was such a chameleon. I always thought it was weakness and self-loathing that kept an abused woman going back for more. I was wrong.

Clara was the strongest woman I had ever known. She had evolved and adapted into a person who could endure anything without losing her inner self. She regularly called up a force that most people only have in extraordinary circumstances. She knew exceptional strength as well as a line on her hand; she could summon it and hide in its shield anytime she wanted. I envied her impervious shell.

I had let the world mistreat me. I felt unfairly chastised by the gods in this life and believed I was a victim of the creator's cruel humor. He made me the weaker twin. Why couldn't I have been the boy? If I were the boy, Daddy would have taught me to work the land and drive a stick shift. If I were the boy, Alvin would have been the twin who had to look after our younger siblings and help our mother keep the house. Alvin could have been the one to wear the stupid frilly dresses and hair bows while I got the overalls and cowboy boots.

My daddy was ashamed of who I was. He was ashamed that a daughter of his could behave like the Bible story of corruption in an evil city. I knew the story well. So did Alvin. He pleaded with me to get a boyfriend when I confided my love for my first girlfriend when we were fifteen years old. He said he wouldn't tell if I would just drop her and act right.

I told him about her long blonde hair and pale white skin and how beautiful it was when the sun shone on her as we lay in the grass behind the hay barn. He said I wasn't supposed to be saying those things about another girl, and if I couldn't stop it for me, then stop it for him. What would his friends think about his twin sister being a lezzie? How would he get anywhere in life with such a stigma?

I wanted Alvin to support me and understand my love of girls and total indifference to kissing boys. I wanted Alvin to help me through my adolescent crushes as he would any other boy pal or even a twin brother. I wanted him to understand that I felt just like he did about girls and that we could talk about it. He wanted no part of it.

I shamed him. I shamed our mother, Daddy, and the rest of the family. Daddy thought no one else outside our house knew, but that was the most comfortable lie he could cloak in. Oh, I tried to hide and lie to protect them every now and then, but I was not fooling anyone. Every soul in Spartanburg knew my business. Every soul in South Carolina knew for all I could see.

The block on the enlistment papers that said something about not being homosexual should have tipped me off that the Army might not be the place to run. But it was the only way out, so I lied as I had lied before, bold-faced and without conscience. I'm glad I joined the National Guard instead of the regular Army because I saw in the first twenty-four hours that I was not a career soldier. I was a good soldier, though, and being surrounded by women during basic training was the best part of the trip. It didn't take long in the midst of all those women to fall for one.

Celeste was the same age I was and drop-dead beautiful. She was about my height—five feet seven inches—with light, wavy hair. She was the fastest runner, held the highest score for pushups, and was a squad leader. I was in love in an instant.

I went from being a marginal recruit to a squad leader myself in just one week. I got the position when my former squad leader washed out for failing her physical fitness test. It just so happened that her position also included being the assigned "buddy" to my new love interest. Everyone in the platoon had a buddy, and squad leaders had to be buddies with other squad leaders. Your buddy was like your spouse; you did everything together, right down to sharing the same punishment if one was disciplined. I would have gladly shared anything with Celeste.

Squad leaders got a little more freedom because we had to monitor our squads all the time. We could be up after lights-out and talk when the others had to be silent, as long as it was about "squad leader business." We spent hours awake together while others slept. I must have gone four solid weeks without a night's sleep.

Celeste had a boyfriend who was also going through training to be a soldier, and they planned to be married after he was assigned a duty station. I planned to change all that.

Celeste and I were the team to watch. We were the best at everything we did. Our drill sergeants would pit us against any soldier in any platoon in any event, and we gave them bragging rights.

All that praise and pride came to a screeching halt one unfortunate evening. Long after bed check, Celeste and I were caught in the latrine in an embrace. Things changed drastically.

We were counseled by the male platoon sergeant, separated and assigned to new buddies, and forbidden to talk to each other. Fortunately, graduation came less than two weeks after the incident, and we left the training post as sad and miserably as we had come. Celeste feared her fiancé might be told, and I feared her fiancé. I'd seen his picture. He was six-foot-three and looked like a Marine-recruiting poster.

Clara laughed hysterically as I recounted my antics from the nine months of military training I endured for the National Guard. She said I was nervy and brazen. I said I was young and stupid. She said I was probably good for people who'd never seen another side of life. I said I was an unwelcome shock to their collective systems. She asked me what had become of my friend Celeste.

"I don't really know," I said honestly. "We went to job training school together after boot camp. Her fiancé was in the same city at the Air Force base, so I had to share her with him occasionally. Her sister was also stationed there as a nurse. She had a big, scary biker boyfriend, and we went to their house every weekend we could get away.

"Another woman lived with Celeste's sister and the biker boyfriend. I thought the whole thing reeked of a love triangle, but Celeste said there was no way her sister was sleeping with a woman. My suspicions were confirmed when we saw the roommate, Christine, at the dyke bar downtown. She implored us not to tell Celeste's sister that she was there. We didn't, of course, but I knew I was right the moment we saw her." I smirked.

"What happened then?" Clara was not satisfied with the ending to my story.

"Oh, we graduated, Celeste married 'what's-his-name,' and they went off to some other country." I sighed.

"So you never saw her again?" Clara persisted.

"No, but I did talk to her a while back. She left her husband and is living with another woman." I told her part of the story Celeste had told me on the phone. "Oh, here's an interesting but sad twist," I recalled the rest of the conversation. "Seems that Celeste's sister was involved with Christine after all. I'm not sure where the boyfriend fit into the puzzle, but they were all pretty lost in the drug scene. Poor Christine overdosed on something and died recently while Celeste's sister tried to resuscitate her." I shook my head. "Sad."

"That is sad," Clara agreed. "Do you ever want to see Celeste again?" she asked cautiously.

"I'd love to, but I bet we're two very different people right now. Besides, the new girlfriend might not approve." I smiled. "Either of them."

Clara loved to hear my stories, and I told her as many as I could recall. She said it was amazing that a twenty-four-year-old could have so much to talk about. I said what was amazing was that she didn't seem concerned with her dysfunctional home life the whole time we were together. She acted as if it were just a cross she had to bear, a handicap that was not life threatening. I believed it was far more dangerous than she admitted, but I indulged her the right to forget as often as she could.

Charlie was always nice to me. I didn't make a habit of going to their apartment, but when I needed to, it was okay. Clara insisted I know Charlie so he wouldn't worry that she was off with another man when we were together. He must have been the only one in town who didn't know I was a lesbian, or else he just felt too sure of his penis to worry that Clara would be with me.

It made me menacingly happy to know I was sleeping with his wife and that she liked it better with me than with him. He gave her pain and bruises; I gave her tenderness and consideration. He crawled on top of her and crudely forced himself on her whenever he pleased, with or without her consent. Fortunately, it was always over in a matter of minutes.

I kissed and caressed her, taking hours to even undress her. I moved slowly and with permission, careful to never lose myself to the force of passion that can so easily render a body out of control. I wanted to lose control, but Clara wanted me to be what she never had before—a gentle and thoughtful lover. I hadn't learned yet the place that is controlled and chaotic synchronously.

We continued to see each other once or twice a week, and I became accustomed to the twisted relationship she had with her abusive husband. I have no idea how I did it, detaching myself as she had from it all, accepting the way it was. It's absurd when I remember it now. He beat her about six more times the first year we were together. I responded to the only other 911 call she made after the most severe of those beatings.

I walked into the apartment with my work partner Jesse, patched her up, and transported her to the hospital with a broken jaw. I wasn't in the body of the EMT taking care of the patient who wasn't my Clara. I wasn't the one who filled out the report and talked to the attending physician. It wasn't anyone I know who agreed with Jesse that she must be crazy. I *was* the one who vomited next to the ambulance as I waited for Jesse to get some coffee.

Chapter Four

"She can't be gone, Jeff." I raised my head toward the light of the morning sun shining through my bedroom windows. I had been crying and remembering my friend for over three hours without speaking a word. From my throat to the top of my pelvis, I felt raw and bruised, and my lungs were as heavy as my heart. My legs seemed useless—like no matter how hard I tried to beckon them, they wouldn't carry me any farther than the edge of the bed if my life depended on it. It didn't matter, though, because I hadn't the vigor to signal them to move anyway. My arms held my hands directly over my heart, as if I were somehow preventing it from bursting through my chest.

"I'm so sorry, Abby," Jeff started. "I don't even know what to say to you right now. This is horrible."

"I just can't believe it," I said hoarsely through my tears. "Clara," I whispered. "How in the world did this happen?" I began crying harder at the sound of her name.

"Clara's friend said she would fax me the police report, so maybe we'll get some answers. I think her name was Laurel." He looked as though he couldn't really remember.

"Where was Evvie?" I asked, wanting a little more than I knew without being sure I could handle it.

"She's away on vacation somewhere in Europe. They don't know how to reach her. She's due in the day after tomorrow."

"She'll go into hysterics." I began focusing on Evelyn's reaction to the news of Clara's murder. "I have to meet her at the airport. She needs to hear this from me."

"That's probably a good idea, but can you really do that?" Jeff was obviously more concerned with my mental state than Evelyn's.

"I have to. There's really no one else she could hear this from," I reasoned. "Who is Laurel anyway?"

"Clara's new girlfriend. She said they'd been dating for a short while. I guess she was the one who found the body." Jeff drew a long breath. "That would be the worst."

"I just don't get it, Jeff. Laurel said the primary suspect is Charlie, Clara's husband." There were many unanswered questions.

"I thought he was in prison." Jeff looked puzzled.

"So did I." I was completely baffled.

"Maybe he got out and Clara didn't know about it," Jeff suggested. "No, that can't be right because I thought they had to tell the victims that they were paroling the offender in these cases."

"Well, technically, she wasn't the victim," I explained. "She didn't put him in prison. Hell, she never even bothered to get divorced from the son of a bitch." I could feel my anger rising.

"So he could have been released without Clara's knowledge," Jeff analyzed. "Isn't that nice?"

"I just talked to her last week." The tears were flowing again. "She said she was well and happy and that she was kind of seeing someone new. That must be Laurel. She said they were going to try and visit me soon." I cried harder than ever.

Jeff was holding me now and rocking me in his arms. "Cry, Abby, it's good to cry."

I used to love Clara's visits when I was away from our town. They always felt like a homecoming and a fresh new start all rolled into one experience.

Clara visited me often at the end of our second year together because I had been sent to Virginia to fulfill an educational requirement for the National Guard. I was away from home for five months, but fortunately, we were only one state apart. We saw each other on the weekends when Charlie was on a drinking binge or a marathon work shift at the factory.

I lived for those weekends. It was the first time we had not a single worry that Charlie would catch us. In fact, Charlie's drinking had become so severe that he had blackouts for days at a time when he was not working. Among the list of things I will never understand is the hard-core alcoholic who is functional enough to hold a job. Charlie was living proof it could be done.

I asked my old friend and ex-lover Evelyn to look in on Clara every now and then, which she did without complaint. The two became good friends, and I suspected by the end of my school obligation that Evelyn herself had a bit of a spark for Clara. Evelyn had been in my life almost as long as I had, and though we had had a brief and turbid relationship of sorts as fledgling adults, we were none the worse for the experience. Our being a couple was nothing if not comical given that more than an hour with her always produced a predictable annoyance in me. It was not something I could palpate—it was simply my lack of tolerance for the naïve carelessness with which she approached life. We were from two different worlds. Mine consisted of chores and discipline, and hers was all about summer camps and vacation choices.

I didn't begrudge her good fortune really, I just wanted her to clue in that the rest of the world didn't live like she did. I also didn't feel threatened by my feeling that she was interested in Clara. I was proud that Clara had chosen me and sure that Evelyn could never win her heart as I had. Clara continued to write me poems and even read them to me on the phone sometimes. I was still forbidden to see the diary she kept, but it was enough to know that I was in her thoughts and her writing every night we were apart.

Clara never spoke of the beatings she endured while I was away, but Evelyn told me of the two she knew about. Neither resulted in broken bones or serious injuries, and I was elated to hear the report. It's sick and demented that I accepted the news of the beatings as a victory because no major damage was done.

The night I returned home from the Army school, Clara prepared dinner for me at her apartment. It was awkward since Charlie and Evelyn were also present, but I was glad to see her, even in the company of others. Charlie was drunk when I showed up and spent most of the evening talking to Evelyn. They had some incomprehensible and frightening kinship that gave me a start, but I was glad he ignored me.

The dinner was marvelous and Clara was radiant. She had a peace and calmness that I had never seen. Looking back, I wonder if she somehow knew about the bittersweet gift we were about to get. That same night, Charlie was involved in a serious head-on collision. He was playing his usual game of drink and drive real fast, but some unfortunate person was in the wrong place at the wrong time. Charlie veered into oncoming traffic and smashed headfirst into the only other car in sight.

The young driver of the other car died instantly, and Charlie was taken to the hospital with severe injuries. He lived, but with his past record, a conviction of vehicular homicide was a walk in the park for the prosecution.

That was the end of Charlie's influence on our relationship. I felt guilty about my delight in his tragedy since it resulted in the loss of another life, but it was such a relief to have him gone. Clara forgot he was alive as soon as he was moved to the prison. She never wrote, never visited, and never planned to see him again.

Finally, we had a chance to be together. Finally, we could live in peace without constant fear of discovery. Finally, Charlie would hit her no more. We could sleep together, we could walk naked around the apartment if we chose, and we could revel in our good fortune. Fate, however, would disagree that our arrangement was such a good one.

One month after Charlie went to prison, my National Guard unit was activated to participate in Operation Desert Shield. I was going to Saudi Arabia. We were assigned to live on the closest military post while the unit completed the required deployment steps.

Now I couldn't see Clara, couldn't pretend she was just a friend from home. The threat that someone might discover our true relationship and punish me for it was too great. I forbid my feelings and retreated inward. In my Army uniform, I died a cruel death akin to drowning and starving simultaneously.

Alvin and my mother came to see me while I was waiting to leave, but Daddy was too busy to be bothered. I think he was still ashamed. He seemed to be more ashamed that I was a "damn lieutenant" than that I was a "damn lezzie." There was no winning with him. He hated officers and let me know right away that he never would have been one. He was an enlisted, working man for his hitch in the service, and that was good enough for him. He said it figured that I would become an officer since I was so much better than everyone else. My mother always said he was just bantering, but I knew damn well that he was serious.

As we approached departure, I felt increasingly patriotic. Clara was finally free, and I was going to war to help keep her that way. I wanted to set a good example for my platoon, so I tried my best to do everything by the book. I had thirty or so soldiers in my platoon when we were deployed, and I pledged before we ever left South Carolina that I'd have thirty or so when we returned.

Evelyn and Clara got together within days of my arrival in Saudi Arabia. They didn't have to tell me; I felt it in the pit of my soul.

Chapter Five

The fax from Laurel arrived around 10:00 a.m. Colorado time. Jeff would not allow me to read it but instead told me the details he thought I could stomach. I tried to explain to him that I had been to war and could stomach as much as he could, but he would not budge.

"Desert Storm didn't take one of your best friend's lives," he rebutted.

"Yeah, well, maybe it did." He looked confused, and I changed the subject. "It took part of mine." I defended my war. "People always assume it was a vacation or that I was on some extended National Guard annual training. It was neither. I was scared every second and responsible for people's lives. I was foolish and inexperienced with no scale to even measure the death and destruction around me. We got shot at and shit on, just like the National Guard always gets when playing with the 'real Army.'"

"Calm down, Abby," Jeff said, following my tirade. "All I meant was that it's different when you're dealing with tragedy on a personal level. Don't get defensive with me, please; I'm not the enemy."

"I'm sorry. Just tell me what happened." I braced myself for the news.

"Charlie got out of prison a while back, but Clara didn't know. He was supposedly clean and sober and not a threat to anyone, so his family didn't see the point in telling Clara to be cautious. It's a little sketchy why she wasn't notified since they are still legally married, but she wasn't." Jeff read on from the fax. "Anyway, a week ago, Clara's house was robbed while she worked. The police were baffled by what the burglar took. The only things missing were her wedding ring and a few other pieces of costume jewelry worth very little, a box of old photos, and her diary."

"Charlie," I said, shaking my head.

29

"That's what Clara thought, too. According to Laurel, she started trying to find out information. His mother admitted he was out of prison but said he was living down in Florida, so it couldn't have been him.

"Laurel said Clara discovered a few days after the burglary that the nightstands on either side of her bed had also been disturbed. Evidently, Clara kept diaries from all the years of her life in the nightstand closest to where she slept. This year's diary, which was taken during the burglary, had been lying on top of that same nightstand. The nightstand on the other side of the bed contained notebooks and loose pages of Clara's writing, mostly poetry." Jeff looked a little confused, but I understood completely. "Apparently, when Clara looked in the nightstands after the burglary, she didn't catch it, but a few days later, she realized the locations of the notebooks and diaries had been switched." He stopped and looked at me.

I had nothing to say. I was listening and remembering how sacred Clara's diaries were to her.

"Clara never reported her findings to the police because she was afraid they would seize the diaries in an attempt to solve the burglary. Laurel said she put them all in a plastic garbage bag and hid them in the house somewhere." Jeff paused. "So here's the really disturbing part, Abby." He hesitated again. "Are you sure you want to hear this? It's not pretty."

"Tell me," I said quietly, not looking up.

"The cause of death was blunt trauma to the head…repeated blunt trauma." Jeff tried to be gentle.

"That's no surprise, Jeff." I was still staring at the coffee cup in my hands. "He loved to hit her in the face," I continued. "The diary was there, wasn't it?" I pictured Clara lying in a pool of her own blood with Charlie standing over her, then tossing the diary onto her body as he left the room.

"Yes," Jeff quietly replied. "The missing diary was lying on her body."

The killer was definitely Charlie. His fingerprints were all over the metal pipe that he used to kill her, all over the house, and all over the diary. The police were attempting to locate him but were not having any luck.

He killed her for leaving him, just as she knew years ago that he would. He broke into her house and found the evidence of her affairs that he needed to justify his actions. I wondered if Clara had used real names in her diaries. Would Charlie go after Laurel now that he had killed Clara? Would he locate and kill every single lover mentioned in the pages of the diary he stole? How many were there this year? Clara and Evelyn broke up a while ago, so Evelyn might be safe. Laurel was recent; were there other lovers Clara didn't tell me about?

"Abby," Jeff touched my shoulder to bring me back. "Are you okay?"

"Of course I'm not okay," I snapped. "Clara is dead and Charlie is running loose," I reminded him. "The police in Spartanburg probably think she got what she deserved for being what she was." A large chip was forming on my shoulder. "They probably don't give a damn about finding Charlie," I said bitterly.

"Abby, I'm on your side. I know this is unmanageable grief for you, but let's stay allies here." He was as soft and understanding as usual.

I nodded, choking back more tears.

"Now what do you know about the diaries that could hurt anyone else?" He was thinking the same way I was.

"I don't know," I said. "Clara kept a book for every year, but I never got to see them, so I don't know what kind of things she wrote. I always wanted to read them, but I couldn't bring myself to violate her privacy. She never offered to show me one."

"Maybe Laurel has already thought about this, but Charlie obviously read the one written this year. It probably contained information about her and Clara's relationship, so he might try and hurt Laurel, too, if he knows who she is." Jeff and I were still following the same thought pattern.

"We need to call her right away." I got up to get the phone. "Let's make plane reservations now, too." I was ready to go home and face the unpleasant circumstances. I was prepared to ignore my parents as they preached salvation in the face of tragedy. I was indifferent to the thought of Alvin, in whom I had confided my affair with Clara, telling me this was a message from God to straighten up. I was ready to meet Evelyn at the airport and ready to face the death of my dear Clara.

"Let me go with you, Abby," Jeff said as I returned to the table with the phone. "You can't go alone." He had an unfamiliar sound of concern in his voice.

I thought about it. "I guess you could if you want." I scanned through our workload to see what was pressing. "We don't have anything scheduled that can't be put off for a while."

"I'm really not too fond of the idea of you walking alone into a potentially life-threatening situation," he confessed. "I'll make our reservations from the office phone while you call Laurel. She said she'd be at Clara's house picking up some things." He headed down the stairs toward the office.

"Is this Laurel?" I asked the voice on the other end of the line at Clara's house. "It's Abby Dunnigan." I was almost whispering. "How are you feeling?"

"The same," she replied in as meek a tone as I had asked.

"We're making the reservations for our trip right now, but I wanted to talk to you, if that's okay." I said.

"Okay." She sounded like a child.

"Jeff told me about the diary that was stolen and how it was returned. We got really worried about you when we realized that Charlie had read it." I tried to be as gentle with Laurel as Jeff had been with me.

"There are no names in the diaries," Laurel answered as if she had read my mind. "Clara never used names." I wondered but didn't ask how she knew.

"I looked at them when she was working," Laurel confessed. "I never told her."

"I'm sure she wouldn't have cared," I lied. "So there were no names or anything to identify the people she was writing about?"

"Not really."

"Oh, good. We were just worried about you," I said again. "Are you alone?"

"No, my mother is here. We came over to get my things out before the family comes in and fights over everything."

"Where are the old diaries?" I asked without thinking about how Laurel would feel.

"Safe," she assured me. "They'll never get their hands on her personal life." Laurel's voice turned strong and determined.

"That's good news." I was relieved. "Do you know when Evelyn arrives at the airport? I'm trying to get there to meet her if possible." Laurel gave me Evelyn's flight information, and I moved on to my next concern. "How is Clara's family taking her death?"

"Not well," Laurel was quick to answer. "Clara's mother told her she had a feeling he was up to something after the break-in, but Clara didn't seem all that worried. Her mother didn't know anything about Clara's women friends; she assumed Clara was dating men." Laurel sounded tired.

"All these years and her mother still didn't guess?" I was amazed by this news.

"Not a clue," Laurel confirmed. "They didn't spend a lot of time together, so it wasn't that hard. I suppose her mother figured we were all just good friends."

"Well, we were." I understood and appreciated why Clara never told her family.

"I'm sorry I woke you in the middle of the night." Laurel broke the momentary silence.

"It's okay," I assured her. "I'm sorry I went crazy and yelled like I did." I was truly regretful but didn't feel entirely responsible for my actions.

"I yelled, too, when I walked in the house yesterday."

"Oh, God, it's awful that you had to deal with that." I didn't know what to say. I was glad it wasn't me who found my slain lover.

"I think I turned into some other person because I just kind of...you know...like called the police and people like that." She was slipping away in the memory of the trauma she endured only a day ago. "I really loved her, Abby." She was crying softly.

"Me too, Laurel," I said tenderly. "We'll get that bastard, okay?" I pledged to see Charlie punished for taking our friend from this world.

Chapter Six

As I stood at the window watching the plane carrying Evelyn taxi into the gate, I couldn't help remembering the last time we had a homecoming.

I was returning from Southwest Asia. She was greeting me, along with Clara and a handful of other friends, at the military post we flew into. That was the night I learned for sure that Evelyn and Clara were in love. I already knew it in my heart, but they had neither confirmed nor denied my questionings. I was so far gone from my experiences in the war that I really didn't even care. They seemed happy, and I felt none of my old feelings. I had blocked my emotions for so long that I couldn't return them to their normal state as easily as I had turned them off.

My first night home, I ate a whole pizza and fell asleep in the bathtub at Evelyn's house. Evelyn was not living with Clara at the time, but they were seeing each other frequently, so she allowed me to stay in her house while I was deciding what to do with the rest of my life.

We were definitely not the same friends we had been before the war. Evelyn felt immensely guilty for taking away my life with Clara, and I was not the same person she remembered. I had so few emotions that I couldn't even convey my initial level of indifference to her being with Clara.

As the days passed and I was finally released from active duty for good, I found myself in a deep state of depression. I could not stand the walls of a house around me after the boundless space in the desert. I insisted on sleeping in my Army cot on Evvie's screened-in porch. Evelyn sat many nights on my cot and cried for me to be myself again. I think she was crying more because she had betrayed me, but neither of us mentioned it.

We never really discussed the fact that I left as Clara's girlfriend and returned as a stranger. I think they were counting on my short attention span to have ended my infatuation with Clara. Whatever the rationale, we all played along for the first few weeks. It was Evelyn who finally broke the ice.

"You need help, Abby," she pleaded, after weeks of watching my strange behavior. "You should talk to someone; at least tell us what happened to you."

"What do you mean?" I snapped at her. "Tell you that it's okay that you took my lover while I risked my life for your country?" I stared coldly into her eyes. The can was opened.

"Abby, look at yourself. You're borderline insane." She held my empty gaze and took no part of the responsibility for my deteriorating mental state.

"Maybe I am, but it feels pretty good here." I walked out and didn't speak to her for a week.

It was just before I moved to Colorado that I sat them down and told them I accepted their relationship and forgave the way they got together. I didn't want to leave with my two closest friends thinking I hated them. I didn't want Clara to think I thought she would wait for me, even though I had. After all, we never said it was going to last forever.

Evelyn and Clara were good for each other, and I could neither hate them nor harbor ill feelings. Who was I to question when it looked as though it was all for the best? Clara finished an associate degree program in technical drawing while they were together and Evelyn was an engineer. Evvie really didn't need to work since she had inherited a large sum of money early in life, but she enjoyed her work. They bought a house and lived peacefully for about four years after I moved. It was Evvie who got restless and started wandering. I was sad to hear they had split when Evvie called and told me. She was kind, though, and walked away leaving Clara everything they had accumulated together, house and all.

I checked back into the present when I heard the passengers deplaning and coming through the tunnel. How was I going to tell Evvie the tragic news of Clara's death? How was I going to explain to her that Clara was gone forever?

Jeff and I had arrived in Spartanburg with only a few hours to spare before I had to be at the airport. I'll never forget the look of relief on my father's face when I introduced him to Jeff. My family assumed he was my boyfriend, and I didn't have the energy to correct them. Though he wanted to help me, Jeff knew I needed to be alone with Evelyn to tell her the news. He stayed at my parents' house while I drove the hour and a half to the airport.

I spotted Evvie coming down the ramp with her carry-on bag in tow. She was unmistakable in her trademark wire-rimmed glasses. Her straw-colored, pixie-bob hair was, as usual, falling forward from where she was still optimistic that it would stay behind her ears. It never stayed, but she never gave up trying to make it. She looked older than when I had last seen her three years ago, but she appeared less thin. I was accustomed to her emaciated look—it was all I'd known of her physical form, so it was nice to see her looking fleshier. She was average height but had been at least twenty pounds underweight since we'd reached puberty. Without fail, in every history class throughout high school, while studying the Holocaust, someone would point to the pictures of the concentration camp victims in our books and ask Evvie how they got her to pose. As cruel as it was, her body often looked like she was starving despite her hearty appetite.

As she approached where I was waiting, I was suddenly overcome by fear and hid among the crowd. I let her go past me and fell into the stream of people hurrying to the baggage claim area.

I watched her from a distance for a few minutes and decided not to approach her until we were out of the airport. I knew I must not look excited or happy in any way, even though seeing her made me both. I had to maintain the solemn sadness that filled my heart so she would not be fooled or caught off guard. I coached myself as I prepared to meet her.

She got her suitcase and headed to the door. I followed.

As soon as she was out the door, I started closing in on her, ready to make my presence known. Just then an athletic-looking woman with short salt-and-pepper hair rose from a concrete bench and approached Evelyn. They hugged and exchanged greetings. Surprised, I did nothing except watch and listen.

The woman led a now puzzled-looking Evelyn back to the bench area where they sat down. Again I followed. I could hear most of what the deep-voiced, serious-sounding stranger was saying as she told Evelyn the news of Clara's murder. Evvie's face flashed horror. I rushed to her.

"Evvie," I grabbed her as she collapsed forward and fell into me. I held her tightly.

"Abby, oh, my God, Abby." She sounded hollow.

"I came to tell you, Evvie, but I couldn't do it at the gate." She held on like she needed no explanation.

Without much further dialogue, the woman who greeted her led us to a car. I assumed she was Evelyn's current lover, but I asked no questions. Still silent, she opened the front door on the passenger's side and steadied Evelyn to sit with her legs hanging out. Evvie bowed her head and again began crying and shaking.

"Oh, God, I feel like I'm in a bad dream," she said finally, wiping her nose on her shirt sleeve and looking up at me. "How did this happen?"

"Charlie," I said. "He got out of prison recently. He broke into her house a while before the murder. He found her diary and took some other little stuff. I guess he killed her for what he read in the diary because he left it on the body." I realized I was not being as gentle as I should, but I felt more angry than gentle at the moment. Evvie sat silent and in shock. I stood beside her, leaning on the open car door with my hand on her shoulder.

When Evvie finally swung her legs into the car and sighed a deep sigh, I gave her another tender squeeze on the arm and stepped back to close the door.

"You doing okay for now?" I asked her as I climbed into the backseat.

"I'm hanging," she said. She was starting to get back the color in her face.

I introduced myself to Evelyn's friend, Pat Archer, who had been standing quietly by as Evvie processed the news. Pat insisted we three ride home together, and frankly, I was relieved not to have to drive. Evelyn, now seeming more alert, joined the conversation to suggest I use one of her vehicles while I was in town, so I turned in my rental car and we started toward Spartanburg.

As we left the airport lot, Evelyn began to regain her full consciousness. I knew once she absorbed the initial blow, it wouldn't take her long to start asking more questions. And she asked all the same questions that I had asked: Where are the old diaries? Were there any names in them? Where do the police think Charlie is now? What are they doing to catch him? How is Clara's mother? I answered to the best of my ability and listened as Evelyn spoke about the Clara she had known for the last few years.

"You know, I've been feeling like something bad was going to happen," Evelyn said as she stared out the window. "Clara acted so odd right before I left on this trip that it made me really nervous. She called me up out of the blue one night and said she needed to talk to me. I figured she wanted to talk about Laurel since they were new, so I told her to come on over.

"When she arrived, she was unusually fidgety and kept looking out the window at the street. I finally got her to sit, and that's when she told me she'd come to make sure I wasn't mad at her anymore." Evelyn took a breath. "I had no idea why she thought I was mad at her in the first place, so I asked her to explain." She maintained her stare through the window glass.

"And then…"

"She said the damn weirdest thing, Abby." Evelyn paused. "She said she knew I was mad at her or I wouldn't have gone out on her, but she never really figured out what she did to make me angry." Evelyn sighed. "We broke up over a year ago, and I thought I explained that it had nothing to do with her. It was my own shit that made me go." Evelyn confessed what I'd known all along and told Clara a hundred times.

"I thought she knew that I just wasn't good at long-term relationships," Evelyn said. "Apparently, she had it in her head that she somehow made me go out looking for a new partner. I was so sad and ashamed for making her feel that way that I didn't even know what to say." I put my hands on Evelyn's shoulders. I knew by the tone of her voice that she was again no longer in her body.

"Relax, Evvie." I massaged her a bit as she breathed deeply.

"Anyway, her whole point of coming over was to apologize to me and clear everything up before I left for Europe. She said she didn't want me leaving angry at her." Evelyn stopped. "Sounds like she knew she wasn't going to be here when I got home."

"Well, did you get through to her?" I asked, hoping Clara had not died thinking Evelyn was mad at her.

"I think so. I explained it all again and again. I told her I was even considering seeing a therapist to help figure out what makes me get bored and take off." I heard the progress Evelyn had made in the words she spoke. "I told Clara I loved her and was never mad at her. I also told her if anyone should be mad at anyone, then you should be mad at us both." She looked over her shoulder at me.

"I'm not mad at you guys either," I quickly assured her. "Clara knew that, too. I understand how things happen. Besides, moving from here turned out to be the best thing for me. I never would have left if Clara and I were still together." As I spoke, I was thinking how the death of a loved one makes all the little hurts of life seem so trivial.

"But if Clara had moved with you, maybe she would still be alive today."

"He would have found her no matter where she was." I was certain.

"You're right," Evelyn agreed. "He would have probably just killed you, too." She stopped at the sound of her own words. "Oh, man. He might be planning to do just that. He might be figuring on taking us all out one by one." Like Jeff and I, Evelyn had concluded that the man who killed Clara was not stopping there.

"Laurel has the old diaries?" Evelyn asked again, now fully alert.

"Yes," I said, "she put them in a safe place." I repeated Laurel's words. "What I didn't tell you is that the old diaries were also at least located, if not read." I tightened my grip on her.

"How do you know?"

"Laurel said the locations of the old diaries and the poems were switched. That could only mean that someone took them and put them back wrong," I tried to explain.

"I don't get it." Evelyn looked baffled.

"Yes, you do. You used to live there. Remember the two nightstands on either side of Clara's bed?" She slowly nodded.

"One for the diaries, one for the poems. Remember?" I knew she did, but like me, I doubted she ever gave them much thought. Clara's private words were off-limits to us.

39

"Well, after the robbery, Clara told Laurel that they had been switched around. In other words, whoever took the poems out of one stand and the diaries out of the other didn't think to remember which was in which," I clarified. "I believe it was Charlie, of course."

"So he's seen them all." Evelyn sounded more than a little concerned.

"Yes, it's likely that he read all of them."

"You said there were no names in them," she said hopefully.

"Get a grip, Evvie." I was not going to let her take herself to a place of false security. "Even a moron like Charlie could figure out who the writing was about by just remembering the dates." I actually believed at this point that Charlie was not at all stupid but extremely dangerous.

"So do the police know he might go after Laurel next?" Evelyn's words explained that she still wasn't getting it.

"Laurel would be the last person he would go after," I started. "I thought that same thing initially but not anymore. The fact that he tried to replace the diaries like he'd never seen them and the fact that he abandoned the current diary makes me believe he's more interested in the past than the present. Besides, Laurel is too close to the whole thing." I may have sounded confident in my theory, but I was grabbing at straws like everyone else.

"Have you seen Laurel to ask her any of this?" Evelyn's voice revealed her fear.

"No, we just got here and came straight to meet you."

"We?" Evelyn questioned.

"Jeff came with me."

"What's with you two?" Evelyn turned the focus on Jeff and me for a minute. "It wouldn't matter to me if you were lovers or something."

"God, Evvie. Like we need to have this discussion now." I began my usual monotone chant to explain my relationship with my housemate: "Jeff is my friend, we live together, we sleep apart, we've never been intimate unless you count sleeping with the same chick. Got it?" I waited for a response.

"Sorry, Abby."

The rest of the drive was relatively silent. We went straight to Laurel's apartment, and she let us in as if she were expecting us.

Chapter Seven

Laurel Greoux was not at all what I envisioned. She looked to be in her early twenties and was a full-figured five feet two inches. Her muddy-water brown hair was halfway down her back and completely eclipsed by her kaleidoscope green eyes. She and Evelyn hugged for several minutes, weeping and rocking in each other's arms. Pat nodded a hello to Laurel, then stood by the door. She was as silent and somber in her expression as she had been all morning.

"This is Abby. Abby Dunnigan." Evelyn introduced me, and I stood staring at Laurel. I was simultaneously astonished by her beauty and saddened by her disregard for her personal bearing. Clara's death must have sent her into a state of paralysis. She looked as though she had not bathed in days. Her disheveled hair and ragged, ill-fitting clothing gave her a look of vagrancy, but her facial expression disclosed a woman who was rock steady.

"You look just like the pictures Clara has of you from years ago." Laurel's voice was as sweet as it was sad.

"I'm sorry. I'm a little out of it," I said, looking through her for what Clara might have seen. "I'm still in shock." I reached out to hug Laurel as if it were a perfectly natural response. It was not. She tensed up at once, obviously sensing my hesitation, as we hugged awkwardly.

"Do you have a place to stay?" Laurel continued to be pleasant and forgiving.

"Jeff came with me, and we're staying out at my parents' place for a few days. Thanks for asking." I wanted to take back my initial reaction to her.

"I have an extra bed and a couch if you need it," she offered. "I'm so glad you could come."

Laurel's apartment was a contradiction of her rough-around-the-edges appearance. Small but immaculate, it was tastefully

41

decorated in bright colors and received a large amount of light from all sides. She invited us to the table for some tea.

Pat, who had previously been standing uneasily by the door, moved to the couch and began thumbing through the magazines in the rack. Evelyn and I sat at the dining table while Laurel went into the kitchen for tea. I watched as Pat picked up one magazine after another, opening each somewhere in the middle, flipping a few pages, then returning it to the rack for the next one in line. The whole time, she was staring at the door or her watch and never once at any of the magazine pages. Her pleated khaki pants were about an inch too short, and her blue oxford button-down shirt was untucking at various places around her brown leather belt. Though not at all heavy, she was a substantial woman with more muscle mass than she seemed to know what to do with.

I assumed Pat was excusing herself from our conversation for her own reasons and imagined that she didn't know Laurel or Clara well, if at all. Her behavior in general struck me as odd, but no one else seemed to care.

"The funeral will be tomorrow at noon," Laurel said as she emerged from the kitchen, tea tray in hand. "It's a closed-casket service, and the interment is for family and close friends only."

"Are we invited then?" I wasn't sure since Laurel had said Clara's mother and sister did not know of her relationships with women.

"You and Evelyn might be, but I've been asked not to attend either service." Laurel's disappointment showed through her grief.

"Who asked such a thing?" Evelyn beat me to the question.

"Clara's sister. She was involved in the police investigation, so she knows everything now. At the police station yesterday, she told me if I really cared anything about her sister that I would have respect enough not to disgrace her family at the funeral."

"If she knows everything, then why would the two of us be invited?" I was not following Laurel's logic.

"The only woman the family knows for sure Clara was with is me," she explained. "I told the police, and the police told her sister. I didn't want to lie about something that might help catch Clara's murderer. Some of the police think he might come back after me next." She sounded unconcerned.

"And you aren't afraid?"

"Not at all. I almost wish he would come after me because I'd love to see him face-to-face."

"Do you have a gun?" Evelyn looked very concerned.

"Yes, and I know how to use it." Laurel sounded as determined as she had on the phone when she assured me she would conceal the remaining diaries, which I remembered in that moment.

"Where are the old writings?" I asked at once. "Are they still safe?"

"Very. That's why Pat brought you two here now, so we can talk about them." Evvie and I looked at each other for clarity as Laurel got up and looked out the windows. She locked the door before returning to the table. Pat stood from her previously isolated position on the couch and moved toward the three of us as she began to speak.

"I'm the one responsible for making sure Laurel is safe." Pat looked as stoic and sounded as emotionless as she had the few other times she'd spoken.

"What?" Evelyn stood and looked at Pat.

"I'm a cop, Evelyn. I'm assigned to this case to protect Laurel and remove Charlie if he tries to come near her." She sounded very authoritarian. "I came to the airport because I knew I could catch both you and Abby there and we could all talk about this together." She pulled up a chair and sat straddling it with the chair backward. Evelyn sat down and looked absent.

"I guess that answers the question of your relationship." I turned as usual to sarcasm. "I thought you might be lovers, but it seems you don't really even know each other." I looked at Evelyn as I spoke.

"Apparently not," she said. "We met this summer. We've hung out a few times, but that's about it." Evelyn looked more stunned by the minute. "Pat's girlfriend, Julie, who was supposed to pick me up from the airport today, is on my softball team. That's why I didn't think about it when Pat showed up." She turned back toward Pat. "You and Julie told me you were a programmer. Why did you lie?"

"I had to," Pat defended herself. "Julie knows what I do for a living, but I can't really make it public knowledge. Do you understand?" She obviously did not enjoy being deceptive.

"You said Julie was working. Is that also a lie?"

"No, she is working, but I really wanted to pick you up because we needed to talk." Pat remained calm. "Since the other diaries don't technically exist to the police, I am in a tough position with you all."

Pat began to explain. "The police only know about the one diary they have—the diary found on Clara's body. When I was first assigned to this case, Laurel told me about the other ones and the fact that they had been tampered with on the promise that I would not tell my department. That information along with that promise has put me in a bad spot." She looked at Laurel with disapproval. "I wish I hadn't made that promise."

"But you did," Laurel spoke up.

"Yes, I did—so now I am in the lonely position of being the only cop who knows the full extent of the danger the rest of you are in." She looked at Evvie and me. "This situation is very serious."

"So what makes you so sure he's coming after us?" Evelyn asked. "He's already killed Clara. She's the one he was married to; what do we have to do with it?" I was a little amazed by Evelyn's naiveté.

"The whole prison experience drove Charlie to this point. He never heard from Clara the entire time he was locked up. He had years to get angry and vengeful toward her for abandoning him. He couldn't figure why she just ditched him, so he started asking questions. We know for sure that Charlie sent a buddy from prison to spy on Clara while he was still behind bars. He paid the guy to find out everything he could about her and what she was doing." Pat confirmed my suspicions that there was indeed a reason for us to fear Charlie.

"How do you know all this?" I asked.

"The man who spied for Charlie lives close by and came forward after hearing what happened. He never thought Charlie was going to kill anyone, and he feared he might be an accessory to murder because he had spied on Clara. He told us everything he knew and everything he told Charlie." She sighed. "His coming out of the shadows was a lucky break for you two."

"When was he watching Clara?" I asked, trying to understand how I could have been a part of anything he learned. I stopped seeing her over six years ago.

"During Evelyn and Clara's breakup," Pat answered, "about eighteen months ago."

"I still don't know what that has to do with me. I was living in Colorado."

"Your brother Alvin." Pat looked at me sympathetically. "I'm sorry, Abby, but it was Alvin who told Charlie's 'secret agent' about your affair with Clara."

The entire room went quiet. How could Alvin have been mixed up in all this? It didn't make sense. Before I could get enough complete thoughts together to make a sentence, Pat filled in the blanks.

"When the man Charlie hired went back and told him about Clara's lesbian affairs, Charlie went crazy. He immediately realized that your relationship with Clara had also likely been sexual." Pat was talking to me directly. "He sent the guy back to verify his suspicions. The man started attending Alvin's church, and Alvin befriended him." I listened in astonishment to Pat's story. I could not believe Charlie knew anyone smart enough to pull off such a deception.

"So what? This guy walks up to my brother and asks if his sister is the dyke who dated Clara Stokes? How did he get this information from Alvin?" I was sick at the possibility of my brother's willing betrayal.

"Something like that," Pat nodded. "The man said he just talked to Alvin at church. Pretty soon they realized they both knew Charlie, then the conversation moved to Clara." She spared me the exact details.

"So Alvin just painted a target on my head." I was very upset. "Does he know what his big mouth has done?" I wondered if the police had told my brother what danger he had placed me in.

"The police don't know enough to know if they think you are in danger," Pat explained. "They don't realize that Charlie read all those diaries and knows what a fool you two made out of him. I think killing Clara might have been enough for him if he hadn't found those books. Seeing his wife's passionate diary entries about being with other women while he rotted in prison fueled his anger.

Worse yet, learning that you were sleeping with Clara right under his nose must have been quite a blow to his ego, Abby." She looked at me to see if I understood. I understood completely.

"So if my theory is right, he could try and get to you while you're in town." She paused. "That isn't going to happen," she assured me.

"So why isn't the rest of the police force over here right now watching my butt?" I was beginning to feel like a victim.

"They are all over this neighborhood." Pat looked at me with a comforting expression. "Every officer in this county is looking for Charlie Stokes. It's obvious why I was assigned to be a more personal contact with you all, but that doesn't mean I'm the only one watching your butts."

I relaxed a little. "So then they are aware that Evvie and I are targets?" This was all too confusing.

"They're aware it's a possibility, Abby, but without knowing about the other diaries, they don't know the whole story. If Laurel would hand them over for review, we could possibly establish a pattern Charlie might follow by knowing what he read." Pat was still hoping Laurel would relent and give the diaries to the police.

Evelyn had not moved or spoken much in the last few minutes. She was obviously paralyzed by her anxiety. I, on the other hand, needed to know more. I did not appreciate feeling helpless.

"I don't get what makes you think the diaries have any bearing on Charlie's behavior. He already knew Clara was sleeping with women before he read them, so what difference do they make?" I could not see her point.

Pat looked at Laurel, then at me. "Are you sure you want to hear this?" she asked.

"Why does everyone ask me that question? Of course I want to hear everything. I'm not going to stay shielded in ignorance and wait for that bastard to come and kill me, too." I raised my voice.

Laurel left the room as Pat began to speak.

"In the diary found on Clara's body, there were various entries circled or underlined. Clara's writing was very descriptive and a bit melodramatic, as you may know." She paused.

"No, I really don't know. I never read the diaries." I waited for more.

"Well, it was." She sighed. "In one of the more detailed entries, Clara wrote about her fear that Charlie would be released soon and that she didn't know how she would tell him she wouldn't be with him anymore. She said she'd have to figure it out, though, because he'd have to bash in her head before she'd let him fuck her again." There was another long pause. "That's exactly what he did." Pat stared hard at me. "Charlie symbolically acted out Clara's written words before, during, or after he murdered her. I think he'll do the same thing with you and Evelyn if he gets the chance."

I didn't want to hear any more. I felt the contents of my stomach rising while memories of patching Clara up after Charlie had beaten her flashed through my head.

As soon as I could speak, I called Jeff at my parents' house to tell him where I was. He said he had been talking to my father quite a lot about our business and living in Colorado.

"He thinks we're involved, Abby," Jeff whispered.

"Good. Let him think that. Let them all think it," I instructed, still nauseated. "It'll make everything simpler. Besides, we have way too much to worry about to be concerned with my parents right now. If they think I'm straight and it makes them happy, good." I'd never had such an attitude toward my sexuality. I'd never tried to cover it up before, except in the Army. I wasn't necessarily trying to cover it up now; I just wasn't striving to make an issue out of it.

"When are you coming back?" he asked in a concerned tone.

"About an hour. Tell Mother not to fry whatever it is she's cooking."

He laughed. "Too late."

"Oh, well." I really wasn't hungry. "I have a lot to tell you. See you in a bit." I hung up the phone.

Evelyn and Laurel were sitting quietly on the couch, and Pat was still at the dining table. I sat next to her.

"Do you really think Charlie will come after us?"

"I think it's highly possible. He's a time bomb. He is definitely going to try and get even for what he sees as the wrongs done to him." Pat knew what she was talking about, and although I didn't care for her callous exterior, I was thinking I might be able to trust her.

"Where would be the safest place for us to stay?" I asked for Evvie, as well, since she was obviously not able to speak.

"In my opinion, all of you should stay together while you're in town. He wants you alone if he plans to carry out anything he read in the diaries. It won't be the same to get you all at once. It also won't be as easy," she explained.

"Evvie, did you hear that? We need to stay together."

"You can all stay here," Laurel offered again.

"I don't know," I said. "I have to see my family at least for a day, so why don't you all stay out at their place? My dad has an arsenal of weapons and half a dozen barking dogs, so I don't think even Charlie could get in to hurt us."

"What will you tell them?" Evelyn spoke at last.

"That we're all a little nervous and need to be together. Anyway, my guess is they are so excited about their idea that Jeff is my boyfriend, they'll ignore the rest of you."

We picked up a car from Evelyn's house and we drove to my parents' with Pat following along. Sure enough, my parents completely ignored Evelyn, Laurel, and Pat and focused all their attention on Jeff and me.

Lying in bed that night, I focused on Laurel. She didn't show the emotions of a woman who'd recently found her lover's bloody and bastardized body. I was deep in my almost contemptuous thoughts when I heard the sound of her stifled crying. I listened to Laurel's sobs until they were drowned out by my own grievous cries of guilt, remorse, and disgrace.

Evelyn, Jeff, and I went to the funeral service the next morning. Laurel, as requested, stayed with Pat while we were gone. The small church was packed with sympathetic community members, family, old friends, and curious onlookers. My family attended, as well. It was the first time I had seen my twin brother, Alvin, in years. He appeared hollow and listless, and I did not speak to him.

Clara's mother looked ready for the grave herself. Small and withered, she sat with an unbelieving expression throughout the service. Evvie and I both hugged her as we filed past the coffin on the way out the door. She did not utter a word to either of us, which was fine with me since I had never felt so speechless.

We met Pat and Laurel back at Laurel's apartment after the service. The apartment was full of lighted candles and burning incense. Laurel sat in the middle of the floor surrounded by memories of her departed lover. There were photos and cards, letters and trinkets; it must have been an intense romance.

She did not move to acknowledge us when Pat let us into the apartment. Evelyn and I immediately and instinctually joined Laurel on the floor for the ritual of Clara's passage from this world to the next. As we sat among the glass, metal, and paper remnants of what was Laurel's lover, we all knew what was happening. Clara was being buried in the ground at the very moment we were lifting her to the heavens with our thoughts and energy.

The diaries were on the floor, within arm's reach. I wanted to pick one up and read from any page. I wanted more than ever to know Clara again as I had when we were new and in love. Out of respect for Laurel, I resisted my urge.

We spent the day in silence, without electric light or manufactured noise. No television, no radio, no stereo—nothing but the sounds of long sighs and muted crying. Remarkably, Pat, while not a participant, was not at all disruptive or disrespectful. She didn't make a noise or a move the entire time we sat our deathwatch.

Some time after dark, Laurel got up and began slowly and systematically blowing out the candles, speaking inaudibly before each blow. When she reached for the last lighted candle, she asked if Evelyn and I would like to blow it out with her. We nodded. She brought it over and sat with us again.

The scene of three people amid the light of a single dim candle is burned in my memory as my last picture of Clara. Tears flowed unchecked as Laurel lifted the candle to her lips. Evvie and I leaned into its glow, and we all blew. Clara was gone.

Chapter Eight

We woke to the sound of Pat's ringing cell phone. It was sometime after daybreak but not long. We had all opted to sleep on the floor in the living room of Laurel's apartment. I was curled up between Evelyn and Jeff, Laurel was in the corner next to the wall, and Pat was still sitting on the couch. I wondered if maybe she had sat there all night.

Pat was on the phone for at least twenty minutes, mostly listening. The news was not good. The man who had been Charlie's informant had been found dead in his car only hours earlier. He had been shot in the head and his tongue had been cut out and placed in his hand. A copy of the first newspaper article reporting Clara's death was found in his other hand. One sentence in the article was circled. It read: *Police are searching for the victim's estranged husband in connection with the murder.*

"This is way more information than any of you should have, so don't communicate with anyone about this case," Pat talked to our startled faces. For the second time in days, we'd been jolted from our sleep by news of an appalling murder.

"He's like a serial killer." Jeff broke the silence. "He's planning to kill every single person involved in this mess with Clara, isn't he?" He stared at Pat for answers.

"Look, you're right to think this is not just a small town criminal who got mad and offed his wife. This guy is really sick and particularly driven to get revenge. He may be a serial killer. He may be anything, but right now we need to focus less on what he is and more on what we can do to keep the three of you safe," Pat said to Evvie, Laurel, and me as she dialed a number on her cellular phone. We all sat with the expressions of those wondering what's coming next.

"Massey, this is Pat. Can you guys come in around nine? Yes, I'll clear everything by then. Thanks." She ended her conversation and looked back at us, still staring at her.

"I need to know who else might be in danger, Laurel. You have got to give me the diaries or at least fill in the blanks for me. I'm breaking my promise if you don't tell me every goddamn woman Clara ever slept with." Laurel's sleepy eyes filled with tears as Pat held her solemn gaze into Laurel's face.

"Wait a minute, Pat," Evelyn spoke up. "You're not going to get anything done by bullying us, so knock it off." She sounded ready for a fight. "Laurel has been through enough, and it's me and Abby who can answer your damn questions anyway." Evvie got up and stormed to the bathroom, slamming the door.

"That's true, Pat," I said. "We know every woman Clara was ever with, so you don't need the diaries. Why don't you try and be a little more sympathetic, okay?" I went to Laurel who was crying in her blanket and held her in my arms. Evvie emerged from the bathroom and joined me on the floor with Laurel.

Pat stared coldly at us as she spoke. "You two just think you know everything there is to know about Clara's affairs."

"What are you talking about?" Evvie asked. "Between Abby and me, we've been with Clara continuously for a good nine years. What could you possibly mean by that?" Evvie was angry, and it was obvious.

"Can we all get along here?" Pat answered Evvie's question with a question of her own. "I don't want to argue with you. I'm sorry, Laurel, please forgive my insensitivity. I just got really angry that he killed another person and extremely worried about who might be next." She looked sincere.

"So what don't we know?" Evvie wasn't giving up.

"There was another woman neither of you knew about," Pat began. "I need to start back a little further, though, before I tell you about her." She had our undivided attention.

"I'm an FBI agent. I told you I was a cop, but you didn't ask what kind. I'm working with other FBI agents and local law enforcement agencies on this case. Less than twenty-four hours after Clara was found murdered, a woman in Georgia was murdered also. Normally, that would not bring in the FBI, but the circumstances surrounding the murder in Georgia changed everything. The other murdered woman had been very close to Clara Stokes at one time. Turns out, they were lovers, but what tied the two murders together is why we were brought in." She drew a long breath.

"The woman was bludgeoned to death like Clara, then raped, but the real link was the piece of paper found lying on her body. It was a page from the same diary found on Clara's body. Apparently, this was a woman Clara had been involved with long before Charlie ever went to prison. The two women had contacted each other only recently. She and Clara had plans to see each other soon, and Clara wrote all about it in her diary. She wrote that this had been her first lover and first true emotional bond. She said in the diary pages that this woman had been her first chance to taste freedom from Charlie. Hell, she even wrote about experiencing her first orgasm with this gal. Charlie never would have known whom Clara was talking about, though, if she hadn't written the one line that gave it all away. That line was circled on the page found at the crime scene." Pat stopped talking and shook her head.

I was struck mute along with the rest of my friends. I thought I was Clara's first lover. I thought we'd done all the things Pat just said Clara wrote in her diary about the murdered woman. I thought I knew everything about Clara's past, but this woman was obviously before my time, and Clara had conveniently left her out of our conversations. This feeling of betrayal swallowed up in terror and sadness was unknown to me. Tears streamed down my cheeks.

"What was the line?" Jeff asked Pat. He was apparently getting all the information he could from this conversation while the rest of us sat in shock and disbelief.

"It was something about Charlie and his brother giving them no other choice by constantly leaving them alone together and afraid." Pat either pretended to forget or really couldn't remember the exact wording. "Anyway, the woman had been Charlie's brother's wife. She and Clara used to stay together while Charlie and his brother binged for days. This all happened shortly after Clara and Charlie first married. The brother died in a car wreck years ago, and the woman moved to Georgia soon after his death. Clara lost touch but apparently had recently located her former lover and sister-in-law." Pat was still shaking her head. "Bad timing for the woman that Clara found her and wrote what she did, when she did."

The doubts as to whether Charlie was a serial killer were gone. He had killed three people in the span of one week, and we were in grave danger. I was finished thinking I knew what was next and finished believing I had known Clara. I knew the Clara that I knew, Evvie knew the Clara she was close to, and Laurel knew yet another Clara, but it was painfully evident that we collectively didn't know the whole person.

"Give her the diaries, Laurel," I spoke softly but resolutely. "You have to protect anyone else who might be in danger." I tried to sound as compassionate as I did firm.

"She's right, Laurel, at least let's see if there are any more torn-out pages. That would be a sign that more killings are imminent," Evelyn added.

"That's a valuable thought, Evvie." Jeff joined the conversation. "If he plans to kill again and didn't copy all the pages, he's bound to have torn the ones he needed for later use."

Pat remained silent as we began guiding Laurel through a thought process that I hoped would result in the surrender of the diaries. Laurel wasn't even looking at us.

"Laurel, it's okay to give them up. Clara wouldn't want anyone else to die because of what she wrote." As I spoke, I suddenly realized why Laurel was so adamantly opposed to betraying Clara's trust and need for privacy. She had known how personal the diaries were to Clara and had read them anyway, without permission. It was guilt and the need to compensate for her own infraction that drove her to hold on tightly to the sacred documents.

"I can't" was all Laurel would say, her head buried in her blanket.

"Laurel," I remained calm. "Let's go in the kitchen and talk a minute."

"That's okay, Abby, we can all go out of here for a minute." Jeff knew me so well. He was already up, motioning the others to follow him. I could hear them beginning to make coffee as I sat on the floor with Laurel, wondering what to say next.

"You know I can't give those diaries to the police." Laurel looked at me with the hope I would understand. "Clara never wanted anyone to read her personal stuff," she added.

"No, but she also never wanted to hurt anyone." I reminded Laurel how Clara was. "She would rather you give them up than see anyone else harmed."

"I feel horrible." Laurel was crying full force. "I let her down in so many ways," she lamented. "I wasn't there when she needed me."

"Sure you were, Laurel. Clara was crazy about you. She told me on the phone the last time I spoke with her that she was excited about her new relationship."

"Maybe she wasn't talking about me." Laurel looked up briefly. "She was planning to see that woman from Georgia, even though it scared me. Why couldn't she just let her go?" Laurel was crying. "That's why I started to read the diaries. I knew she was still interested in her by the way they talked on the phone. She wouldn't tell me anything."

"So you knew about the woman?"

"Yes," Laurel nodded. "Clara said right after we got together that she had recently located an old friend and was planning to see her. She didn't say it was an old lover, but I just knew. When I asked her about the woman, she denied anything but friendship. I listened in on a few of their conversations, though, and they were definitely more than friends."

"So did you tell Clara you were a little uneasy about her visiting the woman?" I asked.

"I told her that I was insecure about the whole thing, but she said I was just young and paranoid. She also said we were only dating and not to get too serious," Laurel told me. "I'm twenty-two years old, and she was forty. I tried to understand, but I was so in love with her that it was hard to accept what she was saying. I read the diaries to try and know what she was really thinking."

"Did you learn?" I, too, wanted insight.

"Yes, I learned that she loved me very much, but I also learned that she had never forgotten any other lover she ever had. She seemed to hold tightly to the past, and that's why her meeting the woman from Georgia scared me so badly." Laurel paused. "That was the last thing we talked about before I left her apartment angry the day she was killed. I confronted her with the truth about her friend, and she accused me of being the one who moved the diaries and poems around in the nightstands." Laurel was speaking very quietly. "I told her I had not touched those diaries but that I might if she didn't tell me the truth. I'm ashamed of myself for the way I talked to her that day. I wish I had just trusted her." She cried harder again.

"Most anyone would have reacted the same way you did, Laurel. It's hard to trust someone when their actions and words are polar opposites." I wanted to reassure her.

"But you never read her personal stuff. Neither did Evelyn," she reminded me.

"But we never had any reason to doubt Clara." I was arguing a side I didn't take. Laurel knew it at once.

"Just say it, Abby. I shouldn't have read the diaries. I know I shouldn't have, but I did, and I can't take it back. I just needed answers. I can't give them to the police because Clara will never forgive me if I break her trust twice."

I knew Laurel was young and inexperienced, but at that moment, I saw what Clara must have been drawn to in her: a strong-willed and determined woman with the potential to bloom into anything imaginable. I realized rapidly that while she was vulnerable and frightened, she was still incredibly savvy.

"Okay, Laurel. You were wrong to read Clara's personal stuff. You were wrong to eavesdrop, and you were wrong to assume the worst of the friendship Clara had with her old lover. You acted out of love and concern for your relationship with Clara, though. Maybe it was not the best action and maybe it was bad judgment, but your heart was in the right place." I rubbed her shoulder. "I would have done the same thing if I were you. You said it; you're twenty-two years old. That's not a lot of time to practice making mistakes and learning from them, so give yourself credit for trying. Clara did love you and you did love her. That's all that matters."

I paused and stared at her. "It's sad that you argued with her right before she died. It's horrible, but people argue, then things happen. That doesn't mean the two experiences are in any way connected." I looked deep into Laurel's face.

"It doesn't?" She looked like a child.

"No. It doesn't. You had no way of knowing Clara's fate. Laurel, listen to me. Keeping the diaries from the police might kill another person. You have to let them go." I held her gaze.

"They're in between the mattress and box spring on my bed," she said, dropping her head. "You can read them, but you can't turn them over to the police until you have gone through them all."

"Why me?"

"Because that's what you want."

She was right that I wanted to read them all, though I didn't know why.

We hugged and cried for another twenty minutes. I looked at my watch and realized the person who had been on the phone with Pat earlier would be arriving in less than half an hour. I thanked Laurel and told her again that she made the right choice. Then I went to the kitchen to tell the others they could return.

Chapter Nine

The kitchen was barely big enough for the three adults milling around trying to calm one another and make breakfast. Pat was poised on the counter with a bowl of cereal and a cup of hot chocolate while Evelyn and Jeff stood over the stove, staring at the French toast in the pan. I stood just inside the door and sighed heavily.

"What happened?" Evvie asked first.

"She agreed to give the diaries to me but under the condition that I read them all before I give them to the police."

"That could take days, Abby." Jeff was not pleased. "We may not have days."

"It's better than nothing." Pat looked up. "When do you get them?"

"I suppose anytime I want them," I answered hesitantly. "I'll start reading immediately and looking for any torn-out pages." I was thinking out loud. "I read pretty fast, and I can give them to you one at a time as I finish."

"Good." Pat accepted the arrangement. "Will you be okay reading them?"

I was a little taken aback by the concern I heard in Pat's usually stoic tone. "I can handle it," I assured her.

"Abby," Pat spoke softly, "I already told these guys, but I need to tell you—I'm sorry I seem so cold and hard about all this. I don't mean to be that way, but it sort of goes with the job. Understand?" She looked at me as kindly as she had yet.

"I understand dissociation very well, Pat," I said, recalling how the Army had taught me to detach. "Just try and be a little more sympathetic to Laurel, would you? She's young and this is overwhelming." I turned to leave the room. No one else spoke.

I went to the bedroom where Laurel was waiting to give me the diaries. She handed me the plastic bag with tears in her eyes.

"You can read them in here if you want," she offered. "I think you'll want to be alone."

"Thank you." I sat the bag on the bed and opened it.

"They're all dated on the spine by year." Laurel reached into the bag and pulled out a book. "See, this one is 1995."

The first book was dated 1978, the year Clara married Charlie. There were twenty books in the bag, and I was wondering how I was going to get through them all quickly enough to help anyone in danger when Laurel again sensed my thoughts.

"There's not much missing from the first ten years of writings. Clara was writing in such code back then that they really don't even make sense." She picked through the bag for a particular year. "Here." She handed me a book. "Start here."

It was 1988, the year I met Clara. I held it as gently as a mother holds a baby.

"What about the woman from Georgia? Is there anything in the early years about her?" I wanted to know everything.

"Nothing that makes any sense or would be of any use," Laurel said. "It was Clara's current diary that told all about her," she refreshed my memory about what Pat had reported.

"Start with this one and go forward." Laurel pointed to the book I was holding.

"Thank you." I wiped my eyes and sat on the edge of the bed as she left the room.

I looked at my watch. The person named Massey would be arriving in less than ten minutes, as Pat had instructed. I caressed and rocked, kissed, and smelled the diary labeled 1988. It felt like a child I had lost but was now returned. I could not understand the gamut of emotion I was overtaken by as I sat rocking and sobbing.

"Abby," Pat's voice broke my trance. "You need to come out and join us for a little while." She was speaking softly. "You can return to your reading after we all talk for a bit."

I tucked the diary back into the bag with the others and returned them all to their former hiding place. I wiped my eyes one more time, fussed with my clothes, and tried to stand up straight. I caught a glimpse of my reflection in the mirror as I approached the door and what I saw forced me to look again. On the second look, the figure changed to the reflection of a swollen-eyed, haggard woman, but the image I saw first stuck like glue in my mind. I had seen the reflection of a soldier. I shook my head and blinked a few times to regain full consciousness, but the soldier was gone and I was standing where she had been.

The doorbell rang as I returned to the living room to join my companions. No one else moved as Pat walked to the door and stood beside it. There was a series of knocks followed by a male voice. Pat peered through the peephole, then opened the door, and three men entered. She seemed relieved to see them all, and they spoke privately by the door for a few minutes before acknowledging the rest of our group.

"Everyone," Pat turned to us, "this is Scott Massey, Marc Jaquez, and Ted Cimino." She pointed to each man as she spoke his name. "We are the entire team assigned to this case, so it's important that you all know us at least by sight." The men nodded in our direction, then moved to take seats.

"We need to talk to all of you about what's going on with this investigation." Massey, the shortest but by far the most muscular of the three dark-haired men, spoke as the others settled into their seats. Massey looked like a body builder. His arms were as big as my thighs, and his neck looked to be just an upward extension of his massive shoulders. "Three people are dead from what appears to be a well-planned killing spree. We have no leads as to the whereabouts of Charlie Stokes, and as far as we're concerned, he doesn't plan to stop until he is either captured or has finished his self-appointed mission. Our profiler believes he won't be finished until he has killed everyone who was ever involved with his late wife. We understand that means all of you." He looked around the room, then noticed Jeff. "Except you, I suppose. Why are you still here?" He was looking at Pat but talking to Jeff.

Jeff spoke before Pat had the chance. "I'm here because I chose to be," he snapped at the man whose name was perfect for his physique, "and I'm not leaving."

"Jeff is very involved in this whole case, Massey," Pat spoke up. "He's Abby's roommate and knows everything going on, so I feel at this point that he is at equal risk."

"I see," Massey sighed. "You're probably right."

"So what about our families?" Evelyn spoke for us all. "Are they also at risk?"

"We don't think so," Massey began, "but we aren't taking chances. Each of your immediate families has a security team watching them. Except yours." He looked at Jeff again.

"I don't have any family, so don't bother trying to find someone to protect." Jeff was nonchalant.

"Abby, your father refused a guard on his property, so we're watching the house the best we can from the public road. We think your family will be fine because you aren't close to them anyway. Charlie knows that. It's your brother Alvin we're concerned about because he was friends with Charlie's informant." I felt sick.

"Is Charlie going to kill Alvin?" I didn't know if I wanted the answer.

"Again we don't think so because you aren't close to him. As far as we know, he had no connection to Clara, but the fact that he was a friend of the dead informant is cause for concern. Alvin agreed to protection for his family's sake." I breathed a sigh of relief. I knew from my parents that Alvin was leaving soon on a church missionary trip to South America. I knew his wife and children would be at risk without him. Maybe he would cancel the trip and stay with his family. I doubted it, though, since the church was his primary family and God was his bodyguard.

"Laurel, your mother is being protected, and, Evelyn, your family is under surveillance, as well. We don't think he will even go near them, but we need to take precautions." Massey sounded competent and genuinely interested in everyone's safety. "As long as you're all together, we feel that you, too, will be safe." He paused. "We just don't think here is necessarily the place for you to stay."

"There's an awful lot of 'thinking and feeling' going on in your plan, Mr. Massey. Do you know anything for sure?" From the tone of it, Evvie's fear was turning to anger.

"We know for sure that Charlie wishes to kill you." He glared at Evvie. "We know for sure that we are going to prevent that from occurring."

"Oh, good, another charming FBI agent to spend an indefinite amount of time with. How about you two?" She looked at the other two agents sitting quietly. "Are you equally as personable?"

"Ms. Mitchell," Agent Cimino, the least imposing of the three goons who'd recently entered our lives, answered, "I'm aware that this is very stressful for you, but our job isn't really to be friendly, it's to keep you all alive." He was polite and his tone was warm. "I'm sorry for all you've been through, but we are here to help. Let us."

"I think when we all get a little more comfortable with each other, it'll get easier," Agent Jaquez added. He was a gruff-looking forty-something-year-old man wearing tight Levis and a black T-shirt. "We know a lot about you and you know little about us, and that's never a comfortable place to start with a stranger." He was right. It occurred to me that Agent Cimino had called Evelyn by her name, even though she had not introduced herself to him.

"What happens now?" Jeff cut to the chase. "Where are we all going to be sent if we can't stay here?"

"We're working that issue now," Agent Massey answered. "We'll let you know as soon as we have secured a location."

The tension eased slightly as we began discussing the investigation and the factors involved in tracking down Charlie Stokes. We learned that the FBI knew a frightening amount of detail about our personal lives and yet knew nothing about us as people. We were interviewed separately by each agent to provide as much information as we possibly could about Clara, Charlie, and the whole messed-up situation. Although the current diary from which pages kept turning up on corpses was mentioned several times, nothing was said about any other writings.

By the late afternoon, we were all exhausted.

Agents Jaquez and Cimino returned from the grocery and a local restaurant as the rest of us were about to fall asleep on the floor in the living room. In my half-asleep state, I wondered if I had dreamed the entire day since I was lying in the same place that I was when it began.

Chapter Ten

Agent Cimino was sitting on the couch reading a book when I stirred awake from my pallet on the floor. He looked to be in his late thirties and had a pleasant face. His eyes were small and round, and his thick black hair was combed to one side. I was the first of the captives to awaken. There was no sign of the other three agents.

I washed my face in the bathroom and started a pot of coffee as quietly as I could. Agent Cimino entered the kitchen as I was scrounging for food in the cupboards.

"Are you feeling better?" He smiled and looked as though he meant it.

"Yes, thanks. I'm more rested and clearheaded."

"I hate to see anyone go through this horror, Ms. Dunnigan. We don't mean to make things worse for you, you know." He looked at me with so much empathy that I patted his arm.

"I'm sure you don't," I allowed. "It's just such an invasion of a person's life to be forced into this situation." I tried to articulate what I was feeling. "I mean, I guess any of us who wanted to leave could, but we're all too terrified to do that. So we're voluntary prisoners." I shrugged my shoulders. "What else can we do?"

"There aren't many options, Ms. Dunnigan." Agent Cimino shook his head. "You're safer with us and each other than you'd be anywhere else."

"Call me Abby," I insisted. "I know I'm safer here, but Charlie will never let himself be captured easily. He will wait it out like he did in jail, until we are forced back out on our own. That's when he'll prey. He's too smart to make his move while we're all here." I knew what I was saying.

"You're right. That's why we have to find him before he comes after one of you. We have to go after him."

"But you said you have no leads and no clues as to where he's hiding."

"We're a huge organization, Abby, and he's one man; we will find him."

I was not convinced.

"And what if you don't?" I had to ask.

"We will." He wouldn't budge.

"I know you guys know about the diaries by now, so why hasn't anyone mentioned them?" My curiosity and distrust of his government-run operation got the best of me.

"We didn't want to upset Ms. Greoux to the point that she refused to give them to us again," he explained. "Have you read any of them yet?"

"You knew all along about the diaries, didn't you?" I asked rhetorically. "How are we supposed to trust you guys if you lie all the time?"

"We don't lie all the time, but this was too significant a piece of evidence to keep a secret. Pat kept it too long as it was. She told us yesterday, but we made no move to forcibly take them out of respect for Ms. Greoux. We do need them, though, Abby. We don't want to get our next look at them through Charlie. The only other missing pages from the current diary are from the time when Mrs. Stokes was beginning to date Ms. Greoux. Since she is safely here with us, we have to believe the next victim is likely to be someone from the past diaries—the ones you are holding."

I started to say that the next victim had to be one of us because there had been no others, but then I remembered the woman in Georgia. I remembered at that moment that I couldn't trust what I thought I knew about Clara anymore. The pain in my heart started all over again.

"I read fast," I promised. "I have to read them before I give them to you because that was the deal I made with Laurel."

I retreated to the bedroom where the diaries were stashed soon after breakfast. I was forced by our security patrol, now three strong and missing only Pat, to leave the door open slightly while I was alone in the room.

I wanted more than anything to know what else Clara had kept hidden from me or lied to me about. I wanted to understand why she told me I was her first true love and first female lover. It made no sense. I wouldn't have loved her any less. It wouldn't have been any less beautiful, so why did she lie?

As I positioned myself on the bed with the 1988 diary, I felt only fear. Fear that I wouldn't understand anyway even after reading, fear that I would only be sadder and more disappointed at what I now imagined to be scores of other women. The first pages of the diary were missing, but when I turned to what was now the first page, all my angst dissipated at once.

Her writing was like a symphony to my eyes. The next twenty or so pages were poems and song lyrics. I knew they were written for me. As I read each one carefully and rhythmically, I heard Clara's voice in my head speaking the words my eyes were absorbing into my soul. I slipped back in time to the all-night restaurant we used to frequent and the feeling of electricity in the air between us as we sat, drinking coffee and feeding on each other.

When I reached the last page of the songs and poems, I was transported to the night I first read the words now in front of my eyes as we lay together in her bed.

You study the bruises. Tears in your eyes, my hands crushed in yours, you plead leave. Please leave. It hurts me when he hurts you. I stop, consider.

Before you touched me, something rose in my chest and reached toward you. Lying on your shirt in the moon, I felt the kiss before our lips met, my body on fire and lifting, longing for you. The first time you placed your hand between my legs, over that thin layer of cloth, everything inside me melted and poured toward you.

After we touch, I trace my fingers along my own smooth thighs, the sharp bone of a hip, discovering the body I never knew was here, the flesh you loved into being, the skin I can no longer hate because you have been here, treasuring me.

I wanted to continue treasuring my time with Clara. I could no longer search for answers that would rewrite this and all the other precious scenes we shared. I wanted no part of knowing anything that would further damage how I remembered my sweet Clara. I closed the book.

Laurel understood why I could not be the one to read the diaries. She handed them over to Pat willingly.

There were other missing pages throughout the 1988 book. Laurel had known it from the start, but the rest of us continued to hope there were none. Charlie had also taken a number of pages from the book dated 1991, the year Evelyn and Clara became lovers. All the remaining years were missing at least a few pages.

The rest of the day was spent discussing our next move. Jeff and I had been in South Carolina for a mere three days, but it felt like an eternity. I phoned my family around 4:00 p.m. to see if they were all right. They were not exactly warm but appeared to be safe. My mother did manage to ask if Jeff was taking good care of me. I told her yes and that we were leaving town soon to flee a possible encounter with Charlie.

My father, listening in from the extension phone, chimed in. "Well, Abigail, we all have to answer for our sins, and I hope this has taught you a lesson you'll never forget. A man goes crazy over his wife. A man can't be anything but crazy when his wife carries on like that." He was referring to Clara's lesbian escapades. "You better fall to your knees and thank your God that Jeff came along to save you. You better pray your pals there find the same kind of healing and forgiveness before they all end up dead and burning for eternity." He sighed and cleared his throat at the same time. "Call us when you get home."

I have no idea how I answered him or how the call was terminated. I sat dumbfounded, receiver in my lap, for over an hour.

Laurel talked briefly with her mother after I got off the phone while Evvie decided not to call her family. She rationalized it by the fact that the less contact she had with them, the safer they were likely to be. The house was silent the rest of the afternoon.

By the end of the day, we were all once again assembled together in Laurel's living room. Pat informed us that a safe place had been secured and that we would leave the following day for a location that could not be disclosed. I could tell that there was a much more complex plan laid out than what she was revealing. Tension was building and patience was thinning, even among the agents.

"This is ridiculous." Jeff broke the silence at last. "You're moving us somewhere and you won't tell us where or for how long." He didn't like the concept of blind faith any more than the rest of us.

"You don't have to go." Agent Jaquez glared at him.

Pat, along with Agents Massey and Cimino answered the glare of their comrade with one equally harsh. "Yes, he does, Marc." Pat was the first to defend Jeff's right to be held hostage. "He is as much a target as the girls now. We've been over this...." She caught herself and stopped. The room remained quiet for the rest of the evening.

Charlie was not going to come after any of us as long as we had the escort of the FBI. That was the one thing I felt absolutely certain about. As I lay on the floor attempting to sleep, I knew the only way they would catch Charlie would be to bait him. I was betting the agents knew that, as well, and I wondered which of us would be their minnow.

By morning, I knew I was the likely candidate. I had military training and combat experience. Of the group, I had the best chance of surviving an attack and the least good sense to say no to the agents when they asked for my help. I didn't give them the chance.

It was remarkably easy to sell Pat on the idea of me helping set Charlie up for capture. I knew ten minutes into the conversation that I had already been their unanimous selection. She never admitted it, though. We agreed that the others would accompany two of the agents to the safe house they were preparing for our group. Jeff insisted on staying with me, and I doubt the president of the United States could have made him change his mind.

The plans were set: Evelyn and Laurel would remain in the protective hands of Agents Massey and Jaquez while Jeff and I returned to our house in Colorado with Pat and Agent Cimino. I insisted it be Agent Cimino and not one of the others because I felt a kinship to him after our kitchen conversation. At least his heart was in the right place. I felt certain that Evvie and Laurel would be safer without us, and I knew they would feel relieved by the hope of capturing Charlie.

By six o'clock in the morning, the small apartment was alive with activity. There was a lot to be accomplished in the few hours before noon, the time we were all scheduled to go our separate ways. We needed to pack, make phone calls, and prepare Laurel's house for an undetermined absence of occupancy. Though we had all been assembled for less than a week, it was a sad parting for everyone involved.

Pat, the only local agent, left around 8:30 a.m. for home to see Julie and pack for the trip. She was to meet us at the airport by 1:30 p.m. Once the packing was completed, I sat with Laurel and Evvie on Laurel's bed to say goodbye for a while.

"This feels kind of like when you went away to the Gulf." Evelyn spoke quietly and looked appreciatively into my eyes.

"Yeah, it does." I felt the same emptiness in my soul. "And the result will be the same, too...No casualties allowed."

"Oh, Abby, how can you say that? You were a *big* casualty of that war." Evvie shook her head in shame as she spoke. "You, your relationship, your friendship with me, your damaged soul; they were all casualties." She was whispering. "Why did you volunteer to be a casualty again? Why don't we all just stay together and wait this out? No one needs to go back to work. You know my grandparents left me enough money to support us all for a really long time. Let's just stay here forever."

I put my arms around her shoulders and pulled her into me. "Our friendship was not a casualty. I forgave you long ago. I love you like I always did, and I will love you forever just like I promised you." I was crying, too. "Evvie, if we try and wait out a man who sat years in prison planning this, we will be waiting the rest of our lives. I refuse to be a prisoner to that bastard forever. If he wants me so badly, he can come and get me." I didn't recognize the voice coming from my own lips.

Laurel joined the embrace by wrapping her arms around us both. "No wonder Clara loved you two so much," she began. "Abby, she said you were the strongest and most fearless of them all. She called you her hero."

I chuckled a little at the triggered memory of Clara calling me "hero."

"Evelyn, she said you were the kindest and most generous-hearted of them all. It's true. Everything she loved about you both is really who you are and not just who she wanted you to be. It's good that you are still the same two people you were when you shared Clara's life with her…It's good." She was trying to help us have peace with our decisions.

It made perfect sense even coming from the mouth of a young woman who really didn't know either of us on her own. She did know us enough to speak with authority, though. She knew us through the diary pages and through Clara's words. If Evvie needed to hide and be protected, that was okay, and if I needed to face Charlie head on, that was fine, too.

"You are the strongest and most fearless of them all, Abby." Evvie looked up at me.

"And you are the kindest and most generous-hearted of them all, Evvie." I kissed her cheek. "Thanks, Laurel." I kissed her cheek, as well.

"You won't let him get you, will you, Abby?" Laurel couldn't hide her fear.

"There's no way he'll get her," Evelyn answered before I could. "He may be looking for another victim, but he damn sure won't find one in Abby's house." It was good to hear her support and confidence in my ability to protect myself.

"Well, you can bet I won't go down without a huge fight," I agreed. "Don't worry, Laurel, I've been in worse situations and lived to tell about them."

"Actually, Abby, you haven't ever really told about them." Evelyn seized the opportunity. "Will you please tell me what happened to you in Desert Storm that changed your life? And don't say again that it was just the whole war." She cut me off. "Something happened to you. Something really, really bad happened, and you've never told a soul."

She was right. I hadn't told a soul. There were people who knew because they were there, but I hadn't told anyone since my return to the United States.

"Why do you want to know now?" I tried to delay the inevitable.

"I wanted to know then, but you sure weren't talking about any personal stuff with me." She was reliving the guilt of her relationship with Clara again.

"I wasn't talking about personal stuff with anyone, Evvie, so don't think it was just you."

"Clara knew." Laurel looked down at the bed as she spoke. "She wrote about it in her diary."

"What?" I felt the cold ache that panic leaves just under your skin. "What did she put in her diary? I never told her anything either." I defended my secret.

"It was war, Abby. She said you had to kill a man to live, and she knew it. That's all," Laurel explained.

"Oh, my God, Abby. What happened? I can't believe you never told me this." Evvie began, as usual, to overreact.

"I never told Clara anything of the likes either." I maintained my position. "Great. She wrote about it in her diary and now the FBI has it for their reading pleasure. Just fucking great." I overstated my disapproval.

"The FBI won't have a clue who she was writing about if they ever even see it." Laurel tried to ease my angst.

"Well, is it true?" Evelyn was fixed on the fact that she had never heard this story.

"I was a soldier in the middle of a war. I assisted in killing thousands of people. I was the one supplying the infantry with fuel and ammunition. Of course I killed people. We all did." I raised my voice for a second, then lowered it to its original calm tone and volume. I dropped my head and stared at my hands.

"It's true" was all I said.

I had been hoping that moment would never come for over six years. I figured if I kept it a secret, it never had to happen. If no one knew, it didn't exist. Now it was no longer a secret. I had said the words I swore would never leave my lips. I said, "It's true." I confessed to murder.

It wasn't actually murder, although I have to say it always felt like it to me. It was self-defense in somebody's reality, just not mine. There had been two others who knew about it at one time. In their reality, it was self-defense, but they are both gone now. One died shortly after our return from the Gulf, and the other is walking around dead, thinking it was all just a dream.

Chapter Eleven

No one ever told me during my military training that the worst enemy in war would be boredom. We sat around the desert for months before the air war started and months again before the ground war kicked in. We had intermittent periods of absolute terror as if to remind us we had a pulse, then it was back to swatting flies and scratching the bites of sand fleas.

It never crossed my mind while I was working my way up through the ranks of the enlisted soldier that I actually would be going to war someday. I sure never thought I'd be leading a group of people from the National Guard around the desert, dodging bullets and looking for a place to sleep safely.

Dodging bullets was fine with me because after a few revolutions of the fear/boredom/fear cycle, I would gladly have run through hell with diesel fuel on my panties just to do something clearly defined. Too much idle time in a place where people want to kill you meant too much time to think about home and eternity. We all saw the start of the ground war as the way home. We tried not to think about it as a way to start eternity early.

Since I never really expected to participate in a war, I didn't expect to do anything important, but we had an important job—to take fuel and ammunition to the soldiers with the big guns. That's what we did. We delivered fuel and ammunition as the forces pushed through Iraq and into Kuwait. We gave them all we had, then turned around to get more. Of course, while we were refueling our tankers at the nearest fuel point, which was often close to a hundred miles away, the unit we supported was moving forward without us. It was always a challenge to find them when we returned. I was not amused by the lack of organization in our little area of the war.

Amused or not, I did the best I could to complete my missions and take care of my soldiers. I really couldn't have cared any less about myself or any of my feelings. I had gone to the Gulf caring about a lot of things, but the night before the ground war started, I became a different person. That was the night that my desire to quell my fear overrode my good sense. That was the night I went where I shouldn't have been and took someone else with me.

It was bad enough that I endangered my own life, but for the last few weeks, I had also been endangering the life of my friend Rachel. She was the only other female around, and she volunteered to go along on our ground-war mission as my driver and mechanic. We were very close. I was her lieutenant and she was my sergeant, and nobody messed with either of us.

On nights when we were in base camp and not running missions, Rachel and I went out into the desert and just drove around in the neutral zone in blackout. Headlights were prohibited. We had night-vision goggles and a global positioning system in our Humvee. Without it, we would have never found the way back to our unit. I tried to rationalize my little roaming game by the fact that I needed to practice nighttime navigation before the ground war began. I suppose it really did help me learn to trust my instincts, as well as my GPS, since I never got lost.

That last night before the ground war, I made some critical errors in judgment. Everyone in my platoon was sleeping or on guard duty in the makeshift base camp when Rachel and I left for our drive. As always, we told Tony that we were planning to go out and be stupid. One of my staff sergeants, Tony had been in Vietnam and understood my need to stay busy.

We said good night to Tony and started out on a northwesterly path into the neutral zone. We knew that the Syrian army was to our west and the Iraqi army was directly north, so we picked the center between them to travel. It was a moonless night, and I could barely see the front of the Humvee without my night-vision goggles.

About thirty minutes into our drive, I spotted something that was definitely not organic to the desert. It looked like a vehicle, but we needed to get closer to tell for sure. I should have said right then to turn around, but instead I instructed Rachel to head toward

71

it. She did so without question. As we got closer, I could see that it was the military equivalent of a pickup truck.

It had the allied symbol painted on its hood, and there was one person standing beside it. He must have heard us coming because he began waving us over to his location before he could have physically seen us in the darkness of the desert.

As we drove toward him, we watched him through the goggles, aware that he could not see my companion or me at all from where he stood. "He looks lost, Rachel. Looks like a Syrian uniform. I wonder what he's looking for out there." I was puzzled by his constant strain to see out into the vastness of the black desert. He was looking in every direction, yet there was no way he could see a thing.

"Maybe he's lost his way and doesn't have such a fancy little gadget to get back." Rachel was referring to our GPS.

"Maybe. We should help him." I never had the sense to be afraid.

"Your call, LT." Rachel drove to within a foot of his vehicle, where we knew he could now see us.

The next five or so minutes is blurry in my recollection even today, but the best I can recall is that he somehow communicated to us that a person who had previously been with him was now lost. He spoke no English, and we didn't even know for sure what his nationality was, so we certainly didn't speak his language. He seemed grateful for the assistance and immediately pointed toward the passenger's seat of his vehicle, then pointed into the desert. He repeated this action along with enough other sign language that we knew someone was missing.

He gestured toward my goggles, then toward the darkness again as if I might look around for his companion through my night vision. It seemed reasonable and he seemed panicked, so I walked a few feet away from where he was standing with Rachel and began scanning the night for a figure.

I spotted a dune close by that I thought might give me view advantage, so I headed toward it to take a look. I didn't think I was gone that long. I didn't even consider that I had left my driver and friend in the middle of nowhere with a total stranger. When that thought hit me, it was like a ton of bricks. I became cold and sweaty, my heart raced, and I rushed back to the two vehicles and people I had abandoned for my search.

When I reached my Humvee, I looked through the goggles and did not see either of them standing where I had left them. I wanted to scream, but I knew no one would hear me anyway, so I began reviewing the area again with my goggles. When I saw Rachel, I couldn't believe my eyes. I froze but did not panic.

The man had her on the ground with a knife to her throat. He was raping her. She looked dead, but her eyes were still open and staring directly at me. Even at my distance, I think she could see me watching her. I stood for another second trying to formulate a plan to remove him without any further injury to her. I could see that the knife was pressed firmly into her neck and her uniform was torn from most of her body.

The next few minutes were all impulse and instinct. I ran to where he had her on the ground and yelled at him to release her while I kicked him in the head. I don't know what kept him from slitting her throat, but he suddenly turned and lunged at me with the knife. Rachel rolled into a ball and wiggled her way to the Humvee while I struggled with our assailant.

I remember him laughing at me as the gun went off and I remember him falling to the ground, but I can't recall clearly what happened in between. I grabbed Rachel and got her into the Humvee, and we sped into the darkness and away from the scene that changed my entire life.

I drove as fast as I could across the deep sand without looking back. When I had the outline of our camp in my goggles, I stopped driving and focused my attention on my bleeding and traumatized comrade.

Never mind the rest of the war. Forget the sniper who attacked us, the dog that dragged an arm to where we were lunching one afternoon, and the stench "the mile of death" at the border into Kuwait produced. Ignore the blown-out vehicles and charred remains of what once were people. Completely disregard the stacks of bodies pushed into graves by Army bulldozers and the knowledge that more Iraqi soldiers were being buried alive in their underground fighting positions. Discount it all because it simply did not matter.

It did not matter that the graves registration van was traveling with us through Iraq. It did not matter that it carried American soldiers whose families had not yet been notified that their beloved were gone from this earth. It didn't even matter when the refrigeration unit went out in 120-degree weather and body fluids leaked from the bags. It was of no concern to me. I was already dead and unable to be affected.

Rachel was going to be okay physically, but mentally, she would never be the same. He bit her breast so hard that it tore her nipple almost from her, leaving it dangling in a pool of blood. Her already hardened exterior became impenetrable. The bruises exposed through her deep black skin were reminders for weeks of the force it took him to subdue her. Why hadn't she screamed? Why had I left her? Why couldn't it have been me?

Evelyn and Laurel had not moved or so much as breathed audibly since I began telling the story that had only left my lips one other time. We told Tony when we returned that night because we needed his assistance in cleaning Rachel's wounds and easing her pain. He had sedatives for his own nerves that only I knew about, and I was sure she would need them. We also needed an alibi should anyone have seen or heard the incident. I imagined it was just a matter of time before someone found the body and started looking for the killer.

Tony argued that maybe I hadn't killed him at all but perhaps just hit him in the leg or arm or some other non-life-threatening body part. He argued that the man probably drove back to his camp and was considered a hero for surviving an Iraqi ambush. He certainly wouldn't have said that an American woman did this to him. He would have lost all face with his countrymen for such an occurrence. Tony was convincing.

Maybe Tony was right because no one ever came. No news story ever broke and no investigation ever ensued. It was my pistol that had been fired, and I knew it could be traced to me by the serial number if I ditched it. Weapons are sensitive items in the military and just "losing" one is not acceptable or excusable, especially in war. I had no idea what to do. Tony assured me we would do nothing until it was necessary to act. I trusted him. I had no other choice. We never had to act.

"Tony was the friend who died shortly after your return, wasn't he?" Evelyn remembered.

"Yes." I kept my head down. "He took my secret to the grave just as he promised he would." It was Tony's memory that finally wet my eyes again. I had no emotion during the tale I was recounting. I had no feelings at all about it.

"Rachel is lost." I answered the question before anyone could ask. "She remembers it as a dream and nothing else. We didn't mention it for the rest of our deployment. Then when we got home, she called and said she'd had a bizarre dream that she was being raped in the desert and I came along and saved her life. I didn't know what to say to her on the phone, so I told her I'd be right there. When I got to her house, she was crying and shaking, remembering the dream and telling me the details." I had to stop for a minute until I could speak again. Evelyn held my hand and Laurel patted my leg. I went on.

"I didn't know whether to tell her it was all true or tell her to look at her breast or what to do. I just held her and told her it was a bad dream and that dreams don't come true. I told her I would kill any son of a bitch who tried to hurt her and there was no reason to be afraid." I sighed. "She's so far gone now I can't even reach her to tell her the truth. She's a hard-core drug addict, and we only talk about twice a year. She somehow keeps a labor job, but immediately after work, she's either high or in a drunken stupor until bed." I was overcome by the guilt of destroying the life of someone who had saved mine.

Rachel very definitely saved my life. During the ground-war phase of our deployment, if left to my own devices, I would have found a way to die. Rachel kept me in the world. She reminded me daily that I had to take care of our soldiers and keep them safe. She was the one who stayed awake and counted explosions while recording the directions of the blasts and their approximate distance from us. She was the one who drove through minefields to get ahead of our trucks when radio communication failed and the lead vehicle went dangerously off course. She was the one who kept the trucks running while babying scared drivers in the middle of the night in the midst of a war zone. We made a pact to leave no one behind, and that's exactly what we did. We pushed, pulled, and dragged those old piece-of-shit tractors through the entire war.

Without us, there would have been no war because without fuel to move and ammunition to shoot, it could not have been.

"She was selling crack in my front yard." I explained why we parted ways after all we had been through. "I begged her to stop. I begged her to get help. I pleaded with her to let me help her. She would only lie to me and try again to protect me from what she was doing to herself. I could not watch her self-destruct. I was not as strong for her as she was for me." I cried the hardest I had since the news of Clara's death came over the phone.

"Have you talked to her lately?" Laurel asked me in a tone so sweet and caring that I looked deeply in her eyes for someone I knew.

"Yes. I called her to tell her I was going to be in town for Clara's funeral, and I said I would look her up. She sounded better than ever and said she had quit using since her father died. I didn't really believe her since she always wants me to think she's okay, but I have hope," I explained. "I didn't want to contact her once we discovered Charlie was out killing people at random because I didn't want to put her in any more danger."

"She lives in Spartanburg?" Evelyn was surprised she didn't know her.

"No, she lives about an hour away."

"Call her now," Laurel urged. "Tell her you need her again. Tell her you're in trouble and you need her to be with you. Abby, you know you need her now." Laurel's green eyes were piercing. The sense of urgency in her voice screamed that she knew something I did not know. I was baffled by what it could be.

"I will not drag her into another life-threatening situation with me. She's already trying to kill herself. I won't help her."

"What would it hurt, Abby?" Evelyn didn't know whether to agree with Laurel or me.

"It could get her killed is what it could hurt. She could end up being another victim of Charlie. She's already been a victim of me. I lost Tony. I can't lose Rachel."

The words leaving my mouth hung in the air for a bit before entering my ears. The dense emotions surrounding me created a screen capable of keeping out time. I allowed myself to be taken into the emotional cloud and drifted to the memory of Tony.

As his platoon leader, I was tasked with organizing and performing his military funeral. It was a moving time for us all. We said goodbye to one of us and a part of each of us simultaneously. We circled the wagons, cried privately, practiced our performance as if it were our own lives at stake, and recalled stories of our dear friend. We stood proudly and protectively as the wake dragged on and performed our duty impeccably as the service stopped time.

When I handed the flag to his wife and son and took a step back to salute it, I lost my composure. It was the one time I broke down in front of my soldiers. I always wondered if I disappointed him with my inability to hold back my emotions.

I shook free from the memory I was trapped in when Agent Cimino called to us that it was almost time to go.

Evelyn looked so sad and lost that I put my arms around her and held on as tight as I could. Almost simultaneously, Evelyn and I reached an arm out to pull Laurel into our embrace. We cried and hugged with no further dialogue until Agent Cimino came into the room and told me we were leaving.

Jeff nudged me awake when the plane was landing in Denver. I had slept like a baby the entire trip. For a few seconds upon waking, I imagined the last week to be a really bad dream. It was when I saw Pat that reality set in.

"There will be a car waiting for us as soon as we get our luggage," Pat announced as we fumbled with our carry-ons.

"You're going to have to call me Ted now," Agent Cimino whispered in my ear as he fell in line behind me to deplane.

"Hi, Ted." I smiled and chuckled a little at the formality we had maintained.

"You okay?" Jeff was in front of me in the slow-moving line and turned his head to see my response.

I leaned my forehead into his back. "Of course I'm okay," I assured him. "We're home."

Chapter Twelve

I may have been the only one who was not underestimating Charlie's stamina when we left South Carolina. Pat and Ted seemed surprised when three weeks went by without so much as a whisper from him, but I knew he wouldn't bite. He might as well have disappeared from the face of the earth.

Jeff and I returned to work the week after we got home, but it was winter and business was slowing to a stall. It was going to be a cold, hard winter from the looks of things, but I was glad for it since we'd be too distracted to work much. For the first time in my life, I was also glad to be relatively unknown in the town where I lived. I had a few friends, but no one close except Jeff.

I used the excuse that I was "too busy" to keep from making friends, but the truth was, I was too afraid of the responsibility. After the trauma I caused Rachel, I made a vow to protect the people around me from my indiscretion. I had enough acquaintances to quell the loneliness and an occasional romantic interest, but no one ever really got through the first few layers of skin.

It was odd having houseguests who never left. Pat and I tried to get to know each other on a more personal level, but we really had nothing in common. We were polar opposites: she liked canned beer and hot dogs while I preferred bottled water and organic vegetables. She watched football like it was the only thing on television. I didn't know anything on television. Still in all, we managed to talk about the only thing other than my predicament with Charlie that we shared—our love of women.

She had been involved with Julie for a few years, but in her opinion, it wasn't serious. They enjoyed each other's physical company and somehow produced an entire relationship based on sex. She told me that if they ever lived in the same place consistently, it would not be such a good arrangement. It sounded to me like they enjoyed the mystery of each other.

Jeff really didn't talk to either of our guests. I think he believed that they should go do something important because he was perfectly capable of defending us from Charlie. Pat teased me relentlessly about how in love with me she believed Jeff to be and how in denial I was for pretending not to notice. I think I just didn't care.

I'm fairly certain that Pat's department was also growing weary of funding a stalemate. I think they were ready to pull the plug when an abandoned car with my name and address in the glove compartment turned up in a grocery store parking lot two blocks from my house. The car was registered to a young man who had disappeared from Florida.

Pat and Ted met with local law enforcement officials and determined that the boy left Florida a few days before the car was called in abandoned. He had been seen with an unfamiliar person just before leaving his hometown. He apparently called his family from the road and said he was dropping out of school to become a missionary and that he'd be in touch. That was the last his family heard.

I was really quite surprised that the car was found here. I immediately thought Charlie was trying to throw us off track with such a blatant display of his presence. Pat and Jeff said I gave him too much intellectual credit, but Ted agreed with me. We were dealing with a very calculating and vengeful person: a bad combination of personality traits.

I still maintained that he would not come after me as long as others were present. He knew the FBI was with me. He knew they were looking for him. I knew when I took the letter from my mailbox the morning after the car was found that he had chosen a more indirect route into my house.

Why I made the decision to keep silent is as much a mystery as why I wanted him all to myself. I did not want the FBI to find him first and possibly let him escape justice in the legal system. I did not want him to have a fair and equitable trial by a jury of unbiased people—people who didn't know Clara, people who couldn't possibly understand the torture she endured at the hands of the monster sitting before them. They would be so preoccupied with being impartial and mindful of his rights that they would never see Clara and her shattered life.

I made the decision to fly solo the moment I opened the letter and saw Clara's handwriting on the page. I would not tell Jeff, Pat, or Ted at this point. I hoped they would understand when it was all over.

The house was abuzz with the details of the car and the missing boy. Local police were involved, as well as Pat and Ted, so they had plenty to do other than notice me. I returned from the mailbox and went to my room with the newspaper and a cup of coffee, just as I always did. I sat at my desk and took the diary page from the envelope.

I knew I should give it to the authorities, but just as Charlie was hoping, I wanted this piece of Clara all to myself. I had passed on the chance to read the remaining pages in the books Laurel turned over to the FBI. I would not let my fear of what I might learn prevent me from a final visit with my dear Clara.

It was everything I hoped it would be. The entry was written the night we first made love, and reading it took me back to the time I was most at peace. The war and the betrayal hadn't tainted my world view. Even the violence I saw on the ambulance crew had not affected me enough to make me into the bitter ball of hate and distrust I became after Clara left me.

I closed my eyes and went to the place we first held each other intimately. I felt her skin and her hair touching my body; I smelled the scent of her perfume in the air around my memory; I wept like a child as we had together that enchanted evening.

I fell asleep with my head on the desk after reliving the glorious night I read about. Jeff came in while I was sleeping and asked me if I was okay. I woke so abruptly that I scattered the papers I had been sleeping on. The diary entry and the envelope were among the papers that fell to the floor.

"Get the hell out of here and stop sneaking up on me!" I screamed at Jeff and dove onto the papers. "You scared the shit out of me!" I shuffled them all together. "Leave!" I screamed again, staring him in the face.

"I'm sorry, Abby, I didn't know you were asleep. I'm sorry." He was backing toward the door.

I burst into tears. "Get out," I screamed again. He obeyed.

My outburst was dismissed fairly easily as an overload of stress and fear. After hiding the diary entry in a book, I stayed in my room and slept for the rest of the day. I wondered if my reaction was exactly what Charlie had hoped for. I wondered if he had the satisfaction of knowing that I was playing right into his hands.

Charlie must have studied hard and planned well during the seven or so years he was in prison. I never thought him to have an IQ higher than a cricket, but I suppose it was because he was always chemically numbed when I saw him. Maybe he just knew all along that if he ever sobered up enough to meet his mind, he would be a dangerous man.

"I'm sorry, Jeff." I sat next to him on the couch when I finally emerged from my room at dinnertime. "I had no right to yell at you. It's just all getting to me." I leaned on his shoulder. "I'll never yell at you again if you'll at least consider forgiving me." He didn't speak, and I looked up at his sad face.

"I forgive you." He pursed his lips and looked skeptical. "You really won't ever yell at me again?"

"Never." I made an X on my chest with my finger. "Is there any news on the car or the boy?" I wanted to go back into my room and read the diary page again. I wanted to burst out with the news that I had received it. I did neither. Instead I sat trying to be interested in the case.

"The boy is definitely connected to Charlie," Pat answered. "He left Florida with him best we can tell. I bet Charlie offed him already."

"Why would Charlie kill him? He's totally unrelated to Clara or our situation. Charlie seems to just like killing people he knows to be involved with Clara…"

Pat cut me off with, "Or people who talk. Like the informant. Maybe this kid was a threat to Charlie. Maybe he knew the kid would blab and he couldn't take the chance."

"We don't even have a body yet, gang," Ted reminded us. "The kid could still be helping Charlie for all we know."

The next few days were uneventful. It was only a week and a half until Christmas, and the FBI was no closer to Charlie Stokes than they had been in Spartanburg. He was simply not making any mistakes. Ted was planning to fly home for a few days to see his family for the holiday, and Pat was planning to spend Christmas with Jeff and me.

I didn't care about the holidays. I went to the mailbox every day hoping to find more memories of a time I longed to live again. We were in my car returning from the grocery after taking Ted to the airport when I noticed the envelope over my visor. The handwritten "Abby" on the outside cover was in the same handwriting as the last envelope from Charlie. I tried to ignore it until we returned home.

When everyone got out of the car, I reached in and grabbed the envelope, stuffing it inside my coat. He had been in my car. He got close enough without being noticed to put something inside my car. I was amazed by his fearlessness and determination to communicate with me. Had I seen him at the grocery and just didn't know it? Had he been the checkout guy the next aisle over or the parking lot security guard? I racked my brain to get a hit off anyone I had seen who was familiar.

Once again, I knew I should give the letter to Pat without opening it. Once again, I retreated to my room and sat at my desk instead of doing the right thing. I opened the envelope and discovered a small piece of paper attached to the diary entry inside. It read: *Things in this life are never as they appear.*

I sat holding the piece of paper and the diary page, wondering what he meant. Was he talking about himself and his identity or my relationship with Clara? Maybe he was talking about the woman in Georgia and the fact that I never even knew she existed. He could have been talking about Evelyn and Clara and how they betrayed me. That single powerful sentence could have meant any number of things.

If I had even considered giving the letters to Pat, the first sentence in the diary entry ended that possibility. I'm sure my face had no color when I finished reading it. I'm sure my eyes were wild and weary. I'm sure I could have stopped my own heart with my fear.

I met a woman my hero served with. She is beautiful, strong, and very devoted. I called her a few weeks ago. I want to understand what happened there. The old spirit would have never given in so easily and so effortlessly, but she didn't even flinch. She would not fight. The fight was all gone from her soul. She just let go and walked away. I saw the pain in her eyes when she stepped off the plane. I saw the emptiness and fear, but I was ashamed of what I had done.

Her friend told me the truth. She said my hero killed a man to save their lives.

It was self-defense. They feared punishment so they told no one. I wish I had been there for her.

All the years he knocked me around left me affected. I needed to be touched tenderly and lovingly like before she went away. I needed it so badly that I couldn't wait for her to return.

I wish I had waited.

I couldn't even think about what to do next. I folded the diary page, tucked away the note from Charlie, and put it all back in the envelope.

Chapter Thirteen

Therapists say you shouldn't worry if you think you are going crazy because it's the ones who don't think they are sick who truly are. I don't buy it. You definitely know when you're slipping away. You can feel the closeness of reality fading into the fog of uncertainty.

I knew without a doubt that I needed help. I sat on my bed the rest of the day and fantasized about killing Charlie with my bare hands. I wanted to torture him first, to know that he was scared and hear him beg for mercy. I'm sure that's how he killed Clara. He kept her in fear for years, then just when she thought it was safe to live again, he jumped out of her worst nightmare and murdered her.

I pictured us face-to-face, Charlie and me. I pictured him drawing his last breath in this world. I delighted at the pain in his eyes and the grimace he wore. I heard him begging me to kill him, and I heard myself reminding him that he was the most evil person on earth. I was no better than he was. I wanted to kill him as brutally as he killed my Clara and the others. I wanted to kill him before he could kill me.

I would survive as I had in Desert Storm, but this time, there would be no guilt, no wondering, no sleepless nights. No visions of the family I robbed of a father or a son—none. This time, I would sleep in the peace that Clara deserved, that Charlie denied her, that I would give her in her departed state.

I snapped myself back and pushed the fantasy from my mind. I had taken a step closer to the edge. I prayed there was a fence there to catch me before I plunged headlong into the blackness of insanity. I knew I was heading there. I had to do something right away. I had to take back the control Charlie was gaining on me with his secret correspondence. I had to tell someone. Charlie was banking on my fear-induced silence, holding the knowledge of the heinous crime I committed over my head. Secrets are power. Secrets are control. Secrets are what my whole life had been based on.

I would not tell Pat or Ted. Maybe I could tell Jeff, but I wasn't sure it was the right move. I had to talk to Laurel. She knew all along that Charlie had the part of the diary that could hurt me the most. She had tried to tell me the last day we were in Spartanburg, but I didn't get it. I never thought about what she meant when she said the FBI might never see what Clara had written of my experience in Desert Storm.

My thoughts were all running together. Once again, I feared myself far more than I feared Charlie.

"Laurel?" Evelyn handed the phone to Laurel after our brief conversation. "Hey, how are you guys doing?"

She sounded particularly cheerful considering she'd been in hiding for well over a month. Pat was reluctant to contact them for me, but I insisted.

"Are you guys celebrating Christmas?" I was suddenly unable to think of anything else to talk about. "We're just pretending it isn't happening this year."

We made small talk a few minutes before I asked her if she still thought I should contact Rachel. She caught on to the uneasiness in my voice.

"Are you thinking about it?" She was careful.

"Yeah, I thought it might be a good idea to check in with her. What you said that last day in Spartanburg really hit home recently." I kept it vague. "We've been through a lot, Rachel and I." I was struggling for a connection that Laurel would immediately grasp. I knew she had read the diary entry, probably more than once. I hoped if I used something from it, she would remember and start to connect.

"I don't know what I'm waiting for. I should just call her up right now." I paused. "People always say they wish they had done something after it's too late to go back and do it again. You never hear of someone saying that they wish they had waited..." I stopped to listen for her response.

"Rarely." Her tone suggested that I might have hit a memory, but I couldn't be sure.

"Yeah, I might wish I'd waited if she's just stoned when I call." I followed the vein I was trying to puncture. "...But Rachel's my hero..." I paused. "...I bet she'll share in my misery no matter what state she's in." That was all it took.

"So call her," Laurel urged. "What are you waiting for?"

"I don't know." I brushed it off.

"I'm glad you're thinking about it, Abby. I think she's just what you need. What made you suddenly decide to listen to me?"

"Oh, I got a letter from another old acquaintance, a couple of letters actually, and he made me remember how much I miss Rachel. The letter said something about meeting a woman I had served with in the Gulf. It really made me think of her." I had given Laurel more than enough. She knew Charlie had been in contact with me. She knew I was keeping it a secret.

"Well." She was cool and collected. "You could just say the letters from your old acquaintance are a sign that you're supposed to call Rachel." She paused and her tone changed. "Don't wait, Abby."

"Yeah, I think I'll call her." I tried to sound nonchalant. "She might be just exactly what I need right now."

"Why don't you guys come here for a bit and hang with us?" Laurel sounded afraid for me. "We really miss you, Abby." I heard Evelyn agreeing in the background.

"Nah, I think I have too much to do around here right now." I thanked her for the concern and assured her we were all safe and well.

"Will you keep me posted?" I knew she was willing to conceal my divulgence for now. "I mean, let me know if you get any more thought-provoking mail." She was careful not to attract any attention from the ears we knew were listening to our conversation.

As I hung up the receiver, I smiled about doing something Charlie had not predicted: I had told someone that he was in contact with me. He was counting on my silence, but I acted in a way he didn't expect. It was a small gesture that netted me nothing in terms of additional information, but to me, it said I was not easy prey. I was not the ball of clay he figured me for this time.

While I didn't learn what else he was holding in the pages of the diaries from talking to Laurel, I learned what he wasn't holding. He wasn't holding the strings to make me dance as he desired. He wasn't holding the knife to my throat by telling me that he knew I was a murderer, too. And he wasn't holding me prisoner.

I was a voluntary prisoner. I was assuming the role I needed to assume to get him where I wanted him to be. He thought he was in control. I knew I was in control.

I really had no intention of dragging Rachel into the mess I was in. I only used the premise of contacting her as a front to connect with Laurel. The more I thought about it, though, the more I knew I needed to give Rachel warning. I feared she might be in danger.

I explained to Pat that Rachel was my closest friend during the time that Clara and I broke up. I told her I was afraid that Charlie might go after her to get to me. She really didn't agree that Rachel was in any danger, but she allowed me to call her and discuss the case a little anyway. I think they all thought I was losing it after my outburst to Jeff, and they wanted me to feel safe at any cost.

"You can only tell her what we rehearsed," Pat coached me as I dialed the number. "Anything else and the phone will suddenly disconnect." She sounded like a terrorist monitoring the communications of her hostage.

"This is ridiculous." I was a little cross with her, but Jeff reminded me that I was lucky to get to make the call.

The phone rang and my heart rate increased. After four rings, it went to voice mail, and I relaxed as I heard Rachel's deep Southern accent.

"I can't get the phone so leave me a message and maybe I'll call you back. If you're calling for money and you're not giving it away, I can assure you, the check is in the mail. Oh, wait for the beep." Good old Rachel. I waited for the beep.

"Hey. I don't want money and I ain't giving it away." For some reason, hearing her voice always brought out the most Southern accent I had. "What are you up to, stranger, and why haven't I heard from you? Call me. I love you. Bye."

I hung up with a lump the size of a racquetball in my throat.

It was almost bedtime when the phone rang. I knew it was Rachel.

"What do you mean *you* haven't heard from *me,* Miss 'I'll call you when I'm in town'?" She was just getting started. "You better be giving away money if this is how you treat all your friends 'cause you ain't gonna have none any other way." I could almost hear her shaking her head at me.

"I was gonna call, but things got a little weird."

"What, you hooked up with some chick and didn't come up for air until it was time to get on the plane?" She was not giving me an inch of slack.

"No, I wish that's all it was." I sighed. "Rach, this is serious. I really need to talk to you."

"You okay, LT?" She had called me LT, short for lieutenant, since the day we met.

"Yes, for now, but some things are happening that you need to know about," I started. "You know I went to Spartanburg for Clara's funeral. You knew Clara?" I waited for her response.

"Yeah, I knew Clara a little. We had a few conversations. It's terrible what he did to her." She said nothing else.

"Well, they haven't caught him yet," I went on. "He's killed a few other people, and they think he might be after me." Once again, I waited for a response.

"Oh, no...he doesn't even need to think like that. That would be a really bad idea." She immediately assumed the old role of taking care of me. "Who's watching your back?"

"Um, the FBI..." I said reluctantly, looking at Pat.

Rachel gave a long sigh.

"So far, they're doing a bang-up job since I'm still here!" I tried to lighten the conversation.

"They better," Rachel remarked. "They damn sure better."

She was always the tough one, always the hard-shelled street kid. Not a day went by in the Army that Rachel didn't piss somebody off with a look, a word, or an action. She came with me to get away from the ones who didn't understand her. She found a home with the rest of the misfits in my platoon. We were the rogues: the unshaven, unpolished, in need of a haircut, "I'll wear my uniform any damn way I choose," country folks.

What did the Army think? We were going to play by their rules and get our asses shot off? No way. We were from the National Guard. That's not the same toy soldier organization that signs on for 24/7. We signed on for one weekend a month and two weeks a year with a promise to go to war if they needed us. That's what we did. They needed us and we went, but unlike the soldiers of the active components, we had another world waiting for us outside the desert. We didn't train every single day of our lives to be miserable. We figured we already knew how to do that.

We loved our country as much as anyone did. Probably more than the active duty soldiers because we did the military thing on our weekends off, the weekends that working-class folks treasure. We got up at the ass-crack of dawn and went to the local armory to be soldiers on our weekends. We took our precious two-week vacations from our predominately blue-collar worlds and went off to some Army post hotter than blue blazes for summer camp. We went to be soldiers and soldiers we were. We may not have looked as good as the active duty or had as many toys as they did, but we could do twice as much with half as much. We had the attitude that the whole Army ought to consider: Don't make a career out of a little task. Let's get this job done and go home.

"What can I do to help, LT?" Rachel was ready to go to war with me again.

"I'm fine, Rach, but it's you I'm worried about. If he finds out how close you and I are, I'm afraid he'll try and come after you, too." I knew no nicer way to say she was in danger.

"Don't worry, LT…I got somethin' for him." She wasn't even remotely concerned for her own safety.

We talked about old times for a little bit longer, and we both avoided the subject of Rachel's drug problem. She sounded present and alert, and that was enough to make me rest easier.

It was Christmas Eve when Charlie delivered his next installment. Pat, Jeff, and I had enjoyed a festive dinner, exchanged a few small presents, and retreated to our rooms for the evening. When I walked through my door, I saw the envelope taped to the outside of the window over my desk. The window was at least twelve feet off the ground, so it was no simple task to place it there, but Charlie had managed. He'd even taken the screen off, then replaced it so the envelope would be easier to retrieve from inside the room.

My first instinct was of course to panic. I froze in my tracks, wondering how long the envelope had been there and if Charlie was still outside my house. I realized that if I alerted Pat immediately, he might be captured. But then again, so would I. I would either have to deny any other contact with him and hope the letter didn't incriminate me, or I would have to produce the other two. Then I'd have to try and convince them all that I wasn't deliberately trying to hamper their efforts to locate and arrest Charlie Stokes.

My thoughts suddenly shifted to how angry I was that Charlie could even get so close to me when the goddamn FBI was supposedly watching for him. Not just the FBI, but the locals, too. Where the hell were the security cops that claimed to monitor my house? Home safely, celebrating Christmas Eve with their families while I was being stalked by a serial killer?

The realization that I was on my own convinced me to fetch the letter from the window and give the FBI no information. I feared that they would assume I was somehow guilty and put me away, just like the Army would have if I had told the truth about that night in the desert with Rachel. I'd heard too many horror stories about doing the "right thing." I wanted no part in being labeled the perpetrator. I would take my chances at being a victim. At least I'd get a running start.

I looked in my closet and under my bed. I checked every inch of my small room as if I thought Charlie a shape-shifter that could fit in my dresser drawer. I turned off the lights and knelt below the window by the envelope, watching the darkness outside my room for anything moving. Nothing was. Everything was still and calm, peaceful and safe.

Shortly, I stood in front of the window in the dark and unlocked the simple top latch. I raised it only as far as I needed to slide my hand inside and grab the envelope. Once I had it in my hand, I quickly closed and relatched the locking device. I dropped to the floor with my back to the wall and breathed like I had just surfaced from the deep.

I might never have realized that there was something very familiar about the way the envelope smelled if I hadn't been sitting in the dark. It was so familiar that it calmed me in the same instant it scared me speechless. I couldn't see the handwriting in the dark, nor could I focus on the envelope specifics. The only senses at work were touch and smell.

I held it up to my nose and took a deep breath, drawing in something I knew at a core level, a smell I had known throughout my existence. I sat with it in the dark corner and continued trying to flush out the faint smell that I knew so well. I could neither place nor name it, but I certainly identified with it.

After a while, I reached into the side drawer of my desk and took out my flashlight. I pulled the throw from the cedar chest and draped it over my head. I had done this same thing in Desert Storm when I needed to read a map or a document and couldn't risk being seen by the enemy. I made a tent over my entire body, using my head and bent-at-the-knees legs as the tent poles. Once I settled into place, I turned on the light.

The red lens was fairly muted, but still it pierced the darkness with startling light. I adjusted my eyes for a few moments, then tore open the envelope. The note began:

We want the same thing. We both want to live. We can help each other. You took something from me; I need something from you. Evelyn took something from you and you did nothing. You killed the man in the desert for less. The score is uneven. You must do the right thing.

The diary pages attached to the note were written the night Clara and Evelyn betrayed me. I could not read them in their entirety. I spent the remainder of the evening and the first light of Christmas Day trying to make sense of what was happening.

Charlie was working to drive me mad. He squeezed every possible trigger and hit with such accuracy that it was as if he had been studying me all my life. It was painfully apparent that Evelyn was his next target. He was planning to use me to locate and maybe even kill her. He obviously believed his mental games were taking effect like a slow-release poison and that I'd succumb to his wishes at any moment.

He had to know I had not gone to the police. I was sure that made him all the more certain that it was just a matter of time until I was in too deep to get out. I knew he had no idea where the FBI was hiding Evelyn and Laurel, and I was grateful they were safe, at least for the moment. I had struggled with the pain of the diary and Charlie's hypnotic message the entire evening and dark hours of the morning, but I was still not his prisoner.

By breakfast, I had an idea about how to thwart his attempts to drive me into the pit of insanity. I knew it would be hard to maintain a level emotional state, but for the time being, I had no choice. Something in this letter screamed that there was more than what I read attached to it. The last message had said it plainly: *Things in this life are never as they appear.* So far, I had not fully uncovered the meaning of that clue.

Chapter Fourteen

I knew Pat would be angry that I had opened the envelope without alerting her and Ted, but I could play it off as a reaction to stress and shock. I couldn't leave Jeff out of the picture or he'd feel betrayed, so I decided to tell him alone before the others knew.

I chose to surrender the diary entry that revealed the relationship between Evvie and Clara because I hoped it would point them all to the fact that Evelyn could need extra protection. I removed the note and stored it with the others. When I showed Jeff the diary page, he read it all, then asked me what I planned to do with it.

"I have to give it to Pat and Ted. I probably should have never opened it, but I did and I can't take it back. Do you think they're going to be really angry?" I looked as confused and ashamed as I could.

"Yeah. They are." He patted me on the leg, then put his arm around me. "It was hard for you to read this, wasn't it?" He knew the answer. "Abby, Clara was just lonely and in a lot of mental pain." He pulled me closer.

"It doesn't matter now." I laid my head on his shoulder.

"What if you were to just go and talk to someone about all this…you know, someone who helps people professionally. Like a counselor or a therapist." He was gentle in his approach to the subject. "I was in therapy for years after my old man ditched. I had a lot of hate and anger, and it really helped me figure it all out." He shrugged. "Just a thought."

I sat quietly without looking at him for a few minutes. I knew I needed help. I'd been scared I was losing it a few times already, and I really didn't know how to steady myself much longer. I feared Charlie might learn that I sold him out to the FBI and stop corresponding with me, but I feared more that he might continue driving me crazy.

"That's not a bad idea." I looked Jeff in the eyes. "Do you know somebody?"

"No." He sounded disappointed. "But I bet we could find someone pretty easily."

"Let's talk more about it after we face the firing squad." I looked at my watch and knew the longer we waited the worse it would be. I stood up. "Let's go do it."

Pat was furious. She paced around the house for a good twenty minutes while Ted sat on the couch looking hurt. She gave me every good reason I already knew for why I should have told her the minute I saw the envelope on my window. She went on and on, finishing her raving spurt with, "We probably could have caught him if you'd done what you should have."

"Probably...maybe...possibly...what the fuck?" I stared back at her. "He was in the goddamn yard on a ladder or something and none of your illustrious security goons saw him, so it's not real likely you'd have caught shit..." I stopped myself. "Look, Pat, I'm a little distressed here. I did what my instinct told me to do. I didn't *have* to tell you ever, so get off my back." I stormed out of the room.

"Let her go..." I heard Jeff say as I left. They obeyed.

"You okay?" Jeff stuck his head in my room a little later that evening. I had spent hours trying to sort out the last few weeks. I was definitely not okay.

"I need help, Jeff." I surrendered to the notion that I was not in control of my emotions. "I've got to find someone to talk to about all this." I raised my head from the desk and peered sideways at him.

"I think that's the best thing for you, Abby." I heard the relief in his voice. "We'll start looking for someone tomorrow." He said good night and closed my door.

The FBI went to work at once on the soiled piece of evidence I gave them. They found fingerprints right away: all of ours, Charlie's, and an unknown set. The missing boy was the obvious possible match; other than him, it was anybody's guess. Pat said the FBI computers could find a match if the prints in question belonged to someone who'd ever been fingerprinted. If the person they belonged to had not, it would be a little harder.

As I watched security around me tighten, I also learned that Laurel and Evelyn were being moved again in case their location had been somehow discovered. I breathed a heavy sigh of relief on hearing of the stepped-up security measures to protect my friends. The authorities were so embarrassed that Charlie got that close to me they weren't going to give him another chance.

I rationalized that the evidence I had turned over was just as good as giving them all three envelopes. It gave them prints, a look into what Charlie was thinking, and increased protection for Evvie and Laurel. It also gave them a reason to keep protecting us all instead of thinking they were wasting their departmental resources on a deadlock again.

I wondered how long it would take Charlie to figure out I had given over any information. I imagined him to be watching the house closely enough to see the stir and wondered if he would just see it as a challenge and try harder.

Also on the list of things to wonder about was what Charlie meant by the last note he sent me. I was pretty sure he wanted me to kill Evvie to "act right," but I was also pretty sure that he was aware of our difference in location. I was hoping and praying he knew as much as I was giving him credit for because I needed time to come up with the rest of my plan.

The agents and I agreed that if any more letters came from Charlie, I would turn them over without opening them. I stressed how important it was to me to get to read them, so we compromised that I could read them in the presence of the FBI.

When I finally had time to focus again on my extreme need for professional help, I remembered a woman I met a year or so earlier. I'd been invited to the home of some women I knew through my work, who had also invited another lesbian couple. The other couple happened to include the most captivating woman I had ever met. I sat across from her at dinner with remarkable interest in simply listening to her speak. She didn't say much throughout our meal, but afterward, we sat around chatting and I learned she was a therapist.

Though I knew little else about her, something in me was drawn to her. She seemed kind and trustworthy, the two most important qualities in a person I have to pay to listen to me. I also considered it a plus that she was dating another woman when I met her. I didn't want to have to qualify my lifestyle before I could get help.

The whole concept of paying someone to listen to my problems felt a little weird. I always thought that was what friends were for, but Jeff convinced me that what I was dealing with was way out of the average person's league. Anyway, my friends were all dead, numb, or involved in this mess, so I had no choice but to look outside the flock.

Once again, Pat didn't like the idea of introducing another set of ears into the case she and Ted were becoming quite sore about. Ted was for it and voiced his concern about my mental health. Pat was concerned, too, but she had really expected to have Charlie in custody by now. I guess he was not as easy as she figured he would be, and she was not only taking it personally, but taking it out on the rest of us.

Jayne Kinderlen was the name of the woman I chose to help me. She remembered me right away when I said my name, and it almost felt like her voice sounded happy to hear from me. I had a fleeting feeling of just dropping the whole therapy thing and asking her to coffee, but I didn't know how I'd pull that one off. Besides, I didn't need a date, I needed help. I tried to explain a little of the situation over the phone, but she insisted on seeing me before hearing any more. We scheduled an appointment for the following afternoon and decided that Pat or Ted would escort me and remain on site during my visit with Dr. Kinderlen.

She was walking down the hall toward the door when I opened it a few minutes before my scheduled time. She was wearing linen overalls in muted earth tones with the legs rolled haphazardly at the ankles. Her bone-colored blouse hugged her slight frame. She had no shoes on her feet, and her light brown hair was pulled back in a single tie, leaving the shorter strands to dangle freely. Dark-rimmed glasses framed the large blue-green eyes I remembered from our previous meeting at the dinner party.

"Come in, Abby." She gestured toward the office with her arm. "I'm glad you could come on such short notice. Did you have any trouble finding me?" She smiled and stood beside the doorway as I walked into the large, mostly empty room.

"No. You were in the phone book." I misunderstood the question, and her smile changed to a grin. "You mean the office, right?" I laughed at myself. "No, your directions were really good."

"Sit anywhere you want." She filled a glass of water from the cooler and offered me one, as well. I accepted and took a seat by the window.

"Do you have some paperwork or forms I need to fill out?" I didn't see any. There was nothing but a clipboard on the small table beside the chair she took.

"Oh, the woman who helps me with paperwork is already gone for the day, but there are papers I need you to sign. We can do that later. Are you comfortable?" She pulled her legs up and crossed them in what looked like a really uncomfortable yoga position as she waited for me to answer.

"More comfortable than *that* looks." I smiled and fidgeted in my seat.

"It's actually really comfortable," she said as she returned her feet to the floor. "Is that better?"

"Much." I was still fidgeting.

"So, what's up?" She began talking to me like an old friend, and I suddenly relaxed in my chair and felt an overall ease.

"Well, I better start slow because this gets a little complicated. I should probably say first that I never thought much about therapy, so I don't know what kind of client I'm going to be." I paused. She continued to listen attentively. "I also better warn you that I'm in quite a mess and you might want to hear about it before deciding to take me on." I stopped and looked at her.

"That's a good idea." She was nodding. "I'll hear you out, then we can decide if we are right for each other in this type of relationship. Fair enough?"

I knew we were off to a good start when she informed me that she, too, had never thought much of conventional psychotherapy. She explained her ideas and philosophies, and I knew right away that I had made a good choice. I was becoming worried that she might decide I was way too much to handle after hearing my story, but I figured I better take my chances and tell all.

"Okay, Jayne, here's the deal: I'm caught in the middle of an intense murder investigation." Her face never changed. "I'm not being investigated or anything, but I am being guarded by two FBI agents who live in my house. The man they are looking for has killed at least three people and maybe a fourth. Have you heard enough to kick me out of here yet?" I was half kidding and half giving her the chance to break and run.

"Is there more?" She still looked calm and interested but not frightened.

"Yeah, there's a lot more." I sighed. "He's been contacting me through letters he stashes in places he knows only I will find them. I told the FBI about one of the letters, but I'm hiding the others for now." She nodded as if she understood and continued to listen.

"Jayne, he killed my former lover—his wife. He killed her former lover—his sister-in-law. He wants to see another woman in the circle dead, but she is also under protection." It all must have been terribly confusing. "See, he found Clara's diaries. Clara was his wife. He found them after he got out of prison by breaking into her house. He knows everything she did while they were married and while he mentally decomposed in prison without so much as a visit from her. He's really pissed. He's really crazy. Oh, and he's really pretty damn smart right now."

I talked for forty-five minutes, explaining how we all got to the place we were now. She listened intently, asking only the questions she needed for clarity and never displaying any signs of distress or discomfort. I couldn't believe she sat there so patiently, waiting for the story to unfold. We were approaching the close of the hourlong session time when she commented that I could continue if I wanted or we could end the session for the day.

"I don't know." I thought about it. "What do you usually do in cases like this one?"

The intensity of the conversation broke with our full-on smiles and open laughter.

"Let me see…" She pretended to be thinking back on cases similar to mine. "I'd say we're just going to have to play it by ear on this one, Abby. You're the first client I've had who came with an FBI escort!" We continued to laugh.

"Can we just finish the shell of the story today, then you'll have the basics for next time?" I asked timidly.

"Absolutely. I think we can bend the time rule a little in this case." She was still looking in my eyes with care and compassion.

I finished the basics in another fifteen minutes, then Jayne asked about my purpose for coming to therapy. I thought that was an odd question, given that I had told her the whole gruesome story, but she explained that everyone deals with different levels of stress and fear with varied tolerances and reactions.

"I'd like to know what you feel your specific goals for seeing me are," she asked after her explanation.

My first genuine response to her question shocked me so much that I almost blushed. At that moment, it had nothing to do with talking about my problems and everything to do with talking to her.

"Let me think about the question for a few days. Is that okay?" I felt my skin flush.

"Sure." She smiled.

As I left the office, I remembered again the night we'd met and the fact that there was something about Jayne that had completely enthralled me. I also left with a momentary feeling of knowing I would get better from spending time working with her. We agreed to see each other once a week and that I could call her if I got into an emotional bind. She said she normally advised clients to call 911 in an emergency. Although I didn't ask for special treatment, she made an exception and made herself available to me.

That evening, I found myself lying in bed thinking about Jayne's hair and wondering what it felt like. It was an odd attraction, emotional rather than physical. I had no identifiable sexual desire for Jayne, just an inexplicable desire to be close. Whatever had come over me in her office was definitely sticking around. Not since the first day I saw Clara, battered and broken in her apartment, had I felt such a strong instant connection to another person.

Those who fail to study history are destined to repeat it. I had studied hard the lesson I learned from my affair with Clara. Regardless of the link I had with Jayne or any other unavailable woman, I told myself over and over that this time I would ignore it.

Chapter Fifteen

"Abby." Pat's voice was barely a whisper. My room was dark.

"What?" I woke quickly and turned toward the door where she was entering.

"Stay really calm and don't get up. There's someone outside your window in the yard." I froze.

"How do you know?"

"The motion detector," she said as I remembered how much I had teased her just days ago when the detector was installed. It went off every time the wind moved a shrub. It had been adjusted countless times, but I still didn't have much faith in it.

"I'm going back to sleep." I rolled over and covered my head.

"No, Abby, there really is a man in your yard. Ted saw him as soon as the detector alerted us. He doesn't know we know he's there." I pulled back the blanket and exposed my face.

"What's he doing?"

"Ted is watching him from the bathroom window. He was trying to pick the lock on your shed when I came in here. The uniformed officers are setting up in the alley right now. I think we have him this time." She sounded confident.

"You don't even know who it is," I reminded her. "It could be some poor bastard looking for a bike to steal and getting ready to have the FBI on his ass." I was tiring of the police routine. "Don't shoot until you know it's Charlie, okay?" I didn't think there was any way in the world it could be.

"You have as much faith in us as you do the motion detector, huh?"

The man trying to get into my shed was in the custody of about nine different flavors of police personnel within the next twenty minutes. He really didn't have a chance; they definitely had him surrounded. As I suspected, it was not Charlie Stokes.

His name was James Helmire, and he was a twenty-two-year-old local. He said he was looking for something he could pawn quickly, tools and the like, and that he didn't know us at all. We sure didn't know him. I didn't feel quite right about his story from the start, but it was only a matter of hours before the FBI broke him into pieces.

His second story was very different. A man approached him at a local bar and asked him if he'd like to make some quick money. The man said he was going through a divorce and needed something his wife was hiding in their shed. The man told James that no one was home, so there would be no chance of getting caught. James had been instructed to remove any Army gear he found from my shed.

The man who hired James was to pick the gear up from him later the same evening. James had no idea how lucky he was that the FBI got him first. I had no idea why Charlie wanted my Army gear. I imagined it to be part of his attempt to drive me mad, but I had no specifics.

More odd than the Army gear was the fact that when James attempted to identify the man who hired him, he did not seem to recognize Charlie's photographs. He was shown more than one picture, but none of them sparked a memory. He also didn't recognize the missing boy from Florida when his picture appeared in the lineup.

We all felt that James was telling the truth in its entirety with his second story, but we did not understand how Charlie could have disguised himself so well. It occurred to me that the man might not have been Charlie, but that didn't seem likely. Composite artists were brought in, and an attempt to sketch the man James met at the bar began as I was leaving.

I went home mid-morning with Ted and Jeff while Pat stayed behind to further interrogate and intimidate James. I felt sorry for him but knew that Pat's routine was nothing compared to what he'd face if Charlie got to him again. I asked Ted if they would protect him from Charlie, but Ted would only commit to trying to determine if in fact it had been Charlie who hired him.

I was surprised to hear a message from Jayne on my machine when we got home. I called her back at once, but she was in session with a client. The receptionist would have her return my call as soon as she finished. I made some lunch and waited.

"Hi, Abby." Jayne's voice was cheerful but hesitant. "Are you okay?" She got right to the point.

"For the most part, I am. Why do you ask?" I was wishing my phone didn't have ears.

"Oh, I was just wondering. Anything new and exciting at your house?" She asked as if she knew the answer.

"As a matter of fact, it has been rather exciting around here." I was not giving up the details. "But everyone is fine."

"That's good. Do you remember that you have an appointment this afternoon?" I guess I could have forgotten, but it didn't seem plausible since she had not left my mind since I left her office.

"Yeah, I do, don't I?" I followed her lead the best I could.

"Four o'clock, right?" She gave me all the information I needed.

"Right. I'll see you then." We said goodbye and I hung up the phone. It was a little after 1:00 p.m. I asked Ted if he could take me to therapy in a few hours, and I retreated to my room to try and rest before seeing Jayne.

Pat called just before we left for Jayne's office to say the sketch was going well and we'd need to have a look at it late this afternoon. I told her I had forgotten my therapy appointment and that Ted would bring me by the police station when I finished. Jeff wanted to be dropped off at the station prior to my appointment so he could see the sketch as soon as it was done. I really didn't care anything about the sketch or Pat or Ted or the lot of them because something was up with Jayne, and I was less than an hour from knowing what it was.

When we arrived at her office, the receptionist was just leaving and Jayne was standing in the doorway. She was dressed in solid black lightweight wool trousers and a slate cardigan with an eggshell silk blouse showing through. Her hair was down, and she wasn't wearing her glasses. Her eyes sparkled and danced, and she welcomed me with a handshake.

"Where's your bodyguard?" She chuckled and looked around behind me.

"Oh, he thinks he's clever, so he hides in bushes and jumps out of trees at my would-be attackers." I had no idea where he was, but I knew he could see me from wherever he might be. "He's around." I walked past her and into the office as she held the door open.

"Do they have a microphone or a homing device on you so they can track your movement?" She was laughing, but I think she might have been serious.

"Not that I know of." I raised my eyebrows. "I wouldn't put it past them, though." I was so glad to see her. She looked more beautiful than I remembered from our last visit, and I just stopped and stared at her for a minute.

"Thanks for playing along and coming in today." We were both still standing in the hallway entry.

"I didn't think I had an appointment until tomorrow, but the way things are in my head these days, anything is possible." I wasn't even questioning why she called me.

"Abby, I woke up a little concerned about you this morning."

I listened without speaking.

"What happened last night?"

"Oh, I had a visitor in my backyard." I told her the story. "Are you some kind of psychic?"

"I never have been." She shrugged her shoulders. "I've always been intuitive with my clients, but that's about it."

I looked at her so intensely that she was the one fidgeting this time.

"Why are you looking at me like that?"

"I just think it's really amazing that you knew something was up." I spoke softly and cautiously, remembering my promise to stay a safe distance. She looked confused.

"Let's go sit down. That's really not the only reason I called you in today." She led me into the room, and we took our same seats.

"Abby, when I arrived here this morning, there was an envelope with your name on it taped to my door. I thought about calling the police, but then I remembered what you told me last time. You said you'd only given them one of the letters you'd received, and I didn't know what you would want." She looked troubled. "So I took it off the door carefully and laid it in my desk drawer." She was getting up now and walking toward her desk.

I felt all the panic I had failed to feel last evening the minute she got up.

"Wait." I stopped her before she reached the desk. "Let me open the drawer." I got up and went to the desk.

"Why? Is there a bomb in there or something?" She was half kidding and half scared.

"I hope not. I just want to see if the same familiar smell that was on the last one is present when I open the drawer." She pointed to the side drawer of her old wooden desk, the one that contained the envelope. "I should just call Ted in here right now." I hesitated. "I promised them I wouldn't withhold any more evidence." I had my hand on the drawer handle.

"Go with what you feel is right, Abby." Jayne touched my arm, and I almost left my skin.

I let go of the handle. "He knows I'm coming here or else he wouldn't have known to leave the envelope on your door. If I don't tell them, they might not know that you're in danger, too." I was thinking aloud. "I'm sorry, Jayne. I shouldn't have come here in the first place because who knows what he'll do to get to me." I felt small and weak. "I'm going to get Ted." I turned toward the door.

Jayne stepped in front of me. "I'm not afraid of being hurt if you don't want to tell." She was standing between the door and me. "Just do what you know inside to be right, and it will be."

I looked her in the eyes. "What is right and what is best are never the same things for me." I felt like crying. "I can't stand the thought of one more person being involved in this horror that started from my indiscretion. This all started because I did what I knew inside to be right. I tried to save Clara. It might have felt right, but it wasn't in anyone's best interest for me to get involved with a married woman." I cleared my throat and tried to feel my legs under me.

"I knew it wasn't the best thing to go screwing around in the desert looking for trouble, but I did that because it felt right, too. But it wasn't either. I even knew it wasn't for the best that I walked away from my life in Spartanburg instead of trying to piece it back together after the war. But it felt so right inside my soul to flee that place that I followed my intuition. Wrong again." I put my head down.

"And what is best versus what is right this time, Abby?" She gently took my chin in her hand and raised my head. She looked deep in my eyes as if she could see the answer in my soul without ever asking the question.

"Not to hurt another person is best *and* right." I felt the tears coming.

"The other person can handle it." She knew I wanted to open that drawer. "Be true to your gut, Abby." She brushed the few escaping tears from one side of my cheek with the hand that held my chin. I found the strength to stop the tears and swallowed hard.

When I opened the drawer, the smell came rushing out from inside it. So subtle and faint that Jayne only thought she might have caught a hint of it. So familiar and comfortable that I had it in my mind long after it left the air. I closed my eyes and searched my memory for its origin. Like a word on the tip of your tongue that just won't reveal itself, the smell remained a mystery.

It's getting harder and harder to reach you.

That was all. No diary entry and no dissertation on our similarities, just those few words on a piece of notebook paper. I had no idea what to make of it.

Jayne said it was a power play. He wanted me to know that he was going the distance to reach me despite the restraints that had been put on him of late. He wanted me to know he was serious about getting through to me and would not be deterred. I wanted him to know some things, too. I wanted him to know how damn hard it was to keep these letters away from Pat and Ted and how guilty it made me feel to deceive them. I wanted to spit in his face and tell him that he wasn't the only one out on a limb here.

"Abby, you *can* tell him. He's going to be back and you can tell him then." Jayne listened to my angry tirade and offered a solution.

"What?" It was starting to click.

"He'll be back here. Leave him a note. Tell him to stop messing with you. Tell him to turn himself in or whatever you want to say. Take back some of the control."

I stood still and tried to fathom what she was saying. He would undoubtedly return to this office to leave me notes; it was the only safe place left for him. I could communicate with him if I chose to. I could say the things I wanted to say.

I snapped back to the world. "If I don't turn this over to Pat and Ted, I'm an accessory or something. They'll never forgive me."

"Will you ever forgive yourself if you don't follow your instinct?" For whatever reason, Jayne wanted me to be in command of my destiny.

"I will never forgive myself if you get caught in the crossfire," I said, not looking at her.

"I'm already in the crossfire," she answered, taking my hand so delicately that I barely felt her grip. I didn't need to ask her what she meant.

I couldn't quell the urge to cry. We were face-to-face when the tears started, and she put her arms around me instinctively. We stood in an embrace for what felt like hours. I must have cried some and she must have wiped my tears, but I just let my soul be lost instead of taking note.

"That feels better, doesn't it?" She brought me back gently with a little pat on the back and a brush of the hair from my wet face. "Crying is cleansing, and cleansing is part of the healing."

"Crying is for babies." I smiled and reluctantly let go of my hold on her body. There were many more tears, but I made them stop.

"Where did that come from?" I wanted to make it clear that it was not my normal behavior.

"You don't always have to be strong." She let go of me, as well, and leaned back on her desk.

"I wish that were true, Jayne, but it isn't. I have to stay tough or I'd never get through this. When it's all over, I may have a nervous breakdown. Besides, if I started crying now, I'd never stop."

"You may have a breakdown whether you think you can or not." Jayne may have known what she was saying, but she didn't know me. "Do you believe you get to consciously decide when you've had enough?" She was looking directly at me, almost like she could take the answer right out of my head.

"Yes. I get to decide. I always have and I always will. I won't be controlled by some inner weakness. I won't break down until there's a good time to do it." The realization that I had already started losing control hit me again like a fast-moving train. "Damn him. I should just lie in the street and tell him to come and get me." The tears returned.

Jayne put her arms back around me and held me while I cried again. I didn't try and stop myself until I felt a little relief, and she didn't say a word while I sobbed openly, my tears wetting her blouse. When I finally forced the tears to slow, we both let go and stood staring at each other.

"Oh, God, I don't know what's happening to me," I remarked as I looked into her kind eyes.

"Just let it happen, Abby." She patted me again on the arm, then reached for the tissue box on her desk. "Here." She handed it to me. "Congratulations on letting some of that out. Are you breathing in there?"

"I think so, thanks." I tried to notice my breathing.

"It didn't really seem like you were there for a minute. You have to feed the far-away parts of your body oxygen, too!" She was trying to lighten me up. "Breathe deep."

"You're an amazing woman, Jayne. I'm so thankful I came here. As long as it doesn't get you in any trouble."

"The only trouble I'm in is with Shannon if I don't get home in the next half hour." She looked at her watch. "She's pretty understanding after all these years, but I have a few issues surrounding timeliness. I should say they are her issues since they bother her. I don't really mind being late for everything!"

"Yeah, I need to get to the police station anyway. The composite artist is sketching the person who hired someone to break into my shed last night," I said.

"Oh, that's what it was." She was nodding. "No one was hurt, though, right?"

"That's right. See, you are psychic." She looked a bit startled. "I'll think about what to write Charlie and get back with you next time." She nodded and turned to the door.

I followed close behind because I wanted to leave at once. I felt uncomfortable hearing Shannon's name and feeling so vulnerable. Jayne stopped at the door and turned back to me.

"Abby. I don't make a habit of crossing into my clients' personal space during therapy, but you really seemed to need a shoulder. I hope you're okay with it." She looked serious.

"I'm more than okay with it, I'm really grateful for your compassion. Besides, I have a hard time talking to strangers about the personal tragedies in my life. That's why I came to you in the first place. You seemed like someone I should know."

"I totally understand what you're saying." She nodded.

She may have understood what I was saying, but I had no idea what I was feeling. If I had said what came to my mind, it would have sounded as stale as a seventies cocktail lounge come-on. I wanted to ask her if I knew her from some other life or if we'd ever been friends. I wanted to tell her she was welcome in my personal space, but I knew better. "I was the one who crossed the line anyway" was all I said.

"We may be crossing some lines, but I'm trusting that it'll all be okay." She had a look of wanting to say more, so I waited.

"Abby, I was really happy when you called me to help you with this..." she paused, "and I shouldn't really have those kinds of feelings about people coming to me for therapy." There was more silence. "I have to tell you that after we met at the dinner party, I thought about you a good bit, then, well, you called for an appointment. I probably should have told you it wasn't a good idea, but I didn't and...." I interrupted.

"And now you wish you had?" I felt very small.

"No," she assured me. "I'm very happy we're working together on this, but I do have a small concern about maintaining our professional relationship."

"Is that what you meant about already being in the crossfire?" I'm not sure why I asked a question I knew the answer to already.

"It is," she confirmed. "And it's my job to keep our relationship professional, so I promise you that I will do nothing to harm you," she pledged.

"I know that," I said. "You don't need to promise."

"Good. So the cat is out of the bag and now we can just get to work." She patted my arm.

"I better get going." I slipped the note in my pocket and headed out the door to meet Ted, who was waiting by the car. We didn't say much, but his silence said that he was keeping something.

As we pulled into the parking lot of the police station, Ted turned off the engine but remained in his seat. I didn't move. After a brief silent period, he drew a long breath and started to speak. "Abby, I have some disturbing news." He let out the breath he was still holding. "The sketch is not Charlie. It's Alvin."

I felt the bottom of the earth drop from under me. A tunnel opened up around what used to be my peripheral vision, and I saw the swirling motion inside the eye of a tornado. The note in my pocket felt heavy, and its smell rose to the present from my memory. The friendly, comfortable fragrance that kissed every correspondence. No wonder it was so familiar.

Chapter Sixteen

There's something different about twins. Everyone knows it. Whether identical or fraternal, boys, girls, or a mix, twins share a bond unlike that of normal siblings. When we were very young, Alvin and I used to tell everyone we were identical. We didn't quite grasp the concept of one egg splitting versus two eggs. All we knew was that we were born on the same day, from the same womb.

We dressed alike most of our preteen years, and with my tendency toward more masculine toys, we shared everything. We climbed the same trees, caught the same frogs, and fished in our pond for anything dumb enough to bite the hook on our homemade poles. It wasn't until puberty that our egg split.

I missed Alvin when he chose to face the world without me. I can't say I blame him for separating us, but I wish he had thought it through a little better before making such a hasty decision. We were seventeen and seniors in high school. Prom was coming up and Alvin had a huge crush on one of the girls from the volleyball team. He was a little shy about asking her out, but with some prompting, he got the nerve.

She accepted and prom night rolled around. I don't remember the exact sequence of events that led up to what happened that night. I do know that I made the first in a lifelong series of bad judgment calls.

I went as the date of the most flaming young gay man in our school. We certainly weren't trying to fool anyone, and we had a great time. After prom, eight or ten of us traveled to our favorite lakefront party spot to continue the festivities. Alvin's date was a fair bit drunk by the time we arrived at the site and full tilt smashed within half an hour. On the car ride out to the lake, she kept falling into my lap, but I passed it off as too much alcohol while Alvin didn't even seem to notice. We made a bonfire and blared music from someone's car stereo, danced, and hung out.

It wasn't long before the first of us stripped to buck and dashed for the water. The time it took for the rest of us to follow suit was even shorter. The water was just cold enough to excuse all our bodily erections and just warm enough to bask in comfortably. I focused on Alvin's date as soon as her dress reached the top of her shoulders. I tried not to notice like I'd been trying not to notice all evening, but she made sure I was watching before she slid her dress slowly and seductively up her firm body and over her head. I followed her into the water but quickly went to the other side of the crowd as far from her as I could go.

She followed me. There was just enough moonlight to see her go under the water but not enough to see where she was going. I knew where she was when I felt her wrap her legs around my legs and her arms around my waist; I sank without her even tugging.

We made our way through the murky lake water with the loud chatter of our companions for background until we reached the dark side of the shore. We had been entangled the entire short swim to the point that I don't know how we ever reached land. I didn't realize for at least an hour that the noise had stopped and the others had gone.

Alvin was kind; he left our clothes and his car. I wondered as we dressed without speaking if the others knew as undoubtedly Alvin had just what we were doing.

That was it for Alvin and me. The end of our lives as siblings began prom night. He only ever said I was sick and needed help. He did tell me that he managed to get the others out of there without them knowing I was sodomizing his date. I know my date was likely cheering me on, but I don't know how Alvin kept it from the others. It was probably more to save his face than my ass.

I don't blame him for his anger, but I wish he had practiced the religion he was always preaching, the one that says forgive and forget. He never forgave me, and while we tried to maintain a shell of the relationship we had shared as children, it was all but gone.

Ted called my name a few times before it occurred to me that he was speaking. I had been away in my head, dragging up the painful memory of my brother's self-guided removal from my life.

"Alvin is in South America." I would not let it be true. "Call the church for yourself."

"We did, Abby. He never went. He sent another man in his place. We think it might have been the missing boy from Florida. We're working on getting a contact to him now."

I couldn't follow all the thoughts that were rushing to my head as the blood rushed away. If it was Alvin, why did he want my Army gear? If it was Alvin, was he involved with Charlie? If it was Alvin, did he kill someone? There were way too many questions without answers.

"Abby, we need your help. We need to know everything you can tell us about your brother." Ted was speaking to me as if I was about to fall apart. I was.

"It isn't Alvin." I knew it was. "It couldn't be." I already knew it could damn well be.

"Abby, don't lie to yourself. It looks bad for Alvin either way. If he is involved, it's likely got something to do with Charlie. If it's voluntary, we'll try and get him help. If it's forced, he's in grave danger and we need to get him help." He knew I was too fragile to press on that moment. "Let's have a look at the sketch. We'll go from there."

We entered the building like we were in a funeral procession. We marched past the front desk, the guards, and all the milling people. We moved into the elevator, then down the hall to the room where Pat and Jeff were sitting around a table with some other men. Jeff got up when he saw me. I didn't even look at him.

There was Alvin's picture on the table in front of me, as big as life.

"Where's the guy who broke into my shed?" I had to stop looking at the sketch.

"He's in jail. Didn't even try and make bail," Pat answered.

"That was wise." I looked at Jeff. "Can we go home?"

He nodded and held out his arm for me. I took it and we walked out the door with Ted behind us.

If they wanted to question me, they kept it hidden. If they wanted me to participate in the conversation, they didn't ask. I am sure that even Pat knew I was at the brink of personal disaster. The moment Ted told me it was Alvin, I left my body and went to the place I go to watch horror from a safe distance. I stayed there with no plans to return to consciousness.

The note in my pocket was all I was really sure of on the drive home. It reminded me that I had made the right choice in keeping the secret. I was glad I had revealed the journal entry because I gave them something, but the probability that Alvin was the author of the other writings made it essential to keep them hidden. I wanted to protect him. How ironic since he might be trying to kill me.

It was almost two days later when I emerged from my room. I was attempting to sleep the pain away, and I might have remained in my room longer had it not been for a phone call from Jayne. She wanted to move my appointment time up an hour due to a cancellation. I agreed.

Pat, Ted, and Jeff filled me in on the happenings, and though they had more facts, they weren't much further along than when I fell asleep. Alvin was missing in the sense that he was not in South America. He had indeed sent a replacement to his mission assignment—the boy from Florida whose car turned up in Colorado. The unidentified set of prints found on the diary entry and in the car belonged to Alvin, as well. The puzzle was forming a picture.

The accidental missionary was certainly not very cooperative when the FBI contact located him in South America. He initially refused any questioning but relented when told he could remain silent and be brought back to the United States to be questioned for his involvement in a serial-killing spree. He knew nothing of any murders, but he certainly knew Charlie Stokes.

Charlie's family had helped put the two in touch while Charlie was still behind bars. Charlie had fathered a boy born to a sixteen-year-old girl two years before he married Clara. The baby was adopted at birth, and Charlie had never seen him again. The boy, named Aaron, began the search for his real parents after high school, against the better judgment of his adoptive family. The search netted him Charlie, aging and serving time.

I suppose blood is thicker than water to some, and the two became pen pals a couple of years before Charlie was released and met in Florida once Charlie was freed. Aaron's adoptive parents knew nothing of Charlie or his involvement with their son. Aaron had apparently stopped informing them of his search when they expressed their opposition.

Charlie left Florida a few days before Aaron left for Spartanburg. Aaron told police that Charlie had said he had to make another stop in Georgia on his way home but that they'd catch up to each other in Spartanburg to begin a trip together. When Aaron arrived in Spartanburg, Alvin met him instead, introducing himself as Charlie's younger brother. Alvin told Aaron that they were all going on a mission trip to South America funded by the church and that he and Charlie had some things to take care of before they could leave town.

Aaron told authorities that he was more than happy to go on the advance party to South America for a mission trip and that he had no reason to believe that the others weren't going to meet him as they said they would. He arrived in South America, met the host family that Alvin was to have met, and began his adventure.

Pat and Ted could not fathom how Alvin factored into the equation but knew for certain that he was as involved as Charlie was. Alvin had provided the opportunity for Charlie's blood son to leave the country and made all the arrangements for his mission. It made sense that neither Charlie nor Alvin wanted this young man hanging around town for whatever was going on with them, but whether they sent him out of the country for his safety or their convenience was anybody's guess.

So many things just didn't make sense. How Alvin became involved with Charlie in the first place was probably the biggest mystery. Why Alvin chose to lie to his family about his whereabouts was equally baffling. Alvin went so far as to send the young man with a stack of letters addressed to his wife to be mailed periodically from the mission site. I was very grateful that the FBI opted for the moment not to tell Alvin's wife or the rest of my family what was going on.

The lies were stacking up. I wasn't telling about the letters I had received. The FBI wasn't telling our family about Alvin's whereabouts. Laurel wasn't telling what I had confided in her. Rachel wasn't telling that she remembered what happened to us in the desert. Jayne wasn't telling about her involvement in the whole mess, and I wasn't telling about my emotional involvement with Jayne. Everyone was lying to someone.

I had only a few hours before my therapy appointment, and I wanted to write a message for Alvin before I got there. I had no idea what to say or where to begin asking him what was going on. I sat at my desk for over an hour, but only one word came: Why?

On the way to Jayne's office, I thought about how I would tell her of the new developments in the case. I knew I had to tell her it was my twin brother leaving me the notes and trying to drive me insane. Despite the conversation we had the last time I saw her, I was sure she would be ready to dump me as a client and go back to a normal safe practice with run-of-the-mill psychiatric situations once she heard the latest. I wondered if I should dump her as my therapist for her own safety and just tell her I made the whole thing up to get her attention.

When we pulled into the parking lot, I forgot about wanting to tell her anything that would mean I wouldn't see her again. She was not in the hallway when I opened the door to her office. I heard her singing from a room in the back somewhere, and I froze to listen. I didn't want her to know I was there and stop the beautiful sound penetrating the building.

When she came around the corner and saw me smiling at her, she looked like she'd seen a ghost. She was mid-note and moderately loud, but she swallowed the rest of what she was singing after seeing my face. We both broke into the same contagious nervous laughter we had the first day I came to her. For those few moments, I misplaced my thoughts just enough to enjoy the simple pleasure of her presence.

"Abby!" She came to me with a welcoming hug. "When did you come in?"

"Only a few minutes ago." I hugged her tightly, then reluctantly let go. "Your voice is wonderful!" I was shaking my head at the raw talent she was keeping hidden.

"It's also rusty and shy."

"Forget therapy; I'll go home and get my guitar and we can sing for an hour. That's kind of therapeutic, isn't it?" I raised my eyebrows and waited for an answer.

"Some other time. We have work to do." She pointed toward the door of her session room. "Shall we?"

"Okay." I drew the word into as many syllables as possible, sighed hard, and walked into the room. "Any more letters?"

"No." She was ritualistically filling our water glasses from the cooler. "You?" She handed me a glass.

"None." I took a drink and thanked her. "Things are really complicated now, Jayne."

"And they were simple before?" She smiled and took her seat.

"It's all very confusing, but yes, it's more complex than before." I began by explaining that Alvin was involved, then telling her about the boy he sent to South America. She listened and tried not to change her facial expression.

"I'm sorry, Abby. This really is more complicated than before."

"I don't think Alvin had anything to do with murdering anyone." My tone suggested I might be unsure. "It's not like him. He could never even watch horror films."

"So you think Charlie kidnapped him?" Jayne cocked her head and looked skeptically at me.

"I think Alvin's in over his head, but I don't think Charlie kidnapped him. I think he's doing whatever he's doing of his own volition, but Charlie is certainly a factor. I just can't figure how the two of them hooked up." I took a drink.

"Is there any reason Alvin would want to kill you, Abby?"

"There are a million reasons, but he wouldn't do it. It's not Alvin. He's peaceful. He wouldn't hurt a flea." Jayne was looking at me as though I were delusional. "Really. He would never hurt a soul intentionally. I know that about my brother."

"People surprise you. They snap for no obvious reason, then they are capable of doing what they were formerly not capable of doing. It is possible that Alvin snapped, Abby." I was listening and remembering what I was capable of doing, but I still couldn't see Alvin as a murderer.

"Charlie killed all those other people. His prints and physical evidence were all over the crime scenes. Alvin didn't kill anyone."

"He may not have killed anyone, but I want you to realize that he could be dangerous so that you'll protect yourself. Do you understand? You could be in danger, and you need to accept the possibility and guard against it. That's all I'm saying." She was calm and convincing.

I compromised with, "Okay, he could be dangerous but not to me."

"Just be aware, Abby, that's all."

I nodded.

"So what are you going to do?" I guess she knew I'd have a plan.

"I have a note for him. I want to leave it on your door if that's okay." I looked at her for an answer.

"Of course it's okay. Can you tell me what it says?"

"It just asks why." I pulled it from my pocket and handed it to her. "Will you tape it to the door after I leave?"

"No problem."

The room fell quiet for a moment. As I sat and stared at her, I wished we could forget what was happening and I could just listen to her sing. I closed my eyes, but I could still see her face. It was just as clear in my mind as it was through my eyes. I wandered away to a place in my imagination where we met under different circumstances. We were both young and I was not yet damaged. It was before I ever joined the National Guard, and so I never did. I did not go to Desert Storm. In the daydream, I saw us sitting on the porch of an old cabin somewhere beautiful, singing together and laughing at ourselves.

"Abby, where are you?" The room was bright when she called me back.

"Nowhere. Just thinking." I closed my eyes again and felt the tears trying to escape. I squeezed my eyelids tightly together. How could just her presence draw out so much emotion?

"Let's talk about what you were just thinking. Is that okay?" She followed my face. "Only if you feel safe with..."

"Desert Storm," I interrupted. "I was wishing I hadn't been to Desert Storm."

"You said something last time about the desert, then mentioned war. It really affected you, huh?" Her face gave away the sadness her calm tone thought it concealed. "Do you want to talk about it?"

"There's not much to talk about. I went, I did my job, and I returned."

"How long were you there?" I knew she was trying to lead me gently into a discussion.

"Four months, three days, seven hours and change from getting on the plane to getting back off again. Plus another four months on either side of the actual deployment spent at the Army post getting ready to go, then getting released. Eight months of my life were wasted."

"It must have been frightening." She concentrated hard on holding my eyes. I was completely with her.

"It was, I guess, but I didn't really have time to be scared." As I spoke, I remembered how afraid I was of being afraid while I was in the desert. I denied myself access to fear for fear it would permeate my existence and render me useless to the soldiers who counted on my leadership.

"So you were busy?" She led me forward.

"Yes. I was in charge of a platoon, and that kept me swamped with work." I began telling her about my soldiers and how much they meant to me. "They were my family."

I had no idea how long I had been talking when I glanced at my watch and realized I was running over my time limit again. I stopped telling my story and started apologizing for holding her over.

"You don't get to be responsible for my time, too." She smiled at me and asked me to please finish what I had started. I talked another ten minutes or so about my platoon, then told her I was finished.

"See, Jayne, after Desert Storm, Charlie's little killing spree isn't much." I stood up and felt hot all over with embarrassment for what I had just said. "I mean, it's not so new to me to deal with fear and death." I looked away.

She stood, as well, and moved toward me. "Is it still okay to hug you?" She was already halfway there.

"I like it when you hug me." We embraced each other as I embraced the realization that Desert Storm was still an open wound after all these years.

"I meant what I said about calling me if you need me." She was holding both of my shoulders and looking directly into my eyes.

"I have your number." I smiled and took a step backward. "There might be a few things left over from Desert Storm that I should maybe talk to you about. We'll see how it goes."

"That'd be great if you wanted to share any of it with me."
She looked at her watch. "I really do have to go now." She made a
face that implied she might already be late.

"Not again." I laughed.

"Afraid so." Her head was shaking as she reached for her
jacket. "She's going to kill me if I don't knock this off."

We taped the note to the door and walked each other to the
parking area. We hardly spoke as she got into her car, and I stood
by Ted's car and watched her drive away.

"She's a handsome woman, Abby." Ted was watching me
watch her. "I might need therapy, too, if my therapist could look
that good." He knew I was paying him no mind, but he continued
to try and divert my attention from her fading taillights. "Does she
have a steady?"

"Very steady." I opened the car door and fell into the seat.

Chapter Seventeen

It was inevitable that I had to become involved in the investigation against Alvin. The FBI had been patient while I slept through the initial shock and kind when I finally came out of my room. Now the grace period was over, and I had to tell them everything I could about my twin and suppose with them why he might be involved in serial killings.

We sat around the kitchen table and began the discussion. Pat, as usual, wanted to know everything without listening to anything, and I was annoyed in record time.

"Relax, Pat." Ted was the only one of us she might take orders from. "We'll get it all, but it just might take a day or two." Pat made a noise that resembled a growl and got up for water.

"Let's go over the part where you told him about Clara. I think we're overlooking something." We'd done this several times already, but Ted was patient and persistent. Pat returned to her seat.

I led into the story the same way I had the last two times they asked me to tell it. "We had been sneaking around sleeping together for about a month when I told Alvin. I think I just needed to tell someone who would disapprove as much as I should have that I was actually having an affair with a married woman. He didn't just disapprove—he totally freaked out. He reminded me that she was married all right, but it didn't stop there. He also reminded me that she was not a dyke like me and said I was playing with fire. He told me I was nuts because if Charlie Stokes ever found out, he'd rip me apart."

"Did he ever threaten to tell Charlie?" Pat asked a formerly unasked question.

I looked up at the ceiling and tried hard to take myself back to that day in Spartanburg when I talked to Alvin about Clara. I stared at the light fixture until I was near blind, but I couldn't get the whole picture. "I don't remember, Pat."

"What if you were to write it down?" Jeff suddenly sat up from his previously slumped position. "What if you write what you know and see if the rest comes? Remember last fall when we decided to start our job journal?" He was referring to the work notebook we began after last season to log all the job specifics for each client. It included everything from the initial contact meeting all the way through the finished work.

"Remember how we sat for days trying to come up with the specifics on the early jobs? Then we just started writing what we could remember, and when you saw it in print, you remembered more. I was amazed at how many little details came back to you while you read the notes. Write what you know about the conversation with Alvin and maybe the rest will come to you when you read it."

"Couldn't hurt anything to give it a shot," Ted agreed. "Besides, writing things down is good for cleaning out your head. I bet your therapist would agree with that, and I won't even charge you for the advice!" He winked at me.

"I think writing is good actually. I kept a journal in Desert Storm because I didn't ever want to forget how I felt." I caught myself revealing more than I wanted to and stopped talking. My mind kept moving, though, and I realized I couldn't have known back then that there was absolutely no chance I would ever forget that experience. Clara used to try and inspire me to write. I squeezed my eyes tightly together again and relaxed in the safety of my thoughts. I would give anything to have the rest of her writings: the ones my brother and Charlie were using against me.

"I don't see how Abby writing a story is going to help us any." Pat was her usual skeptical self. "If she can't remember it to tell us, how could she remember it to write it?" She stared at Jeff.

"You didn't hear a word we just said, did you?" He shook his head in disgust. "We agreed it feels like the right thing to do to help her remember. Do you ever get feelings, Pat? Or should I say do you *have* any feelings, Pat?" His voice rose. "If we can try something new that sheds light on this case and gets your negative, sorry ass out of our house, I am 100 percent for it. You're pissed because a white-trash man with a ninth-grade education has you chasing your tail." Jeff was the one who got up to leave the room this time.

"You're pissed because you're in love with a lesbian." It was out before he left earshot. I heard Jeff returning slowly to the room.

"I may be in love with a lesbian, but at least I have enough respect to keep my feelings about it to myself." He looked at me. "Sorry, Abby, but she's a bitch." He left again.

"Good one, Pat. You have such a way with words. Maybe you should write a story." I went after my friend.

"Knock, knock." I eased the door to Jeff's room open. "Can I come in?"

"As long as it's just you." He didn't look up from his desk.

"Don't worry about her. She's just high-strung." I put my hand on his shoulder.

"I am in love with you, Abby, but you already knew that. Everyone who knows us knows it. I never meant for it to be a surprise or anything." He took my hand and squeezed it. "You're not upset with me, are you?"

"No way." I wrapped my arms around his shoulders and hugged him close. "If I ever wanted a man, it would definitely be you." I kissed his head.

"I know."

"Stop letting her get to you. She's just upset because of the way the investigation is going." I wanted to change the subject to one a little less personal.

"She hates me because I'm a threat to the strength of her team." He looked at me. "She's afraid you might actually have the capacity to care for me the way you would another woman, and that makes her nervous." He was not letting my eyes wander.

"Jeff, I love you like family. You are the one sure thing I have in my life right now, and if I could fall in love with you the way I have with women, it would be great. I don't know why I couldn't have been bisexual, but I'm just not made that way. I don't find men attractive the same way you don't find other men attractive." I didn't want to hurt his feelings, but the topic was on the table.

"I could wear a dress and lipstick every now and then!" He faked an excited face.

"Then I'd think you were a freak." I hugged him again.

"Hypocrite," he teased.

"Maybe I am. I don't understand men in dresses any more than I do women with big belt buckles, but I guess it takes all kinds. I'm just saying that I personally don't find either particularly sexually appealing."

"Whatever." He rolled his eyes and shook his head. "I'll take the love you have for me in whatever form it comes in, Abby."

After dinner, I retreated to my room again and sat with a notebook on my desk and a pen in my hand. I began writing the things I could remember about telling Alvin of my affair with Clara. The one-line memories filled up half a page. I sat with my words and thoughts for nearly an hour before deciding I needed a rest.

Jayne had been in the back of my mind ever since I left her office, but now her presence shifted to the forefront of my thoughts. I closed my eyes and saw the outline of her energy just as I had during our earlier session. It was a comforting sight in place of the usual darkness in my head.

She wanted to know about Desert Storm, and I wanted to tell her. For the first time since my return, I wanted to talk about my experiences. I wanted to tell someone who wasn't forcing me to talk and didn't just want to live a little safe horror through me. I don't blame people for being curious; I just never liked being on display.

It's human nature to want to hear about things that you've never experienced yourself. I remember wanting to talk to other veterans long before I knew I would go to war. I was fascinated by the Vietnam veterans in my Army unit. I wanted to hear the stories of their experiences without having to feel the pain, wanted to know all the gory details of war and survival.

I wanted to know because I had no idea what it could be like. The media glorified war and made heroes of all the soldiers; I wanted to know some heroes. I could not conceptualize the realities of such an experience. I didn't know about the mental anguish and recurring nightmares they lived and died with as part of just surviving. I didn't know of the guilt they bore simply for the act of breathing. I didn't see the others who hadn't been so lucky.

Jayne, on the other hand, wanted to know for different reasons. She wanted to know because she wanted me to know. I guess that's what therapists do; they want to hear the entire trauma replayed so their patient will hear it also and start to let it go. I wanted to let it go. I wanted Jayne to help me.

I was surprised by my earlier remarks to Pat and Ted. I hadn't mentioned the journals I kept in Desert Storm because I never wanted to see them again. I saw no point in ever reading the words that captured the raw emotions of some long-dead person who used to live inside me. I might have thought when I began writing them that I would want to see them again someday, but that was another time, another place.

I started keeping a written record of my experiences in Southwest Asia the day I arrived. I figured if I never came home, at least someone would hear my story. I wrote bits and pieces as I had time and mailed them to the post office box in my hometown where the mail was on a hold order until my return. A friend from school who worked at the post office made sure they were kept safe; he knew that if anything happened to me, he should take them all to Clara. Given her love for writing, I knew she would want to read them if I didn't return. I did return, though, at least in body, and I collected the journal entries with the rest of my mail when I visited the post office.

For the first three-and-a-half years following my return from Southwest Asia, I did not open a single envelope to read what I had written. I placed the envelopes with my military gear and packed it all away. I was afraid of what buried emotions would escape if I ever opened the bag they were stored in.

I was sure that the entries were a roller coaster of utter confusion. They could be nothing else. They contained the mixed-up emotions of a young, brand-new second lieutenant during a combat scenario, the lieutenant I no longer was but still remembered in my worst nightmares: someone other than me.

They tell the story of a war: my war. They also tell the story of a war endured by the brave soldiers who served with me: the soldiers who tolerated, baby-sat, supported, trained, annoyed, and protected me and my career along with the freedom of this thankless, reckless country.

I couldn't read the journals because I didn't want to put myself back in the place of that young scared lieutenant. I knew those pages could force me to remember.

After three-and-a-half years, I tried to open the bag a time or two and read a few pages, but I just couldn't do it. I'd start reading at random and immediately begin to shake and feel embarrassed— embarrassed that I was shaking over a little piece of paper and embarrassed that reading an apparently innocuous line or two about a convoy could evoke such fear.

Anyone else reading the journals might wonder why they induced such fear and panic. I didn't have to wonder because I could read from any page and be there in an instant, feeling it all over again. It was the things that weren't on the page that brought me the most anxiety. Maybe it wasn't as bad as what the Vietnam veterans endured, but when it's the worst thing you've ever dealt with, it's damn bad enough.

A chill that shook my whole body brought me back to the desk where I was sitting and the half-blank page in front of me. It suddenly hit me like a lightning bolt out of a clear blue sky. It wasn't something Alvin said when I told him of my affair with Clara, but rather something he said when I was leaving to go to Saudi Arabia.

We were standing with our family members in one of the buildings at the airbase just before I boarded the plane. I was sad that Clara couldn't be there and mad at Alvin for not bringing her with him as I had begged him to. They called us to board, and I said goodbye to everyone. As I began to walk away, Alvin followed me out of the others' earshot. Walking beside me, he took my hand. I scarcely acknowledged his gesture since I was half-numb and furious with him.

"She's easy to forget, Abby. Just let her go, she always does anyway." He spoke quietly as I continued to move past him and out of the building.

I pondered what Alvin meant for a bit as the plane left the airbase headed for uncertainty. We weren't even out of the United States before the metamorphosis changed me into a different animal. The new animal didn't care what Alvin was saying. The new animal was all about survival and not at all about looking back.

As I sat with my own page of notes before me, there was absolutely no doubt in my mind what had happened: Alvin and Clara had been lovers. It must have happened right before I had an affair with her. I don't know how I let it go unnoticed. I had no way to express the anger and betrayal I felt toward Clara as yet another layer of her mounting lies peeled away.

Clara never mentioned that she knew Alvin by anything more than sight. I talked about him some since I was always trying to think of new ways to get him to love and forgive me, but she only listened. I remember crying to her more than once that I missed him and wished we could understand each other, but she just held me and said nothing.

Clara and I spent all the time we could alone. We certainly never spent any time with my family. We rarely socialized as a couple, mostly because it was too dangerous to be public, but partly because we preferred the company of each other to the company of anyone else. At least that's how I thought it was. I suppose now it was just that Clara preferred the company of whoever happened to be her current interest.

I was red-faced and hot from the humiliation and anger coursing through my veins. In my head, I saw Alvin and Clara naked and twisted in a heap of melding flesh. I imagined all the raw animal passion I tried to coax out of Clara coming to the surface with my brother.

He probably didn't care about her emotional frailty or the abuse she had endured. He likely only cared about himself and never gave her needs a second thought. I'll bet that's why she liked him: because he couldn't touch beyond the physical side of her. She could keep her real self bottled and shelved with him. It was me who brought that side out in her. I got credit for that—if nothing else, at least I got credit for unlocking the deep-seated passion in her soul.

The reality of what was running through my mind slapped me at the moment of my last thought—the woman from Georgia—the one Clara had been with before me, the one who died for her involvement with Clara. She got credit for all the things I thought were Clara's and mine alone: all the firsts, all the newness, all the freedom.

I had always felt peace in knowing that at least I did something special for Clara by showing her real love, the love of another woman. That was when I thought I was the first woman. Clara's lie was so convincing that I never gave its validity a second thought. Clara told me about the wonders I had done for her mentally and physically, but then again, she told her diary the same thing about the woman from Georgia. I could no longer believe in the comfort that I had given Clara. My heart was crumbling inside my chest with the knowledge that I couldn't separate reality and truth from fantasy and lies.

And now, Alvin—my twin, my blood, my male equal. We were cut from one mold. We share a bond bestowed only on those born at the same time of the same womb. We had identical environmental influences that bred parallel belief systems as children. But we weren't children anymore, and while we were as different as two people could be, it seemed that we were still as alike as when we came into the world.

I was sure that Alvin met Clara just as I did, on the ambulance crew. He responded to a call and instinctively wanted to help her. He had to have seen in her the same childlike qualities that needed protection. He had to have seen the wise old soul that gave the child strength to continue in spite of her bleak circumstances.

It never occurred to me back then that Alvin had picked up Clara when he worked for the ambulance service. I never asked him; he never told me. I just assumed he knew her from around town like he said. Everyone knew Charlie Stokes, so it wasn't out of the question for Alvin to know his reputation, as well.

Alvin's wife might have found out about the affair. That could have been why she insisted he leave his job at the ambulance service. She probably caught them and gave Alvin no other choice. Maybe she threatened to tell Charlie herself. Maybe she *did* tell Charlie. The conversation Alvin and I had the day I told him about my affair with Clara suddenly rang through my head in its entirety. It contained everything I needed to be completely convinced that the two had been lovers.

I wanted to talk to Jayne. She said I could call in an emergency, and this was as close to one as I had felt yet. I wanted to hear her soft, reassuring voice tell me we could figure it all out. I wanted her to know what I had discovered and what it could mean. Alvin could absolutely be involved in the killing of Clara. He could certainly have participated in the hideous crime simply to save his own ass from Charlie Stokes. I wanted to tell Jayne she was right and that I now believed her. I wanted to tell her that now I feared Alvin, as well as Charlie.

To appear so needy as to call her for help was out of the question. I would sit at my desk and deal with it as I had dealt with everything else, alone and silent. I couldn't call her every time I felt afraid and confused. I had to stay in control of my emotions. As I sat in the dark and pondered what I could do to feel better, I remembered again that Jayne offered to help me with my turmoil over Desert Storm. It was apparent to me that I still needed help.

I decided to give the Desert Storm journals to Jayne the next time I saw her. I would give her the tattered red backpack they were stored in, and we'd sort them out in her office during my sessions. It wouldn't solve the mystery of why Alvin was involved with Charlie Stokes, and it wouldn't bring Clara back from the dead, but maybe it would be a start to holding my waning sanity intact.

Chapter Eighteen

"Are you awake, Abby?" Jeff whispered. It was fully light outside and the winter sun was shining through the curtains in my room.

"Sorta."

"Jayne's on the phone. I thought you might want to wake up and take the call." He was already coming toward my bed with the cordless in his hand. He winked and put it beside me.

A wave of relief and thankfulness came over me. He touched my forehead and smiled before he left the room. I picked up the phone and said hello.

"Good morning, Abby." Jayne's voice was soothing. "Did I wake you?"

"No, Jeff did." She laughed a little at my words. "I was awake already."

"I wanted to check on you since our session yesterday was a little tough. I was also wondering if you have lunch plans." She sounded nervous all the sudden. "I had a cancellation and an opportunity to take a lunch break for a change, so I thought it might be fun to see you outside the office again." She paused and I listened for when to speak. "That is, if you're okay with it."

"I'd love to see you—have lunch with you—whatever." I stumbled. "It would be great for us to hang out. Thanks for calling me." I had so much nervous energy I feared I would explode. "What time and where?"

"That depends on your entourage. I figure that at least one of the spies will accompany us, so you can pick the place, but the time is between noon and 2:00. Does that work for you or do you need to check with them first?"

"They can just deal with the time or leave me alone today." I already knew I was going regardless of what Pat or Ted said.

"How about the new deli over by your office? Do you know the one?"

"I do. I've been meaning to go there, but I rarely leave for lunch, so it's perfect!" She sounded as excited as I felt about our lunch plans.

"See you there at noon then."

"Abby," she broke in before I started to say goodbye. "Was everything okay last night?"

"It was troublesome, but I'm okay." I heard her release the breath she was holding. She sounded glad to hear I had endured whatever it was unscathed. I remembered just then what I was thinking before going to sleep. "I have something I want to bring you to hang onto for our next office session. Is it okay if I bring it today and leave it in your car?" I wanted to take her the backpack full of journals before I lost my nerve.

"Whatever you need. Do you want to talk about it now?"

"No. It's some stuff I wrote in Desert Storm that I think we should maybe look at during our sessions."

"That'd be great. I'll see you at noon."

I wasn't yet ready to face the world when I set the phone beside me on the bed. The same cloud of confusion I had fallen asleep with still hung above my head, but at least now it had a silver lining. Just hearing Jayne's voice brought me peace. I couldn't exactly pretend it would all be okay, but I felt a momentary foothold under my sliding feet.

Jeff was on the couch reading the paper and Pat had gone to the police station when I emerged from my room. I hadn't decided what I would tell Pat and Ted about the affair I hypothesized between my brother and Clara, but I knew I had to tell them something eventually.

Jeff, on the other hand, needed to know more than I was telling him. I suddenly felt as though I had betrayed him just as my family and Clara seemed to have betrayed me. I got my coffee and sat next to him on the couch. He put his arm around me, and I sighed heavily as I fell into his embrace.

"It's going to be fine, Abby." He kissed me on the head. "I know it's hard right now, but this can't last forever."

"I think I'm more afraid of the outcome than I am of the waiting game." I sipped my coffee. "Alvin is in a heap of trouble, and I just can't imagine how he got involved in this. He's my brother. Why is he doing this to me?"

Jeff pulled me a little closer. "There has to be an explanation. A man doesn't simply wake up one day and decide to get involved with a serial killer. Alvin didn't just happen to run into Charlie. There is definitely something we don't know."

"I might know." I started to cave.

"What?" Jeff sat calmly.

"I was trying to remember my conversation with Alvin like you suggested, and I started remembering other things that might be relevant." I paused.

"Like?"

"Like that he might also have had an affair with Clara." I shook my head. "I don't know how I missed it for so long."

"What makes you think that?" Jeff sat up on the edge of the couch and looked at me.

"I remembered something he said before I went to Desert Storm that kind of implicates him." I told Jeff the story of our conversation in the hangar.

"Are you going to tell anyone else?"

"Jayne," I answered.

"I mean Pat or Ted. They need to know this information. It changes things a little." He realized as I had that Alvin might be a bigger player than we originally suspected.

"I don't know, Jeff. There are too many variables; there's too much gray area. I still don't think he killed anyone, but I have to think now that he is involved as more than a hostage." I knew from the letters that Alvin was in deep.

The front door opened, and Ted returned from his morning sunning ritual on the porch.

"Good morning, Abby," he greeted me. "Are you feeling better today?"

"Yes, thanks. I'm meeting Jayne for lunch, so having a good day is a given." I smiled and Ted rolled his eyes. I really did think I might have a good day for a change.

"I thought she had a steady."

"That doesn't change a thing," I assured him. "She obviously wants to be friends, so big deal. Besides, it's only lunch."

"Do I get to eat with you or do I have to stay in the car again?" Ted continued to tease.

"Hey, I have an idea," Jeff joined in. "Why don't you and I get a table in the same restaurant and just stare at them the whole time?" Ted was already nodding in agreement.

"Great idea! Your friend doesn't know us anyway, Abby, so you can just pretend like you don't either. We'll listen in and tell you if she's interested or just bored with the old ball and chain at home!" The two guys were thoroughly amused with themselves.

"Not." I got up to go for more coffee. "You two can eat outside in the car." I tried to sound annoyed, but I was secretly enjoying the lightness they brought to the air.

The teasing continued until we heard the garage door opening, signaling Pat's return and the end of the fun.

Jeff got up immediately. "I'm going to finish reading the paper in the office."

Pat was more silent than usual when she came through the side door from the garage. She opened the refrigerator and took out a soda. Ted and I stood and stared at her from the living room.

"What are you two looking at?"

"Nothing," Ted answered as I walked in the kitchen to get more coffee and look for food.

"Are you two still mad at me?" She sounded as though she didn't care if we were, but I wouldn't give her the satisfaction of knowing she annoyed me.

"I'm not." I walked past her. "I think Jeff might be a bit upset, but he'll get over it."

"Is he home?"

"Why? Do you want to torture him some more?" I smiled at her to break the tension, then patted her arm. "Pat, I know you're stressed out. We all are. But we need to give each other room." I shrugged my shoulders. "Besides, after you opened the can of worms last night, it occurred to me that Jeff might just be my best bet for getting laid these days." I tried to keep a serious face. "I can't go anywhere without you two hanging on my coattail, so maybe you did me a favor!" The corner of her mouth started to give way to a grin she couldn't control.

"Jesus, Abby. If it's sex you want, I'll be more than happy to do the selfless thing and help you out." She patted my arm the same way I had hers and raised her eyebrows. "Anything for a friend."

"What a totally unselfish sacrifice, Pat. I'm touched. I'm sure Julie wouldn't mind." She made a face that suggested I had spoiled her fantasy.

"I've been a jerk all the way around here lately, haven't I?"

I hesitated, but only for a second. "Yeah. You really have."

"Do you think Jeff will forgive me?"

"Why don't you ask him?"

"I will." She started toward the office.

"Watch for flying furniture," Ted added as she disappeared down the steps.

"Wow. What do you suppose came over her?"

"Maybe she saw an orphanage burning on the way home and it brightened her spirits." Ted grinned and winked at me. "The stress is a little overwhelming, Abby. We're under the gun to end this stalemate. Pat's reputation for being a good agent is on the line if we don't wrap this up soon."

"You mean she gets in trouble for not solving cases fast enough?"

"It's not about solving things, it's about not looking like a fool. Charlie and your brother have danced circles around us, and we look like idiots," Ted explained. "We're going to be pulled off if things don't change soon."

"What do you mean? The case closes? We're on our own?" That didn't seem possible to me.

"No, nothing like that. It's more likely you two will get sent to a safe house and the intensive manhunt will begin. We've been lying on our backs waiting for Charlie to move first, but he's not budging. We know Alvin is involved, but we still don't know why or to what extent, and we have no way of knowing what they might be up to. We need a break in a big way." Ted rubbed his eyes. "This gives me a migraine."

"What if I told you I know for certain that Alvin had an affair with Clara?" It was out before I could stop it.

"Are you telling me that?" He removed his hand from his face and looked up.

"Maybe." I wished I could take it back, but it was too late.

"How do you know?"

I was afraid he would ask that question. "Oh, shit." I sat at the kitchen table and put my head down. "I just know."

"You're not going to tell me how you know?" He was right beside me now, hanging on my words.

"Last night when I was trying to remember the conversation Alvin and I had about Clara and me, I remembered something Alvin said when I was leaving to go to Desert Storm." I told Ted the story I had just told Jeff. "I know it's a long shot from where you stand, but I see it in clear view. He met her just like I did— working on the ambulance crew and picking her up when Charlie knocked her around."

"So Charlie might have found out and threatened to kill Alvin or his family if he didn't cooperate." Ted was thinking out loud but then looked at me directly. "He could be selling you out to save his own ass, you know."

"I don't think he's selling me anything." I felt defensive. "I don't know what he's doing any more than you, but he could actually be trying to help me."

"You know we have to tell Pat this information, Abby. It's also likely going to result in the need to involve Alvin's wife."

"I figured as much." I was sick in my stomach over blurting out my recent discovery and felt that my honesty had further endangered Alvin.

"Do you want me to get Pat now or do you want to wait until after lunch?" Ted smiled just enough to say he understood how I was feeling. I must have been an easy read because I was feeling that I needed to wait a while. Long enough to talk to Jayne, anyway.

I hated myself for deceiving Ted, who seemed so understanding, about the letters. I could make no sense of all the emotions flooding over me. I wanted to kill Charlie. I wanted to help Alvin. I wanted to hurt Alvin. I wanted to hold Alvin as we had held each other when we were scared children. I wanted to tell the whole truth to the agents in need of it. I wanted to punish them for invading my life. I wanted to fall in love with Jeff and live happily ever after. I wanted to run to Jayne and tell her I could be everything she needed. I wanted to talk to Clara.

The chill that overtook my body shook me back.

"Let's wait," I said. Ted nodded.

Ted drove me to meet Jayne without ever questioning the contents of the red bag I had slung over my shoulder. Strangely enough, Jeff and Pat were having lunch alone together. I didn't have time to talk to Jeff before leaving the house, but he and Pat actually looked like they didn't want to hurt each other when they emerged from the office. Ted assured me he'd get the scoop. He figured lunch with Jayne would keep me dreamy and useless for the better part of the day, so he'd have time.

She was sitting cross-legged on a bench by the door of the deli when we pulled into the parking lot. Her hair was pulled back neatly and she wore the same glasses she had the first day I saw her in her office.

"She is a looker," Ted commented as we pulled past her. "Is her steady as good-looking?"

"I guess she is to some people. I never really noticed." I usually didn't notice if someone was attractive until I got to know her, but Jayne's beauty couldn't go unrecognized. "Why don't you come meet her?" I asked Ted as I was taking off my seat belt.

"You sure it's okay?"

"Yeah, as long as when she asks you to join us, you decline gracefully." I smiled and raised my eyebrows. "Deal?"

He nodded. "Deal."

She was looking in the opposite direction when we walked up to where she was sitting. "Jayne?" I said softly when we reached her. Her whole face smiled when she turned and saw us standing there. She immediately stood and hugged me.

"Hi, Abby," she whispered in my ear and continued to hold on.

"There's someone I want you to meet," I whispered back. She righted herself at once and cleared her throat.

"Oh, a friend?" She was suddenly nervous at being caught off guard.

"Uh, yeah. A friend." I looked at Ted, who was as puzzled as I was. "I guess you're a friend. I never really thought about what our relationship is."

"Well, whatever else I am, I am Ted, and it's a pleasure to meet you, Dr. Kinderlen." He extended his hand, and Jayne took it at once.

"The bodyguard." She smiled and nodded as though it just clicked. "It's certainly a pleasure to meet you, as well. And please, it's Jayne." She still had a light grip on Ted's hand.

"Okay, Jayne. Yes, I am sort of the bodyguard here, I suppose. Well, she's definitely the most entertaining job I've had yet!" He nudged me and I blushed.

"Are you joining us for lunch?" Jayne let go of Ted's hand.

"No, I have to sneak around out here while you guys eat," he lied on cue. "But Abby agreed to buy my lunch today and deliver it when you two are finished." He snickered and looked innocently at me.

I shook my head at him and smiled. "Tuna salad?"

"Philly cheese steak, all the trimmings. Fries, too. Thanks, Abby. It was a pleasure to meet you, Jayne." He turned and walked back toward the car.

"The pleasure was mine," she called as he was leaving. She turned to me. "Nice guy. Shall we go in?"

"Can I have your car keys to put this in your car?" I turned my head to look at the bag hanging off my shoulder. She watched me all the way to the car and back to where she was standing.

We ordered, found a seat, and fumbled with our coats without saying much. It was not uncomfortable at all, but I felt there was more than just lunch and friendship to be discussed.

Jayne confirmed that feeling after we took our seats. "I have another envelope for you." She dug in her blazer pocket for it.

"Not yet." I reached across the table and held her arm so she couldn't draw the envelope from her pocket.

"Is that why you wanted to meet today?" I was a little disappointed since I had hoped it was merely to see me.

"Actually, no, not totally. I wanted to see you anyway." She convinced me with her eyes. "It was in my car this time, Abby." She looked pale all the sudden.

"He likes to leave them where he knows they'll be seen. Remember the one stashed above my visor? But you did know something was up with me last night?" I waited for her response, but she only nodded.

"It's hell being psychic," I said, trying to lighten the conversation again. It felt so heavy and serious. I wanted to just forget the case and focus on talking to her.

"Remember, I've never been psychic before."

"But you are now. I was in a pretty big panic last night. You must have felt it." I gave in to the inevitable discussion, thinking I'd get it over with and we could just eat lunch in peace and denial.

"What happened?" She looked hard at me.

"Oh, shit, here we go again." I felt the tears welling up. "What is it with you and making me cry? I've told this story two times today without emotion, then you come along and suddenly I want to cry like a baby." I fought the tears back and forced laughter in their stead.

"You're good at that." She marveled at my emotion replacement. "I wish for your sake, though, that you'd just let go and cry sometime. I promise you'll stop when it's out."

"I'll stop before it's out and save all that energy." I moved the conversation along before she could question me about my detachment techniques. "I realized last night that Alvin most likely had an affair with Clara before I did."

"Is there any way to be sure?" She, like the other two, clung to the words I was speaking.

"Not without asking him, but I'm quite convinced of it. They could have easily met in the same way I met Clara. Alvin and I are just enough alike that I can see it happening. They say lightning never strikes twice, but it sure struck poor Clara." I unexpectedly felt pity for her having to deal with both Alvin and me.

"That explains how Alvin got involved in this, doesn't it?" Jayne was staying right with me. "I bet he either tried to protect Clara or himself from Charlie and somehow got caught in the volley. He could have even gotten himself involved to protect you, Abby. You've maintained all along that he would never hurt you."

"And you've maintained that he would." I felt a flash of anger.

"I just wanted you to be careful." She paused. "I was worried."

I sighed so hard it made me dizzy.

"Yes. He could be protecting me in some sick and twisted Alvin way. He may be a Jesus freak, but he's not a bad person." I wished I could explain to Jayne the weird dynamics of Alvin's and my relationship, but it was not possible. She, like anyone else who was not born a twin, could never understand it.

"So you already told the agents about this discovery?"

"Not both, only Ted. I told Jeff, too. I had no intention of telling Ted, but it just came out. We're going to tell Pat this afternoon."

"How did you figure out that they had an affair?"

"I was trying to remember anything I could about telling Alvin I was involved with Clara when I suddenly remembered a conversation we had when I was deploying to Saudi Arabia. He told me to forget her because she always leaves anyway. There was something in the way he said it that smacked of experience." I paused. "I just know they were together."

"Then they probably were." She supported my theory. "What do you think caused him to get involved with Charlie?"

"I can't be sure, but I don't think he intended to hurt anyone." I told her the only elements I knew for a fact. "He wants my Army gear for some odd reason, and he also wants me to turn against Evvie. I can't figure how those two things factor into the equation, but they are unmistakably relevant."

"Maybe in Alvin's mind, if Charlie can kill Evvie, you'll be spared. I can see that as a fair trade in the mind of someone who is already not thinking clearly." Jayne was hypothesizing with me. "What I can't see is where your Army gear would be of any use to either of them."

"Me neither." I shrugged and changed the subject. "Did you get in trouble for being late yesterday?"

"Only a little." She smiled. "Don't you worry about it. I can handle my own time problems. You really shouldn't concern yourself with them."

"But if I start creating problems, you might not want to see me anymore." I spelled out my cause for concern.

"That's just not likely." She patted my hand as our food arrived.

"Do you talk to Shannon about your clients?" I had to keep present in my mind that unlike me, Jayne was involved in a monogamous relationship.

"I rarely talk to her about the specifics of my clients. That would be against my confidentiality rules, but I do sometimes talk to her about things related to my work. We keep it very vague, though. Sometimes I have to explain things to her if they are particularly consuming. It's courtesy, you know. It's a way for me to vent and she never gets too personally involved." Jayne seemed nervous again.

"Sounds like a good system. So who do you lay all the heavy stuff on?"

"I have a therapist, of course. You think I could deal with all this and my own life without someone to listen?" She was laughing at my face, which must have registered my surprise that she, too, had a therapist.

"I just thought all you therapy people took care of yourselves. You know, 'Doctor, heal thyself.'"

Jayne laughed out loud at my comments. "It would be more like 'Doctor, kill thyself' if I had to treat my own problems! I prefer to subscribe to the 'first, do no harm' theory. That means under no circumstances would I treat myself!" She had an expression of fake horror at the thought of having to take care of her problems alone.

"So are you Shannon's therapist?" I don't know why I asked such a question.

"I was." She looked uneasy again.

"Oh, I get it. That's how you met."

"Yes. That's how we met, and it was ugly." She was fidgeting.

"There's no reason for us to talk about this."

"Yes, there is. You asked, and I need to tell you. That's our deal. You always answer my questions, so I can answer yours."

"You've answered everything I asked so far," I reminded her.

"Oh. I did. Well then, this is a good time to change the subject." She was a little red-faced but cracked a grin. "What about you? Any noteworthy recent romances?"

"I really suck in the romance department, so if you mean anything that lasted more than a few months, no." I picked at my food.

"When was your last serious relationship?" She, too, was playing with her half-eaten sandwich.

"Before I moved here. It was Clara actually. I've had a lot of 'intimate friends,' but I just never wanted to put anyone else through what it would take to really have a relationship with me. I'm damaged goods, Jayne. It wouldn't be fair." I looked down at the table.

"That's not true. You may need some tuning here and there, but I bet you have a lot to offer someone in a relationship." She smiled sincerely and touched my hand again. I jumped, and she felt it.

"I'm sorry." She pulled back. "I didn't mean to startle you."

"That's okay…it wasn't startle…I mean it was, but it was, more, um, you know, electric shock." I stumbled for an explanation. We both laughed.

"I know what you mean." She touched my hand again, and this time held on. "I feel it, too."

I couldn't speak.

"Abby, I think I can help you get over whatever it is that makes you think you don't deserve to be happy. I want to help you if you trust me."

"Of course I trust you. I trusted you the first time I looked in your eyes. I knew in that moment you could help me. That's why I keep coming back."

"I think our becoming friends is part of the plan, as well." She let go of my hand and began playing with her food again, waiting for my response.

"I told you, if you weren't someone I knew I could be friends with, I wouldn't have any faith in you or your ability as my therapist. I just wish you weren't in the middle of this murder investigation."

"And I wish you weren't in the middle of it. But we both are, and we can both handle it."

"Reality sucks." I shook my head. "Let's have a look at the letter."

I felt a little distraught as she took the envelope from her pocket, but I concentrated on my breathing and kept my fear at bay. I took it from her, closed my eyes, and held it to my nose. It was Alvin's smell—nothing else smelled like that.

"Should I open it now or wait?" I felt like a little girl asking for advice.

"Whatever you think is best."

"What the hell." I tore it open and took out the contents. There was an entry from Clara's diary with a small note attached. It read: *To answer why would take more time than either of us has. You might merely need to read your own hidden words to derive the why you're looking for. Please believe me when I say, like you, I hurt no one who didn't deserve it. Don't sell me out, Abby. Just because you don't understand now doesn't mean you won't ever.*

I handed it to Jayne and sat quietly while she read it. I held the pages of Clara's diary to my face, using them to cover my eyes.

"Are you going to read that now or later?" Jayne's voice was kind and soft.

I just shook my head and said nothing.

"It's almost two o'clock, Abby," she said after a few long minutes of silence.

"I'll read it at home tonight."

"Will you call me?" She looked concerned.

"Can I?"

"I told you already that you could. I want to help you." She forced my eyes to focus on hers. "Let me."

"I'll call."

"I'll be calling you if you don't call me," she threatened as if that would be a punishment. She had no idea how much I needed to hear her voice. She really was the only reason I was clinging to the life raft because my ship had long since capsized.

I changed the subject. "I put that bag on your back floorboard."

"Should I just leave it in there until our next appointment?"

"No, I'd rather you take it in your office or somewhere a little more secure."

"Do you want me to wait until I see you to open it?" I appreciated her respect for my boundaries.

"I don't care. You'll see the contents soon enough. Read if you want. The journals are all numbered and dated, so help yourself." For the first time since I wrote them, I really wanted to share the memory of those days with someone I knew would understand.

We hugged for a long time beside her car before she unlocked the door and got in to drive away. "Don't worry, Abby." She opened the window. "You're not alone." She almost looked as though she would cry this time, but she held it in.

"I know." I smiled and touched her sleeve. "Thanks."

"Remember to breathe."

"I will." I sure felt alone as I watched her drive away.

Chapter Nineteen

Ted shook his head as I got into his car empty-handed.

"Where's my lunch?" He held off a smile.

"Oh, shit. Wait. I'll be right back." He tried to stop me as I dashed for the door of the restaurant to get him something to eat.

It was the same need I have to make everyone in the world happy that got me involved with Clara in the first place. It also sent me to Evelyn when she seemed so lonely and propelled me toward a friendship with Jeff despite my awareness of his ultimate intentions. It pushed me many times in my life to seek forgiveness when I wasn't wrong, help when I wasn't needy, and shelter when I wasn't cold or afraid.

For the first time, though, I was in love with someone who didn't need me. She may have had an interest when she first met me, but now she wanted to be my therapist, my friend, and nothing more. Jayne didn't need my strength, my wit, or my ability to survive. She had all that herself. She didn't need me for physical pleasure or mental stimulation. She could live without my opinion or my input into her daily transpirations. She was totally self-sufficient and adequately equipped to deal with her life and its idiosyncrasies.

Furthermore, she had Shannon, a bright and charming independent partner. They had been together for many years. Jayne had all she needed. She wasn't looking and she wouldn't be. I was the one who needed this time.

For all the lovers I dragged along because I couldn't stand hurt feelings and all the would-be suitors I kept just a little out of reach, this was the payment. This was the restitution for all their pain and suffering. My love for Jayne was all the love they wasted on me and my selfishness.

She would never need me as I needed her. She would never want to touch me in the way I longed to merely brush her hair and stroke the skin on her cheek. Those things would simply never cross her mind with me. I was her client, her friend-in-the-making: someone in whom she might someday confide her deepest thoughts and fears. Today she was the person I entrusted with mine.

There has to be a reason that some people live life solo. I must be one of those unfortunate souls destined to learn from my loneliness what I will need to help others who are lonely. I would not wish this emptiness on another human spirit because in it lies the ability to displace the life from the creature it inhabits.

I went to my room when we returned to the house. I knew Ted was going to tell Pat what I had revealed about Alvin and Clara, but I wanted to be alone for a bit. I needed to wallow in my self-pity and bathe in my regrets a while longer before dealing again with the obligation to protect my brother.

It was almost dark when I pulled the envelope from my pocket to read the diary entry inside it. I did not have a feeling that I held in my hand anything that could make me happy. I was right. The entry was from the same book I could not bring myself to read in Spartanburg. This was undoubtedly one of the missing pages from the beginning of 1988.

It was penned before Clara met me and explained in detail her initial encounter with a person who I innately knew to be my brother. It was the first day he picked her up in the ambulance. I thought up to that point in my life that I had experienced every emotion possible. I was wrong.

Pat knocked on my door just after dark and asked if she could come in and talk to me. I called her in, and she sat next to me on the bed. The diary entry was on the floor in front of us, and I knew she saw it before I had the chance to try and hide it. The note from Alvin was safely out of view, although I really didn't care right then.

I leaned down, picked up the pages, and handed them to her.

"I know I promised not to read any more without telling you, but I couldn't help myself." I confessed part of the truth. "It's about Alvin and Clara. Take it." Pat took the pages and read them by the dim streetlight coming through my windows.

"Abby, are you okay?" I was shocked that she actually sounded more concerned for my well-being than for the furtherance of her case.

"Not really."

"Should we talk later?" She started to get up.

"No. Let's do it now. Where are Ted and Jeff?" I wiped my eyes.

"They're in the kitchen waiting for us." She patted my arm, then pulled me into her body. "I'm really sorry you have to do this."

It was easy to let her hold me since I felt so alone and afraid. We sat another ten minutes in silence, then left the safe darkness of my room for the all-too-bright light of the world outside it.

Jeff handed me a cup of coffee as I walked into the kitchen and led me to a chair at the table. Pat passed off the diary pages to Ted and whispered something I could not hear as I seated myself and took a sip from the cup.

"Abby, we should talk about these diary pages." Ted looked up after he finished reading. "When did you get them?" He was gentle.

"Is that really important?" Jeff had no idea what the pages even said. Maybe he just wanted me to feel I had a voice in my silent shock.

"It's not the most important thing. No, we don't have to go there now. Okay with you, Pat?" Ted was ready to yield if Pat would agree.

"Fine." She sat next to me. "So you figured it out from the diary pages or before?" Pat kept a soft and kindly tone.

"Before," I whispered. "It hit me last night when I was trying to remember my conversation with Alvin about me and Clara." My voice was lifeless and monotone. "I remembered something he said to me before I went to the desert."

Jeff spoke up again. "Let me help you, Abby."

I nodded as he repeated the story I had told him earlier in the day. He missed nothing in his almost word-for-word recital of our conversation.

"So since Charlie also knows they were lovers," Ted theorized, "he might be holding Alvin hostage. You know, forcing him to help in trade for his life."

"Or Abby's life," Jeff stepped in. "He might have told Alvin he would kill them both if Alvin didn't cooperate."

"Why this entry, though?" Ted handed it to Jeff.

"Because he wants Abby to know her own brother deceived her just as Clara did. He wants to pit them against each other. It goes right along with sending the entry that detailed Clara's affair with Evelyn. He wants to debilitate her. He wants her to feel alone. He doesn't want Abby and Alvin to unite against him," Pat answered while Jeff read.

"So you're saying he's using Alvin to get to Abby and weaken her?" Jeff didn't get it, and I was only half able to listen.

"Maybe." Pat looked skeptical of her own speculation. "But something about it still doesn't smell right. It's too easy an explanation, and it's dropped right in our hands."

"Not exactly," Ted argued. "Maybe he wasn't counting on Abby giving us the pages. I think it's more likely that he was planning to get Abby's attention and keep it to himself."

"Could be, but it still doesn't add up. Why did Alvin or Charlie or both of them send that kid after Abby's Army gear? That really makes no sense."

The brainstorming continued as I sat with both hands around my cup. They were all wrong. I knew it was Alvin's choice to send me the diary entry. It was a confession and nothing more. I suddenly felt sick in my soul at what I feared he was trying to tell me. He was confessing to more than the affair with Clara. He was confessing to murder.

At that very moment, it was all as clear to me as if I had subconsciously known it all along but not been able to bring it to surface. He wanted my journals, not my Army gear. He just thought they might be stored with my gear. He suggested in the letter today that I look at my own "hidden words" for answers. The journals I kept from Desert Storm were the hidden words to which he was referring.

Alvin was with me the day I picked up the journals from the post office. For all I knew, the same friend holding them for me told Alvin everything I requested he keep silent. He was Alvin's friend also. It was feasible.

Alvin knew I had been mailing myself letters during the deployment. I'm sure it wasn't hard to figure out that they might contain details of the story he read about in Clara's diary: the story of the soldier who threatened my life and the life of my companion in the desert.

I remained silent as the three sat around the table shooting in the dark for a hit on what was happening. I was glad Jayne had my journals. I was even more pleased with my last-minute decision to put the diary pages and letters from Alvin that the FBI didn't know of in the backpack. I laid my head on my crossed arms and fell asleep. I slept through the call from Jayne and the rest of the noise surrounding me. Jeff woke me and put me to bed sometime after midnight. He told me that they had decided to send a team to Alvin's farm early in the morning. Ted would be flying to meet them.

It was still dark when I first awakened from my stress-induced sleep trance. I thought I must have slept for more than the six hours between midnight and first light, but the clock read 5:30. I didn't want to wake anyone else, but I was overcome with hunger and thirst.

When I stepped from my room, the house was lit and I heard voices in the living room. I stopped mute when I recognized Jayne's as one of the voices. I looked back into my room again at the clock on my desk and realized it was 5:30 p.m.

I had slept for more than seventeen hours. I hadn't dreamed, gone to the bathroom, rolled over, or noticed the light coming through my windows. The room fell quiet when I entered from the hall, but I kept walking until I reached the sink for a glass of water. My mouth was a wasteland, and my head pounded from the lack of liquid in my body.

"Well! We're sure glad to see you back among the living!" Jayne was the first to come to me. She threw her arms around my body and kissed my cheek as we embraced. "Don't scare me like that again, Abby," she whispered in my ear.

"Like what?" I whispered back, surrendering my whole self to the grip of her arms.

"I was afraid you had decided not to wake up." She squeezed me again.

"But I did wake up." The child in me was speaking to her. No one else spoke or moved from their seats. They all sat staring at my swaying figure in the arms of the woman I loved more than anything in the world.

"What made you come?" I looked into Jayne's beautiful eyes.

"You called to me and I came." She kept it brief. "We'll talk about it later. Can I make you some food? You must be starving."

"I am starving." She let go and I refilled my glass, chugging it as I had the last one.

Pat and Jeff remained seated while I drank another two glasses of water. "I'll be right back," I said as I walked toward the bathroom.

Jeff helped Jayne put together a simple quesadilla and green salad, which Jayne brought me when I returned and sat at the kitchen table. Pat had moved to the table also and was waiting to talk to me. I could tell by the look in her eyes that it would be a serious conversation.

"Where's Ted?" I vaguely remembered Jeff saying he was leaving for somewhere I thought was Alvin's farm. "Is he in Spartanburg?"

"Yes. He met a team of agents there to visit with Alvin's wife, Janis." Pat stopped and awaited my reaction.

"And?"

"Abby," Jayne joined the conversation again. "Why don't you eat and wake up for a few minutes? All this can hold until later." She set a cup of tea in front of me. Jeff joined us at the table while Jayne stood behind my chair.

"What's going on here? Why does this feel like a setup?" I looked over my shoulder and up at Jayne. "Just tell me what's happening, okay? I can handle it. I know it's about Alvin, and I know it can't be good. Is he dead?" I turned to Jeff this time, hoping he would see the anxiety in my face.

Jayne put her hand on my shoulder as she spoke. "Tell her, Pat. She's tough, she can take it."

"Okay." Pat sounded reluctant but began to speak. "The agents went to Alvin's house and talked to his wife. She was pretty shaken by the news that Alvin is not in South America, but she was aware that something was going on." Pat paused as her voice took on the same tone it had in Spartanburg before she told me the details of Clara's barbarous murder.

"Go on, Pat," I pushed.

"As usual, the details of all this are a little sketchy, but before Alvin left, he gave Janis a map of a wooded area on the farm. He told her if anyone such as the police came there asking questions to give it to them. He instructed her to keep the kids and herself away from the woods. She followed his instructions." Pat looked at the table and stopped talking again.

"Pat," I urged. "Finish the story."

"They found Charlie's decomposed body in a shallow grave in the woods. The map led the agents right to it. It looks like Alvin killed him, Abby."

Scenes began to flash in my head as I reached up behind me and took the hand Jayne was resting on my shoulder. She offered the other one, and I took hold of it, as well. As I began to fade, I saw in my mind's eye the scene of myself killing the Syrian soldier. As I continued to be pulled into the memory, the scene changed from me to Alvin, the soldier to Charlie, then back again. I pushed my whole body into the wooden chair as hard as I could push. I planted my feet firmly on the floor and impelled them to go through it and into the ground below. I felt the shaking begin at my legs and work its way up into my soul. My eyes were open and fixed on the wall in front of me. I was aware of the very moment I turned to stone. So was Jayne.

"Abby, come back...Don't do this...Stay with me," she pleaded as I removed myself from the here and now. "Abby, you're hurting my hands." I felt her tears on my neck, but I could not move.

Jeff stood and helped her release the grip I had on her hands. My hands remained in the same position even after she was free. I was a statue. I was finally a rock. The world continued around me as I sat in the chair unencumbered. I could not break down when I so desperately needed to in Desert Storm. I could not turn hard and untouchable there, but I certainly could now. I made a clear choice to allow it.

Jayne continued to call to me, as did Pat and Jeff, but I simply would not respond. Maybe it was that I could not, but it was fine with me either way. I had told Jayne that I would wait until it was a good time to break, and this was as good a time as any. I registered the call to 911 after I felt Jayne's fingers on my neck and heard her screaming that there was barely a pulse. Still I chose to remain silent and motionless.

I've seen movies and read books about people who have died and left their bodies. I didn't feel dead, but I absolutely left my body. I wasn't hovering above it, and I didn't see white lights or tunnels anywhere. There was no one hanging around waiting for me and no sign that anyone might be coming.

I wanted to concentrate on what was happening in the kitchen, but at the moment, I was more interested in where I was and why I felt nothing bad anymore. Only minutes before, there had been a wave of pain flooding me and now it was totally gone. I felt only peace and ease.

I was singing the songs we used to sing as children in church when the paramedics laid me on the floor and tore open my shirt. I was singing as loud as I could and laughing all the while, but no one seemed to hear me. They were frantically working on my body while my mind took no part in it. It was only when I saw Jayne huddled in the corner of the room that I stopped singing and felt sadness.

It was not my sadness, though I felt it as if it were. Still, I wanted to make it stop as I had my own. She looked so frightened and alone. Her legs were bent and her arms were wrapped around them as she swayed gently and sobbed quietly. I never went far from my body, so it was easy to go back into it. I just stepped inside myself as effortlessly as I had stepped out and retreated to the place that I knew was safe.

Once inside again, I could still hear everything going on, but I could no longer see the room. The trip back was worth it just to hear Jayne leap to her feet and scream with joy.

"Thank God," she cried out. "Oh, Abby, please stay with us!" I felt her touch my forehead before everything went black.

Chapter Twenty

I remember the exact moment the coma began and consciousness ended. The picture in my mind faded briefly to a foggy haze involuntarily replaced by the faint light from a single, bare bulb. It was a transition as easy as an extended eye blink. While I was unaware of the happenings outside my head that included Jayne, Jeff, and the team of paramedics, when the fog lifted, I could see clearly the picture inside my head.

I was seated at a small table located in the center of a sparsely furnished room. In front of me lay the tattered red backpack containing my numbered and banded envelopes of Desert Storm journals. As if I knew what I was doing, I began pulling envelopes from the bundle and placing them in order on the table.

I took the first one, then the third one. I skipped a few and took a few in a row. I paused to touch one now and again, then passed it by like I knew it wouldn't be needed. I selected the entries that formed the new stack slowly and methodically. I didn't break my stride until I reached the last envelope in the bundle. It was the writing from my final day in Southwest Asia.

I separated it from the others as I returned the unchosen entries to the backpack. I tore open the envelope, removed the contents, and unfolded the pages. I may have intended to read it all right then, but I stopped after the first few lines.

I'm having trouble remembering what day we came here or what day it is in this stinking country. I think it's day 121. We leave for home today. The words bounced off the inside of my head like ricocheting bullets.

I took a deep breath, turned the paper face down on the table, and picked up the first envelope I had removed from the bundle. It was the right time and the safest place to begin my tour of the memory I only thought I had forgotten.

Day 1 / 5 January 91

I've been in country 24 hours, and I'm in a weird state of shock. We landed at 2130 Saudi time, and when I stepped off the plane, it was like stepping onto another planet. The air was cool and very dry. The sky and stars looked closer than they do in South Carolina. I've never felt so strange.

Before deplaning, we got a briefing, during which the speaker said, "Welcome to Saudi Arabia; you are at Threatcon Level Charlie. That means terrorist attack is likely. Last week, two Marines were found slaughtered in a military truck. It appears they were killed for their chemical protective masks, going rate— $1,000 on the black market."

The plane got quiet as everyone stared ahead. I wanted to yell or scream or cry or do anything to know that I could actually feel, but no emotion would come.

When he finished talking, we filed off the plane down a long metal staircase to a rally point. When I got there, my platoon was standing around as if wondering what to do. I didn't know what to do either, but immediately some instinct kicked in and I started giving orders to squad leaders. "Get accountability. Get a sensitive-items check. Physically look at all your people...look at their masks...touch their weapons." I went on and on.

We moved to a holding area by foot, carrying everything. We were given bottled water and shown to a latrine. We had been sitting in the white sandy rock for hours when the buses came for us. We packed the buses standing-room-only and rode an hour and thirty minutes to the Port of Dhahran. We were dropped at a drafty old warehouse where people appeared to be living. We stood outside the building and waited for the equipment truck to arrive. When it did, we unloaded the bags.

After unloading, we moved into the warehouse. There were so many soldiers in our building that we had only a space about the size of my front porch to put 143 people.

We're crammed in here like sardines, 1,300 bodies in a drafty building that is only a roof with sheet metal sides. There is a maximum of 12 to 18 inches of space between each cot, and I heard right away that theft is a big problem. Maybe someone will steal my job.

We learned the rules within the first hour: you never go anywhere without your protective mask and weapon, even to the latrines.

Speaking of the latrines—they are disgusting. I can't even write how detestable they are. They are wooden outhouses with only partial sides; your butt is covered and your head peers over.

The showers are a little cleaner by virtue of the fact that there is no shit on the walls. This is just a holding area, though, and from what I hear, the best facilities we'll have. It's a goddamn refugee camp. There is laundry hanging everywhere, filth, stench, and more troubled people than I ever cared to see in one gathering.

Day 3 / 7 January 91

Last night was hell. I'd gladly go back to port to be crammed into the warehouse rather than stay here in the middle of nowhere. I'm pretty sure we'll all die out here. We were in the port for less than 24 hours before suddenly we were the most deployable unit there. I don't quite understand how, but for some reason, we were ordered to take what equipment we had and head to the desert. Here we are.

After driving all night to get here, everyone is exhausted. Once we finally arrived, we pitched our only three tents and circled our tractors together like pioneers in an old Western. As we were preparing our guard duty roster and eating cold meals from plastic bags, headquarters sent a messenger to alert us of activity. Intelligence sources reported that Saddam plans to attack only 78 km from us in the next 24 hours.

The news made a bad night worse since there are only 66 of us with limited ammunition in the wide-open desert. The rest of our company had to stay back at port and await the remainder of our trucks and equipment. We have no foxholes to jump into, no perimeter security around our camp, and no radio communication to the outside world. The desert is pitch dark—we're freezing and frightened.

Headquarters says we'll know eight to 12 hours before we get attacked, but I don't believe them. If we get attacked, only 66 people—we're all dead.

Day 9 / 13 January 91

Today is Sunday and the rain is pouring down. It reminds me of how godforsaken this place really is.

The chaplain came from headquarters to give us services a while ago, and I actually thought about going. I didn't because I'm afraid I'll break down and not regain composure if I participate in anything spiritual. I'm so scared of falling apart.

If I could talk to God and know that someone other than the voice in my head was listening, I might give it a try. I'd ask God to keep Clara safe and Evelyn sane. I'm more frightened of never seeing the people I care about again than I am of dying. I know I have to die someday but not here and not now. I'm going to do whatever it takes to get out of here alive.

Day 11 / 15 January 91

It's D-day: the end of the grace period for Iraq. We told them to go and they refused, so now we have no choice but to force them out. We here at our modest and undermanned camp can only wait and wonder what will happen next.

I need to rest, but I doubt I'll sleep since I can smell burning shit outside the tent. It's a job that has to be done for sanitary purposes, but it is abhorrent. The soldiers pour diesel fuel on the shit pile and burn while stirring. The smoke smells so bad that I can't imagine standing over it to stir. Lieutenants aren't worth much, but that is one benefit of being an officer in this deployment: no shit burning.

Day 42 / 15 February 91

I've lost track of all days and time. I think this is day 42, but I can't be sure. I know it's Friday, the 15th of February, and it's damn dark out.

We are positioned approximately 8 km from Iraq. When we moved here, we were told not to pack our tents. We packed only our personal gear and left in the middle of the night. We have no toilet facilities at this location and are short of water and rations.

There is definitely no bathing water, so I am filthy. I suspect my next shower will be a long time off.

It's already dark, and we still have a long blackout move into an unfriendly area. There are no massed forces around us, but scout patrols are everywhere. I don't imagine it will be a fun trip. I hope all those nights Rachel and I spent trekking in the desert looking for trouble taught me how to get around in this hellhole. I really don't want to get lost and go a mile too far north.

Day 46 / 19 February 91

We got our first incoming artillery round today. No one was seriously injured, but we did have a minor burn victim from my platoon. I value my emergency medical training more every day.

This place is unlivable. The lack of facilities is not only embarrassing, but also unsanitary. People are just going to the bathroom anywhere and everywhere. I never thought my job would entail teaching people not to shit where they sleep. I'm tired and frustrated.

Rachel and I returned to base camp today to get a GPS navigational device put in my Humvee. I'm glad she volunteered to be my driver—we're a really good team. We picked up some M-203 grenade launcher rounds while we were there, and Rachel helped me steal some flak vests. They were earmarked for troops in the rear, but there aren't any bullets flying around back there. I got tired of waiting for someone to process my request for them. I don't consider protecting my soldiers to be breaking the law. What law applies to this operation anyway?

I should find out tonight what is going on with us for the next few days. I hate the nights around here. They last an eternity. You can sit and wonder all night what's out there or you take control of your fear and go find out. That's what I do. I go find out.

I laugh now at how scared I was when we first arrived in the desert. What the hell was I scared of then?

Day 51 / 24 February 91

I have been sleepwalking for the last four days. I can't eat, I can't think, and I am barely breathing. It seemed like the right thing to do at the time. It seemed harmless enough to stop and help a fellow soldier. Tony is the only one we told, and he says everything will be fine. I'm not so sure. Rachel says nothing, and I am fighting the urge to turn to stone.

I feel as if someone siphoned the marrow from my bones while I wasn't looking. I'm hollow and covered in a dull ache. I try to focus on the mission and nothing else, but when I do, I see past the world. It looks like maybe there is a pinprick in the view I used to have and suddenly I can see to the next level. I don't know how else to explain it.

Tears are burning to escape while I hold them at bay with all the strength I have. I will never forgive my selfish wandering. I have no idea why I let that happen. I deserve whatever comes next.

When the hammer falls, it hits all that are close—not just those in its sight. Tony stopped by and talked to me a minute ago. He says move on. I wish Rachel would talk to me—be mad at me or something—but she says nothing.

Everything has changed. We are preparing to move out as I write. I'm sitting here watching the platoon pack their belongings and load their trucks as I struggle to remain human. The ground war has started, and our next move is into Iraq. The timing is unbelievable.

I had a talk with the platoon, and we agreed that no matter what happens, we'd take care of each other. It's a pact. I'm ready. So are they.

Day 52 / 25 February 91

We're on the verge of being in Iraq. Our next jump or two will put us there. Last night was quite a light show. It's damn hard to sleep when the sky is lighting up and you're sitting bolt upright freezing your ass off. Every time I woke up, Rachel was counting explosions. The B-52s bombed the shit out of Iraq all night and they're still at it.

Smoke is billowing over the large berm in front of me. It's all that lies between Iraq and us. The Iraqis built the berm on the border, then mined it with explosives. Our trucks will go through there when the division rolls.

Choppers are flying all around as the sun is going down. The chemical report said Saddam threw chemical today at Hafar al Batin, Saudi Arabia, about 40 miles from here. I have traveled through there many times with my convoy. I wonder if I'll ever again see places that I've been before.

Day 53 / 26 February 91

We spent our first night in Iraq. It was noisy as hell and not very restful, but we're moving up again in about 30 minutes, so I need to try and clear my head. Three American soldiers blown up by land mines were brought to the graves registration point in our area last night. It was not reassuring to learn that they died where we are about to go.

I was also in a minefield today, but fortunately, the outcome was better for us than for the soldiers in body bags traveling with our convoy. Rachel and I stopped to assist a driver whose truck was stuck in the sand, then took a shortcut to catch up. When the other lieutenant came on the radio and asked if I knew we were in a mined area, Rachel stopped immediately and looked at me like I actually had a plan. She still has so much faith in me in spite of what happened. We managed to get out, but it was certainly due more to luck than skill.

Day 54 / 27 February 91

I hate Iraq as bad as I hate Saudi. Sandstorms, windstorms, cold and rainy weather.... Only here you can add the elements of minefields, enemy bunkers, blown-out tanks and vehicles, airstrike scares, and people just plain old shooting at you. Why the hell are they shooting at us?

We're heading for Kuwait by way of the east along the border. We're at least 20 or 30 miles into Iraq now, but I can't be sure where. I'm sitting up here in the "mine-sweep" position again about to lead a column of tankers from a place I can't find on a map to a place I don't have a map for. Who planned this operation? I bet whoever it was has the only map.

Day 56 / 1 March 91

The last 24 hours have been awful. After traveling across Iraq with the 1st Infantry Division through burning bunkers and blown-up tanks, hordes of dead soldiers, and even more surrendering soldiers, we arrived in Kuwait.

Our tankers were drained within 45 minutes, which left us no choice but to return to Iraq for fuel. It was a 96-mile drive one way back to the logistics base. It was also a totally different scenario at night since we couldn't see the enemy very well and they certainly weren't surrendering.

We were cruising at about 5 mph in total blackout drive when the first two rounds came in. I saw only the muzzle flash in the darkness to the right side of the convoy, and I knew it had to be enemy fire. I looked through the night-vision goggles in the direction of the flash, but I couldn't see anything. I looked over to see if Rachel was okay at the same instant that two more rounds came.

I felt them hit. They landed in the rear quarter panel of my Humvee. I radioed the front of the convoy to speed up and informed them that we were being fired on. One of the terrified drivers broke ranks and tried to take off on his own.

With minefields all around us, I was worried that he might detonate one or more mines in his panic. Rachel went after him before I could say a word. She pulled up next to him and forced him back into line as if herding a calf while I continued to monitor the convoy on my radio.

I called to all drivers to close the spacing and drive bumper to bumper as fast as they could. I called to the maintenance team to locate the sniper and radio me when they had him in their night-vision scope. We couldn't risk leaving him for the next convoy that happened in his path.

Despite the radio chatter, my mind was focused on what might come next. I knew from years of military training that a sniper is often a prelude to an ambush. With a convoy of empty fuel tankers riding so close together, I shuddered at the repercussions of a heavy round hitting even one tanker.

Our options were extremely limited. If we scattered for safety, someone would surely detonate a mine, not to mention that we'd all be lost in the blackness of the desert with no headlights. If we stayed in a column and opened up spacing, someone might get stuck in the soft sand while slowing down to spread out. And if we maintained our current position and simply increased our speed, we had momentum on our side to keep everyone moving.

I was not about to take the chance of losing or leaving anyone, so I opted that the gain of staying together was worth the risk. We maintained our zero spacing while increasing our speed.

As crazy as it sounds, something touched me on the shoulder those seconds I was struggling and seemed to say, "You're OK— you know what to do—trust your instinct." So I did. "Hesitate and die" rang through my head while I hastily gave orders.

We arrived at our destination, Log Base Nelligan, just after sunrise, exhausted and shocked. We had been stopped less than 10 minutes when some officers from a medical unit approached us to escort them back to Kuwait. I refused the direct order from a higher-ranking officer on the grounds that my soldiers were dangerously tired and needed a break. I ignored his threats as he wrote my name and the bumper number from my Humvee in a small notepad and stomped off. We fueled our tankers, rested briefly, then headed back toward Kuwait.

At the same approximate latitude and longitude where we'd been fired on the night before, there was again hostile activity. A medical unit had been ambushed in broad daylight, with serious casualties. A rocket-propelled grenade launcher round hit a Humvee, killing at least one and wounding several. There were Medevac choppers, smoke, fire, and commotion. I know it was the unit I refused to travel with. I knew it would have been us. All I could think was thank you God it wasn't us. I don't have words to explain the relief.

Day 71 / 16 March 91
We've been in Kuwait supplying the division with fuel for weeks now. The fuel point keeps getting farther away, but today we were able to travel a paved road for a change. About 10 miles out of our base camp is a two-lane road that leads through Kuwait City and down into Saudi Arabia.

The road is lined with blown-up vehicles. They are stacked on top of each other, totally demolished. The horrid smell that I have become so familiar with hangs in the air—it is the true smell of death.

War is so senseless.

Day 109 / 23 April 91

We moved back to Iraq a while ago. We've been running fuel missions to support the troops monitoring the civil unrest around the Tigris and Euphrates River areas. We have fought flies, mosquitoes, malaria pill illness, heat, the smell of burning shit, cold showers, chicken and rice every day for chow, and bad attitudes. We have feared terrorist attacks, land mines and sniper fire, battled among the platoons, hated the chain of command, and tried to merely exist.

Anyway, it looks like we'll be home within a few weeks, so I'm closing this journal for now. I'll close the final page on the airplane.

I've changed a lot. I've grown up, and I've felt and seen things I never wanted to feel or see. But the soldiers I was responsible for are all well. They aren't happy and they aren't unaffected, but they are alive.

That was my goal. To get every single person in my care home safe and sound. I've not failed in the safe mission, but none of us are of sound anything. We are all affected in our own little worlds.

Day 121 / 5 May 91

I'm having trouble remembering what day we came here or what day it is in this stinking country. I think it's day 121. We leave for home today.

Once I'm home, I'll have to somehow begin my life again, but I don't know how that will be possible. I've seen and done things that will remain with me forever. I fear my reaction to seeing my family and the people who used to be my close friends. I also fear my reaction to hearing the truth I've known all along about Clara and Evelyn.

I doubt it will affect me like it would have before this war. I doubt anything will affect me ever again in this way. It will be hard to look at everyday life and find something exciting after the adrenaline I've experienced here. My perspective has totally changed.

I've never really wanted to go backward, but if I could undo some things that happened here, I would. The things I wish I could erase will haunt me forever. Some people cracked under the pressure because they weren't prepared. I simply let my strong need to be in control of my fate lead me astray.

Anyway, in retrospect, we all know we made some mistakes. I messed up, but I learned as I went. At least I always had the best interest and safety of my soldiers first and the mission second.

These journal entries have been cleansing to me in this place. I have written mostly the negative, but there were also times of happiness. Though it may not be evident in these pages, the camaraderie of my platoon is unquestionable.

I used to think soldiers saw an officer as the enemy and nothing else, but I have learned another way to be seen. They respect me and I respect them, and from that primary exchange, we built a team.

They taught me that if I listened to them and took care of their basic needs, gave them the tools to perform their missions, and defended them from higher headquarters, they would follow me anywhere, anytime, and for any reason.

It is for them and because of them that I would again risk my life for my country. I would again take the same chances as before. I would again walk blindly behind the lead of the United States Army into uncertainty.

Not because I am not smart enough to think for myself or not radical enough to protest, but because I am not yet bitter enough to stand idly by and let my country be captive.

I will leave these people, this place, and this bond behind when I get on the plane, but it will live in my heart and in these journals forever.

Chapter Twenty-one

The next feeling I had was the heat of the sun on my face. Jayne was the only one in the room when I opened my eyes.

"Abby?" She squeezed my hand. "Is that you?" Her voice cracked. Cracking or not, it was the most wonderful sound I had ever heard. I couldn't force a tone from my throat, but I blinked to focus on her face.

"Don't try and speak." She must have sensed my struggle. "I need to get the doctor, okay?" I felt her grip loosen on my hand, so I tried to hang on. "It's okay, I won't go anywhere. Just let me hit the nurse call button." She reached for something over my head but didn't let go of me.

Within minutes, my room was full of activity. I heard Jeff's voice through the crowd, then saw him standing over my bed. He smiled when I looked at him.

"Nice nap?" He was purely Jeff and nothing had changed. I attempted to smile back to say hello.

He wept openly as he stood across from Jayne and took my other hand. It was a wonderful sight to wake up to. I felt drowsy and drifting for the next few hours, not really knowing where I had been or what I had been doing. All I knew for sure was that I was out of immediate danger.

When I woke again, Jayne was asleep in the chair next to my bed. It was quiet in the room, and I felt very peaceful. I could see her face clearly, and she looked like an angel. She was draped in a jacket with her head leaning on a pillow. She wore an expression of total tranquility, and her open, relaxed sleeping posture agreed wholly with her expression.

I didn't want to wake her. I wanted to know what had been happening while I was away, but I wanted more to study the lines on her beautiful face. Many times in my dreams, I had seen her in restful slumber. I savored this precious opportunity to enjoy such an innocent, simple pleasure for real.

As I watched her, memories of my own extended stillness began trickling back. I remembered the mostly empty room and the wooden table—the red backpack and the envelopes containing my journals from Desert Storm. I recalled in its entirety the task I had completed while in my suspended consciousness.

The nurse peeked in the room and saw I was awake.

"Good morning, Ms. Dunnigan," she said in a half-whispered, half-conversational tone.

Jayne stirred and I felt almost violated as my unfettered moments with her were stolen.

"Hi." My voice was weak, but I was looking in Jayne's now open eyes. I compelled all the sound I had to come forth and let her know I was grateful for her presence.

She gave a long and triumphant sigh. "Hi." She came to my bedside, leaned over the rail, and kissed me on the forehead. "How are you feeling?"

"I'm not sure." My voice was quiet and throaty.

"It's so nice to see you." She had tears in her eyes and a wide smile on her face.

"Have you been here long?"

She chuckled and shook her head. "Not long enough to make me go away." She tousled my hair and kept her smile.

"How long?" I persisted.

"A while," she maintained. "Can I get you anything?"

"Ice, please." As I spoke, my memory registered how dry I had been the last night I woke at home and found Jayne in my living room. I was struggling to remember more of that night when she touched a few small chips of ice to my lips. I don't know if it was the ice or the touch, but something about the act halted my trifling.

"Is that better?" She stroked my cheek with her cool, wet fingers.

"Yes, thanks." A calm swept over me again, and I closed my eyes.

It was a few more days before I regained full consciousness. I learned that I had lapsed into a diabetic coma the night I was brought to the hospital. I had no idea that I was even diabetic, which might account for winding up in a coma for two weeks.

My remembrance of the events leading up to the coma was slower to return than my consciousness. No one talked to me about the case or the fact that my brother had murdered Charlie Stokes, but those memories finally came on their own. I wasn't ready to talk about them, though, particularly not in a hospital. It took most of my energy to heal my shrinking body and all my concentration to walk, talk, and perform other normal daily functions.

It was the start of my third week in the hospital when I felt strong enough to pick up the life I had left behind. I was getting out in a few days and wanted to prepare myself for going home and handling the stress of the case again. The doctor told me I would be an insulin-dependent diabetic for the remainder of my life but that I should be able to live with little more inconvenience than a daily injection.

I completely understood the physical part of my diagnosis and treatment, but the issue of how to heal my troubled mind was another situation entirely.

For the first time since my return from the Persian Gulf, I remembered everything that had happened there in vivid detail. I had placed it all in an untouchable region of my consciousness, then retrieved it while I slept. I didn't quite understand how, but I knew that I had not only touched, but full-body embraced the memories during my stillness.

Jeff came into my room and forced me out of my head and into the world.

"You look good!" He hugged me as I sat on the edge of my bed. "Are you supposed to be sitting up?"

"I can do anything you can do," I teased. "As long as it doesn't make me dizzy."

His expression softened. "I won't touch that comment." He looked at the door, then back at me. "'Cause what makes you dizzy is coming down the hall."

"What?" I squinted at him.

"Knock, knock," Jayne said as she entered the half-closed door to my room.

"What'd I tell you?" Jeff shrugged his shoulders, raised his eyebrows, and moved over to let her near me. I couldn't suppress a laugh.

"Hmmm." I rolled my eyes at him, then smiled at Jayne who was already about to put her arms around me.

"Careful," Jeff cautioned. "You'll need to lie down if you feel dizzy." He tried to sound concerned.

"What are you two up to?" Jayne stood and began taking off her coat. "Have I interrupted a private conference?" She looked at Jeff, then back at me.

"No, Jeff was just leaving." I flashed him a grin, and he halfheartedly obliged my hint.

"See you after I get some coffee." He left the room, and Jayne sat on the side of the bed with me.

"Are you ready to go home?" She put her hand on my leg.

"Maybe." I leaned my head on her shoulder. "But maybe not."

"Why the not part?" She slipped her arm around my waist.

"I'm scared," I confessed.

"Of what?" She stroked my hair. "There's nothing to be scared of there."

"I'm scared of me. I feel so different since I woke up. So many things are still unclear, yet too many other things are painfully clear." I was confusing, but she was with me.

"You mean sleeping woke you up." She hit the nail on the head.

"Yes. That's exactly what I mean. I remember things from the past that I haven't thought of in years," I explained. "Is that normal?"

"I've never been in a coma, but I have read quite a bit about the experience. I'd say it could be. What do you remember?"

"I went through the pages of my own journal entries from Desert Storm..." I paused to compose my explanation. "Well, not all of them...but the highlights or something." I felt confused. "I have striking memories of those days right now." I looked up at her.

Water slowly filled her eyes. "I read some of your Desert Storm journals while you were away. It's so sad you had to endure that horrible experience." Her face showed her sadness full-on. "I hope it's okay that I read them." A tear escaped.

"Of course it's okay. That's why I gave them to you. I wanted you to know. I think I even needed you to know." I let the tears come. We sat on my bed and held each other, crying freely.

Jeff peered in the door but did not enter. I became very aware of my unrestrained tears when I saw him and forced them back. Jayne and I stayed in the safe grip of each other's arms for a while longer before we came around again. We didn't speak a word, but the communication was unambiguous.

"Did you read the pages from Clara's diary that were in the bag? And the notes from Alvin?"

She nodded and held me tighter.

"Abby, I'm not surprised the memory came to you while you slept. I can explain all that later. You're going to need a lot of time to heal from everything you've been through." She paused. "I want to help you." When she looked at me, her face was again overcome with sadness.

"I'm counting on your help." My look betrayed my attempt to hide my confusion. "Why do you seem sad?"

"Oh, Abby. This is very complicated." She was shaking her head.

"What's complicated?" I was afraid of the answer she would give.

She drew a long breath and began to speak. "I'm in a relationship, Abby. With someone who has been my whole life. She was the center of my universe until you walked into my office, and now suddenly, I have no idea what I feel for anyone. I wouldn't trust my feelings right now if I did know what they were." She stopped abruptly. I said nothing.

"I tried to talk to you while you were asleep." She smiled through her tears. I maintained my riveted posture. "I don't want to mislead you. I want to put it all on the table before it gets any more convoluted."

"Go on."

"I can't leave Shannon. I can't break her heart. There is absolutely no way I can hurt her. Do you understand?" The tears were pouring down her cheeks.

"I understand, Jayne. It's exactly why I love you." I wiped her tears and fought my own. "I understand."

"Did you hear anything I said while you slept?" She reached for a tissue on the bedside table.

"I heard you reminding me to breathe." I took the tissue she offered me and wiped her face with it.

Jeff came to the door again and stood just outside it. He was waiting for someone to tell him it was all right to enter. I did.

"Do you need me to disappear?" he asked as he entered cautiously.

"It's okay, Jeff." I looked at Jayne, who nodded her approval. "I need to discuss some things with you both anyway."

"That's cool." He pulled a chair over to the bed and pretended to ignore us as we blew our noses and wiped our eyes.

I'm grateful that Jeff interrupted my conversation with Jayne. I had learned enough for the moment. I knew she loved me, but she had made it painfully clear that she had no intention of expressing that love in a physical realm. I could not process two discoveries of equal and opposite intensity in the same short span of time. I didn't know which emotion to feel first.

I settled for a general question. "What's been going on?"

They looked at each other, then away. Jeff was the first to seek clarity. "What do you mean?"

"Is anything new going on in the case?"

"Well, it depends on what you mean by 'new,' but some things have changed a little." He was careful.

"Like what?" I persisted.

"Like Evelyn and Laurel aren't being hidden away anymore."

"They just let them go home?" I felt a little pained that they hadn't tried to contact me if they had indeed been released from their protective-custody prison.

"They didn't really let them go home." He looked at Jayne for help.

"Abby, they're at your house." She took my hand and held it in hers.

"They are?" I was pleased with the news but still grasping for clarity. "Why haven't they come here?" Jeff looked at Jayne again.

"Because I thought it might be too big a shock for you to see them before you were released from the hospital," Jayne began to explain. "They wanted to come, but I advised against it."

"Are they doing okay?"

"They seem to be just fine," Jeff answered. "They're anxious to see you."

"Wow. I can't believe they're at the house! That's great news. I really miss Evvie." I felt warm and comforted knowing she would be there when I got home.

"To answer your other question, there's very little happening in the attempt to locate Alvin." Something in Jayne's voice screamed that she was withholding information. I accepted it as truth, though, and guided the conversation back to Evvie and Laurel.

Going home felt foreign, yet very much part of the overall design. I had physically been away for only three weeks, but in my mind, I had been away since I left for the Persian Gulf in 1991. Evelyn and Laurel, along with Pat and Jeff, were waiting on the lawn when Ted and I pulled into the drive.

It was an emotional reunion. I stood surrounded by Evelyn and Laurel in a clinch so tight that it meshed us into one being. I was already tired from the day's excitement by the time we went into the house, and I fell into my own bed sometime before 8:00 p.m. I thought briefly about why Jayne was not around, then slipped easily into sleep.

In my deep sleep trance, I heard a phone ringing. I knew I had unplugged the extension in my room shortly after learning of Clara's murder, and even in my groggy state, I was aware that I never reconnected it. I waited to see if anyone else in the house would wake and answer, but no one did. The machine didn't connect either, so after about ten rings, it was up to me to pick it up or continue to listen.

When I reached for the phone at the side of the bed, it occurred to me that it wasn't the one ringing at all. The soft ringing was coming from under my pillow. I fished around in the dark, and to my surprise, I found my cell phone, lighted and ringing. I answered.

The words, "It's me, Abby," jolted me completely awake.

"Alvin. What are you doing? Where are you?" I whispered. I couldn't believe my ears.

"Listen, Abby. I only have a minute or two. If anyone comes in, turn off the phone and hide it. Do you hear me? You have to or you'll get Jayne in big trouble." He had my undivided attention.

"I hear you." My heightened senses absorbed the instructions like a sponge and stored them for later use.

"Are you feeling better? I was worried about you."

"Yes, I'm better."

"Abby. I had to take him out. You know I had to…don't you?" He sounded desperate for me to believe him.

"Yes."

"I didn't hurt the others."

"I know."

"If they find me, they'll kill me. It was self-defense, Abby. Just like you. Self-defense." I heard the emotion begin to infect his voice.

"What can I do?" I pledged my loyalty.

"Jayne knows what to do. I'm sorry for everything." He sounded overcome with regret.

"I'm sorry, too. I'm sorry we've never understood each other, even though we're so very much alike." I hadn't the words to describe my sorrow over our fifteen-plus years of separation.

"I still don't understand you, Abby." He made his opinion clear. "But you're my sister, and we're both in trouble. We both loved her, and we both lost her. I couldn't let him get away with it." Alvin sounded like he was about to break.

"I know. I'm glad it's over." I wanted to tell him that I yearned to kill Charlie with my bare hands and that I was really glad he did it instead, but it wasn't the right time. "Why did you call me?" I was split down the middle on how I interpreted his intentions.

"We need each other." He reined in his straying emotions. "Jayne has been very helpful. Is she your new lover?" His candor shocked me.

"No." The word stung as it left my lips.

"Good. Don't make that mistake again." His voice was almost a warning.

"When will I talk to you next?" I sensed the need to disconnect.

"I'll be in touch. Be strong." He hung up before I could say anything else.

I turned off the phone and sat with it in my hands, wondering if I was dreaming. Had I really just talked to Alvin? Did anyone hear me talking to him? The sound of footsteps coming down the hall suspended my internal questioning, and I quickly stashed the phone in the headboard bookshelf.

"Abby?" Jeff's voice pierced the silence. "Are you awake?" He was halfway in the room before I spoke.

"Sorta." I tried to sound asleep.

"I heard something in here and thought I better check on you." He sat on my bed.

"I think I was dreaming."

"Probably. Can I get you anything?"

"Jayne." I laughed quietly.

"I'd deliver her right to your bed if I could." He sighed. "She has no idea how lucky she is." He rubbed my shoulder, then leaned down to hug me. "No idea."

"I'm the lucky one." I held tighter to him as I spoke. "Lucky that you stick with me."

"I'd stop a speeding truck for you. Want some tea?"

"Nah, I'm going to take a stab at sleep again." I stretched my arms and settled back into my nest of blankets.

"Mind if I hang in here with you until you're asleep?"

"Be my guest. Crawl in if you want, and we'll freak them all out when they wake up." I was startled by my own suggestion, but it felt okay.

I fell easily into Jeff's comfortable and familial embrace. He kissed my head, and I kissed his cheek as I drifted back to the safety of sleep.

Chapter Twenty-two

It was odd waking to Jeff sleeping beside me. I felt a little disoriented at first, but I remembered the chain of events leading to his current location as I sneaked quietly from the bed. He didn't move.

Evvie was on the couch when I entered the room. I fell onto her body, and we snuggled in the silence of the morning. Laurel turned our couple into a group when she woke. We must have looked like a pile of children at a slumber party. Ted stood in the doorway and laughed aloud when he saw us.

"I need a camera," he called toward Jeff's room. "Jeff, you don't want to miss this."

"He's in my room, Ted." I somehow managed to speak through the heap of bodies. "He's still asleep."

"That's interesting. I won't ask."

"I was dreaming or something, and he came in and woke me last night. We slept together the rest of the night. No big deal," I explained to the three curious and too-close faces hanging on my words.

"I wonder about you two." Evvie shook her head.

"What about *you* two?" I had sensed the energy between them in the short visit we had on my return from the hospital.

"I don't have a dog in this race." Ted excused himself as we all sat up.

"Tell her." Laurel punched Evelyn in the ribs with an elbow.

"No need," I smirked at Evvie. "Another one bites the dust." I winked at them and started toward the kitchen.

"It's not what you think, Abby," Evelyn called after me. "We're just dating."

"Laurel?"

"Yes. Dating." She grinned and kissed Evvie on the cheek. "No strings."

"Good God...Lesbians," I said with as much fake disgust as I could muster in my voice.

"We are an incestuous lot, aren't we?" Evvie quipped as I turned away.

"No comment."

We spent the entire morning catching up. I wanted to know everything that had happened while I was asleep, and as it turned out, it wasn't much. Alvin had not made a detectable move. He hadn't tried to contact his wife or our family, he hadn't tried to see me in the hospital, and he hadn't stuck his head out of the hole he was in to risk anyone identifying him.

Jayne must have been his only contact, and my curiosity was maxed out as to how he managed to hook up with her. I didn't know when I would see her again, nor did I feel comfortable calling her after our conversation in the hospital. I wanted to respect her relationship and her unspoken decision to distance herself from me. She knew Alvin was calling me last evening, though, so I was betting she would come around.

I had barely completed my suppositions about her next move when the phone rang. It was Jayne. She wanted to come over after dinner, and I happily agreed to see her.

My parents called just before dinner. I was surprised to hear my mother's voice. She sounded a hundred years old. It was apparent that Alvin's predicament had taken a toll on her health. My father asked only if I was all right and if Jeff was with me. He said nothing about the case or Alvin. I couldn't help feeling he somehow blamed me for all that Alvin was involved in now. He surely knew that Alvin had been with Clara, as I was, and he surely knew that Alvin had killed Charlie.

Mother said they were praying for my health and for a speedy end to this nightmare that had destroyed our family. She said God would know what to do and that I should join her in a prayer for us all. I sat close-lipped at the other end of her long-distance prayer connection, waiting patiently for the "Amen."

The ring of the doorbell couldn't have come at a better time. I was trying to play cards with Jeff, Laurel, and Evelyn when Jayne arrived, but I was going out of my mind with concern for what would become of Alvin. Ted filled my place graciously while Jayne and I retreated to my room.

I closed the door behind us and immediately took my cell phone from the bookshelf. She sat in the chair by my desk and put her head in her hands to rub her face, as if she had dealt with this situation all day and was already exhausted from it.

"Did anyone else wake up?"

I took a seat on the bed facing her. "Jeff. But he didn't hear anything other than noise. He had no idea what was happening."

When she looked me in the eyes, I melted. I had coached myself all afternoon on keeping a safe distance, but it was all in vain when she reached out to me with her hands. I fell to my knees in front of her. She wrapped her arms around me and leaned forward to engulf my whole torso in hers. I felt her legs pull me even closer as I surrendered entirely.

It was our first passionate, whole-body embrace. The lines separating us ran together. The multiple relationships we maintained all fused at once, and we were at that moment totally connected.

I wanted to stay there. I wanted to be clay for her hands and food for her soul. I wanted to denounce my singularity at once and pledge my commitment. I wanted to scream through the house that I had finally been reborn into a being that knew its way in life. I could accept her relationship with Shannon, and I could embrace her need for autonomy as long as I could just be near her.

It was the most self-effacing act of spirit I had ever allowed to roam through my veins. I gave in. I let down my shields the instant I felt her energy encompass me. I transformed. There would be no way to ever call up the stone soldier that once lived at my core. In my mind's eye, I watched as the rock image was reduced to a dust pile and carried away in a windstorm so violent it left no trace of the powdered ruins.

I had thought that since I met Jayne, I had learned to cry, but I was about to learn that I knew nothing. I sobbed unabashedly for so long that I lost track of all outside influences. It wasn't any kind of crying I had ever known before. I let go of all the pent-up sadness I was hoarding, along with all the other emotions I had forced to obey my rule of indifference, and they came out with a vengeance.

Jayne held on. She tightened her grip and let me wail. I didn't hear my door open when Jeff came to investigate, so I had no awareness that words were ever spoken around me. My eyes were closed and my fists were clenched, but the rest of my body opened up to release the burden it was tired of carrying.

Three hours later when it was finally over, the world hadn't come to an end. It was all as I had left it. I was still on the floor in Jayne's arms; she was still in the chair at my desk. The tears simply stopped when there were no more. Just as I hadn't started them, I had no hand in their fading. Jayne was right.

It was the most intimate experience of my life. She was smiling and brushing the hair from my face when I looked in her eyes. She held me solidly and kissed my cheek as I faded slowly into the present.

"I need to sleep." I laid my head in her lap.

"Good idea." She rocked me.

"Will you stay until I go to sleep?"

"Gladly." She helped me into bed and sat beside me. "I just need to use the phone."

"You'll need to plug it in first." I pointed toward the phone jack, then to the cord dangling from the night table.

She must have thought I was sleeping when she finally dialed the number to her house, but I heard every word. I also heard the uneasiness in her voice as she tried to explain to Shannon why she needed to stay with me just a while longer.

She kissed me on the hand she was holding moments before sneaking quietly from my room. I didn't move for fear she would stay and further complicate her life.

I could have easily reached out to her and pulled her into my bed—I could have held her in my arms as I slept the rest of the world away, but I could not take any more from her. In the darkness of my room, I could feel that she had left behind all the energy in her soul to comfort me. To introduce her to my own private reality would have been beyond selfish, past self-centered, and into self-absorbed.

I was wide awake from the moment the door shut behind her. The darkness that used to scare me was now my close companion. I couldn't say I liked it, but I certainly needed it to hide while I sorted out the thoughts slamming against the inside of my skull.

Like being in the coma, I felt suspended in energy and dependent on autonomic responses to support my life as I drifted into subconsciousness. There was nothing I could do to alter the state of my awareness, but I allowed it to be, as if I had a choice.

I returned easily to the pit of memory I had climbed from while in the hospital. As before, I moved downward at a steady pace nearing the bottom. Unlike before, this time, I was not free falling. I was roped in for safety. As I rappelled the slick, gray walls toward the cavern floor, Jayne stood fastidiously on belay.

It was as it should be, as I had designed it to be. I wasn't about to transcend my comfort zone without her. With her, I was completely safe in my memory world. The first thing I saw once my feet touched the ground was the vastness of the desert surrounding me.

Like a dance we had polished to perfection, Jayne and I began to move around— me from the bottom, her from the top. I was the mirror image in the reflecting pool she was standing over. She could turn away and I wouldn't exist anymore. I was there only because she was there.

In the distance of the desert, I saw a lone, still figure in the sand. As soon as I acknowledged it, I felt my body being pulled closer to it. I did not fight. When I was close enough to make out a shape, I knew at once that is was the Syrian soldier. My panic was replaced immediately by the touch of Jayne's hand on my shoulder. I looked up; she was reaching toward me with both arms. I reached back before I had time to think. It was enough.

I was suddenly standing over his body, which was decayed beyond recognition. I could have vomited, but I did not; I was frozen in place above his rotten corpse. I could smell the stages of wither his human shell had crossed through and saw before me the product of my indiscretion as big as life and as black as death. My skin began to feel hot and pallid, and my nerves began to defect, but my feet remained resolute. Fixed to the ground and in no position to flee, they were holding us all together.

Jayne was holding us, as well. I pleaded with her to let me turn away, but she insisted that I endure it instead. I tried to close my eyes, but the vision would not fade. At the moment, I believed I would return to the comatose state I had relinquished control of myself to while in the hospital. I saw the knife.

Still clenched in his skeletal hand was the knife he used to rape Rachel. It was the one I saw at her throat through the green

174

glow of my night-vision goggles. It was the knife in his hand when he lunged at me—the one he would have used to kill us both. I was as surprised as someone who had only made up the story of a knife to cover an act of cold-blooded murder.

I was ascending the pit before I knew what was happening next. Jayne steadied the rope as I dragged my body up the dark sides and into the light at the top. I was almost to the lip when I stopped and looked back on the scene I had just left. It was not the same. It was no longer the desert, but rather a place I didn't recognize. I wanted to return and investigate, but I urged myself up instead.

I closed my mind when Jayne took my reaching arms and pulled me over the top. I was back in my bed in the dark of my room, alone.

Chapter Twenty-three

When I opened my eyes, Evvie was sitting in the chair by my bed, reading a book and drinking coffee. She put them both down when she caught my eye.

"Good morning, Sunshine!"

"What are you doing?" I smiled back.

"Hanging out with you." She rolled the chair closer to my bed.

"That's cool." I reached my hand to her, and she took it.

"I'm sorry I couldn't come to the hospital." She shook her head. "I tried to make them let me, but Jayne was a bulldog about your recovery." She chuckled but kept her transparent thoughts away from words.

"I understand. She didn't want me going into shock from seeing you or something like that." I never really got the full explanation. I just accepted that she knew what was best for my mental health. "Anyway, I wasn't all that talkative."

"So I hear." She leaned back and took her cup from the desk.

"Are you and Laurel heading back to Spartanburg pretty soon?" I somehow knew that was the plan.

"Right as usual," she remarked. "I know that you're in good hands here, and we haven't been home in forever. We really need to go back and try to sort out our lives."

"Makes sense," I agreed. "I'm just glad you came."

"Wild horses, my dear Abigail." I hadn't heard that in years. "Wild horses with naked women on their backs couldn't have dragged me away from seeing you in person." She smirked. "I let you down once. I wasn't about to abandon you again." Her look turned serious.

"Come on, Evvie. Knock it off. You didn't let me down. You just had lousy timing." I didn't care about the past at the moment.

"Do you really forgive me?" She looked desperate for me to say yes.

"I really forgive you." I squeezed her hand. "Will you forgive yourself?"

"I'll try."

"Try really hard." I pulled myself up to a sitting position so we could hug.

"You're such a sap," I said as I looked into her almost-teary eyes.

"And you're such a rock."

"Not anymore." I smiled. "Not like I used to be."

"Jayne softening you up?" Evelyn raised her eyebrows.

"She's trying." I drew a deep breath.

"Are you in love?"

"Head over…" I sighed, "pointless though it is."

"What's with this 'pointless' crap? No one in history has been able to refuse your services, in case you forgot. It's you who never bites."

"Well, this one has no trouble refusing me. She has a partner, a life, and a home. She won't be needing my 'services,' as you call them. What does that mean, anyway?" I looked as puzzled as I felt.

"You need me to spell it out for you?" She grinned. "I still haven't forgotten."

"Never mind." I halted her in her tracks. "I can't take another stroll down memory lane this morning. Suffice it to say, she's not interested."

"Then she's foolish." Evvie wouldn't give. "Want me to scope it out for you?"

"No, thanks. Don't help me." I fished around on the floor for my sandals as I spoke.

"I give you two a month and you'll be in the sack." She extended her other hand. "Want to bet?"

"Yeah, I'll take that bet because it ain't happening." I shook with her. "You have to stay faithful to Laurel if I win. Deal?"

"What a weird bet. Okay. I can do it. How long?"

"As long as she wants." I firmed up my grip. "Understand?"

"Okay, but that's an awfully easy bet for me to follow through with."

"Why so easy?"

"Because I'm also in love." She made a silly face.

"Really?"

"Really." I'd never seen such sincerity in her eyes.

"My, my, my." I was glad for her. "So what was with the 'just dating' front you pulled out yesterday?"

"We don't want to jinx it, Abby. We just want it to be."

"I wish you luck and support you every step of the way."

"You don't think it's too weird since we were both with Clara and all that?" Evvie was obviously uncomfortable even talking about it.

"Our whole life has been weird, Ev. Why worry now?" I patted her arm.

"Coffee's on." She got up first. "I'll call you every day until this nightmare ends. And I'll be here if you need me."

"I know." We headed toward the smell of fresh coffee.

"Well, if it's not sleeping beauty!" Jeff greeted me as I walked into the kitchen.

"I don't know about the beauty part...." I hugged him. "Where's Laurel?"

"Shower. And Pat flew out of here like she was going to a fire after a call on her cell phone a few minutes ago. I have no idea where Ted is hiding out."

"You don't know who called Pat?" I knew it had to be case-related and damn important for her to leave when Ted was not around. "What'd she say?" I suddenly felt a little troubled.

"She didn't say anything except she had to go and for me to stick around until she came back." He shrugged. "Don't worry, Abby. Alvin is too smart to get caught by those clowns." I was shocked he was so candid, but I relaxed a bit just the same.

We were almost through with breakfast when the phone rang again. Jeff answered and handed it to me.

"Abby. It's Shannon, Jayne's partner." The voice on the other end was soft.

"Hi, Shannon. Is something wrong?" I knew it was, and I wanted to know as fast as I could what had happened.

"Yes. Jayne has been arrested by your security guards and the police for obstruction of justice or something like that."

"What?" I raised my voice.

"She called me right before they took her from her office. Apparently, your brother met her there, but she was being

178

watched. She managed to get him out without him being apprehended but then refused to cooperate with the officers who burst in unannounced. They told her she could talk or they could arrest her. She wouldn't talk."

"Shit," I said. "I am so sorry, Shannon. What can I do?"

"Meet me at the station and let's get her out of there as quickly as possible. Maybe you can talk some sense into your friends." She sounded rightfully annoyed with me.

"Of course, I'll be right there. I'm really sorry."

"Tell that to Jayne. She's never been in trouble in her life. This is probably the most terrifying thing she's ever personally experienced." I knew better than that, but I agreed that it must be horrible for her.

Jeff and I arrived at the station in time to see Jayne being booked for the charges against her. I saw Ted sitting outside the room where Jayne was being held. Shannon was already arguing with him.

"What's going on here, Ted? Are you out of your mind?" I interrupted.

"Goddamn it, Abby. Why didn't you tell us she was involved?" He looked at me with total disdain. "This is serious."

"Damn right it's serious. Let her out of here or you get no more cooperation from me ever."

"We haven't had anything but interference from you, Abby. What do you mean cooperation? Why would you start now?"

"Ted, listen to yourself. This is my brother you're trying to arrest. My brother. He killed a murderer. A murderer you couldn't catch. You should be glad. He's not dangerous. He's just scared you'll shoot him if he shows his face. How the hell do you know he wasn't going to Jayne for help in turning himself in?" I was screaming while Shannon stood by speechless.

"Well, she helped him escape, not turn himself in." He spewed the facts at me.

Shannon looked him in the eyes and shook her head. "Wow, you are a big asshole, huh? Jayne said there was one reasonable cop. It certainly isn't you." She walked off.

I stared him down. "Let her go, Ted. You know she doesn't deserve to be put in jail for anything."

"It's not up to me." He looked away.

"Can I at least talk to her?"

"Not alone," he snapped back.

"I don't give a good goddamn if you broadcast it on the news this evening, I just want her to know we're here." I pushed past him and into the glass cubicle where Jayne was being processed. Shannon followed.

They embraced and kissed as Jayne fell into tears. As I watched Shannon tenderly comfort Jayne, the pain in my chest felt like a cardiac arrest. It was obvious that Shannon loved her more than anything on the planet.

I knew that feeling. I loved her that way, too.

When Jayne finally realized I was standing there, as well, she put her arms around me, and we hugged like old friends. Shannon didn't seem the least bit interested in the dynamics of my relationship with her partner. She knew there was no need to worry. Her only concern was getting her beloved released.

It was four hours later when we finally got Jayne freed. Pat and Ted impeded the release process every step of the way. I spent the entire four hours with Shannon. I could never have known so quickly under any other circumstances what a wonderful woman she was. It was a bittersweet discovery.

It was comforting to know Shannon deserved the love Jayne gave and reassuring to watch them and experience the commitment they shared. Shannon was calm but firm in her demand that Jayne be treated to standard by her captors. I admired her way and condoned her role as Jayne's mate with an odd, contradictory sense of approval.

I was furious that Jayne had been subjected to such harsh treatment, and I let everyone in earshot know it. Ted tried to talk with me as Jayne was being released, but I wouldn't even listen. When he said I shouldn't encourage her further involvement in the case, I said I wanted him and Pat out of my house immediately. He said I was making a big mistake, and I pointed out that he had already made one himself.

Jayne seemed undamaged as she and Shannon prepared to leave the station. We sat briefly in the lobby before departing.

"Why did you let yourself go to jail for this?" I asked as Shannon sensed our need for privacy and went to the nearby soda machine.

"It was worth it, Abby. He's really scared, and I couldn't let them take him today. He's not ready. Besides, I didn't want him to think I set him up. They've obviously been watching me for a while now, although I had no idea."

"Aren't you scared?"

"Of what?"

"Of Alvin? Of the FBI? Of me?"

"No, to all the above." She kept her smile. "He's going to turn himself in to you and me." She lowered her voice. "I have the time and the place all arranged. We'll pick him up a few counties over. I have a friend in the police department in La Junta who can assist us when we get there. I'll contact him tonight to give him the details. It will also prevent these local cops who've been frustrated by this case from giving Alvin a worse time for making them work so hard. He's really afraid of the police, and from this incident, I can see why."

"You're going way beyond the call of duty, Doc." I smiled through the sadness I felt for Alvin and his situation. "This could have been me. I feel so bad for him." I dropped my head.

"Me too. That's why I'm committed to facilitating his surrender." She patted my leg.

I felt like falling on my knees in front of her again, but I saw Shannon out of the corner of my eye, so it was easy to quell my urge.

"I'll be in touch. It's the day after tomorrow, but they're going to be watching us closely." She looked around the lobby. "They probably are now."

Jeff was standing by the door waiting for me as Shannon came back.

"I'm really sorry I caused all this, you guys," I said as I stood to leave.

"You didn't cause anything." Shannon spoke for them both as Jayne nodded agreement. "I'm sorry I was a bit antsy on the phone earlier. I was just really annoyed that this was happening."

"Understandably so," I agreed. "If all her clients are this labor intensive, you probably never get a moment's rest."

"They aren't, so you don't have to worry." Jayne answered this time. "Besides, they aren't all my friends." She touched my arm.

"Thanks for protecting him," I said as I turned to go. "I'll be in touch."

"So will we." Jayne put her arm around Shannon as they left for home.

I was quiet most of the drive home, and Jeff shared my silence. A few blocks from our house, I told him that I had thrown Pat and Ted out. He laughed aloud.

"Way to go, Abby! It's about time we get our life back. When are they leaving?"

"I said immediately was good for me." I laughed with him. "They better be out by morning."

"Evvie and Laurel leave tomorrow, too, you know. We have to take them to the airport by 9:00 a.m."

"No, I didn't know. Evelyn just said soon."

"Well, it's tomorrow."

"That's pretty soon."

"Can you tell me anything that's going on?" he asked timidly.

"Yeah, Alvin is giving himself up to me and Jayne the day after tomorrow," I answered as softly as he had asked.

"That's great news. I know it must be hard, but if they find him first, who knows what they'll do."

I agreed.

"How are you going to pull it off without being followed?" I hadn't really thought that far ahead.

"No idea," I answered honestly.

"Let's put our heads together in the morning and see what we can come up with," he said as we turned into the driveway.

The confrontation with Pat and Ted was emotional but unequivocal—they had to leave our home by morning. I saw no reason to remember the good times as Ted had suggested because the end result was still the same.

I found it tragic that after all the time we spent in the same house, we still had no trust for one another. I wanted to say I would miss them, but I honestly could not. They had crossed a line, breached a confidence, and fatally injured any hope we had to maintain a relationship. I used to think it was just Pat and that Ted was really okay, but I had learned that Ted was just better at masking and manipulating. That was the saddest part.

As agreed, Jeff saw them off in the early hours of the morning. I watched from the window in the office. The house fell peaceful as the door closed behind them. Just like that, they were gone. None of the drama and intensity that accompanied them when they came into our lives saw them out. Just the sound of the door followed by the sound of the car engine followed finally by the sound of silence.

We didn't mention the plan to Evelyn and Laurel as we took them to the airport and saw them onto the plane. I didn't want them to have anything to worry about as they began the trip home and started the journey toward rebuilding their disrupted lives.

On the way home from the airport, Jeff and I discussed the likelihood of our house being under voice and video surveillance. We even toyed briefly with the paranoid notion that our car or even our bodies were bugged. I wasn't so sure about the car, but I knew I had nothing on my body.

It was a little shocking walking into an empty house again. It was November when this nightmare began, and suddenly, February had come. The altered state of existence we had been forced into had begun to feel almost normal. Jeff and I just looked at each other and fell onto the couch.

Jayne called at noon to remind me of my afternoon appointment. She didn't say much else on the phone, but I confirmed our regularly scheduled time. She sounded unusually nervous, which startled me, but I didn't ask questions. Something was strained.

When I hung up the receiver, it occurred to me what was different. I had met Shannon. I knew the dynamics of their relationship, as well as the depth of Jayne's feelings for me. I was the only one privy to what she must see as her fatal flaw. Of course things had changed. There was absolutely no way they couldn't have.

I struggled to believe it was almost over. The months of fear and anxiety, grief and mourning were coming to an end. I would soon be able, like everyone else, to begin rebuilding my life. I knew Alvin was in for a long ride, and I was committed to see him through it, but I also knew I would rest easier when he was no longer on the run.

I was in for just as long a ride. My ride involved traveling back through time into my desert hell. I didn't know if I could survive it without Jayne, but I also didn't know if I could continue to see her. The pain in my chest returned as I thought about what lay ahead.

When I arrived at Jayne's office, there were no other cars in the parking lot and no sign of the eyes I knew were watching. I fought the temptation to wave and smile in all directions in defiance of the invasion of our privacy. Instead I walked quickly into the building to find Jayne sitting in the waiting area, reading a magazine.

"You look like the patient today."

"Maybe I am."

"Okay with me."

"Only I prefer 'client.' 'Patient' connotes illness."

"Then I'm the patient." I claimed the label.

"How's your blood sugar?" She stood and put the magazine down.

"Fine," I lied. I hadn't checked it as I was instructed.

"You think..." She was on to my deception.

"Yeah, fine, I think," I admitted.

"Will you check it when you go home?" She hugged me as she asked, knowing I couldn't refuse such an intimate request.

"Yes, Doctor." It felt good to be in her arms. I held on way past the allowed time for a greeting hug. She didn't seem to mind.

When I finally let go, we went into her room, got a drink, and took our seats.

"Are we having therapy or discussing Alvin?" I was confused.

"Both," she answered. "If that's okay. I want to check in with how you're holding up in there." She pointed to her head.

"Well, it's a lot to deal with all at once, but I believe I'm hanging," I said, almost afraid to be okay. "And I really am taking care of myself. I'm definitely not going back into a coma."

"You're doing better than okay for someone who has been where you've been."

"I'm just relieved that it's almost over. Did I ever tell you how much I appreciate all you've done for me?" I didn't want another day to go by without telling her what an impact she'd had on my life.

"It's mutual," she almost whispered.

"How can that be? You help me and I send you to jail? Doesn't seem very equal to me."

"I didn't go to jail for you, Abby. I went for what I believed was right. It was worth it."

"Then what, pray tell, have I done that has been anything but draining to you?"

"It's more of an intuitive thing than a describable incident, Abby. You walked in here the very first day and opened your skin. You showed me your soul, and it was familiar. I'm not sure I can explain it any better."

"But everyone who comes in here asks you to find their soul, don't they? That's kind of your gig, isn't it?"

She laughed at me lovingly. "That's just it. You didn't ask me to find your soul; you showed it to me. You came in here knowing I could help you, and I helped you knowing I was supposed to. Don't you get it?" She really wanted me to understand.

My face spoke for me.

She sighed in disappointment but did not give up. "Okay." She rolled her chair closer to me. "Look in my eyes. What do you see?"

"I see my own reflection."

"Exactly." She was pleased. "Have you ever heard that the eyes are the windows to the soul?"

"Yes."

"So if the eyes are the windows to the soul, then maybe the soul is the true mirror. You know, the place the reflection really comes from." She paused to let me think. "You said you looked in my eyes and knew I could help you."

I nodded, remembering my words.

"Well, I looked in your soul and knew you could help me." I felt her looking in my soul at that very moment. It was suddenly comprehensible. I continued to stare at my reflection in her eyes until my mind faded to the image of her holding the rope above the pit of memory I had descended recently. I recalled how I had been simply a reflection of her, how she could have turned away and I would have vanished.

I came back when she touched my leg. "Help you what?"

She shrugged. "I don't know yet. We'll find out, I guess."

"Whatever it is, count me in."

"I know. I do count on you. Now we have work to do." She smiled and rolled her chair back a little.

"Not too far." I felt panic.

"How's this?" She stopped a few feet from me.

"Good." I breathed again.

We spent the next hour bouncing between the past and the present, the real and the imagined, the feeling and the physical. We tied a rope to every straying emotion I had lost out there in the time zones and pulled them all together. I was awed by her ability to weave all my broken parts into one person whole enough to deal with the current crisis. She assured me it would take more than an hour to put me all the way back together but explained that she wanted me to feel both feet on the ground for the next few days.

We spent another half hour passing notes back and forth to plan the rendezvous with Alvin. It was less than twenty-four hours away. It was my idea to write our communication just in case the walls had ears. We planned our strategy to the finest detail, covering every base we could fathom. Jeff would be needed to maximize security, but I knew he would be loyal to the end. By the time we were through, the plans were set. The rest was up to fate.

"Are you going to be okay tonight?" Jayne asked as I started to get up from the chair.

"Of course I am," I assured her. "You?"

"Just fine. Remember to breathe and call me later if you want to."

"I'll be breathing, but I'm sure Shannon would rather I minimize the phone interruptions." I turned red and hot from embarrassment.

"She's really okay with it, Abby. I had to tell her what was going on, though, since it was becoming so personal. You understand, don't you?" She looked a little uncomfortable.

"I expect you to tell her why your patients get you arrested." I tried to make it light.

"Clients."

"Whatever. The people who traipse though this office and disrupt your life." I couldn't help feeling bad for what I had caused her.

"Please stop that. You're not like everyone else who traipses through this office. You took a detour through my heart on the way." She smiled and laughed a little. "Jesus, how sappy can I get in one afternoon?"

"I thought it was sweet." I put both arms around her and pulled her in to my whole body. I kissed her cheek and thanked her again before leaving without saying more.

The house felt twice its size with all our guests gone and our world only a day from some semblance of normal. Jeff was making dinner while the television played to no one. If I hadn't known better, I could almost have been convinced that the last four months never happened.

Chapter Twenty-four

We had arranged to meet at a place just outside the county line. Jeff would take me there and Jayne would pick me up. We gave ourselves enough time to mobilize plan B in case anyone forced us to abort plan A. Plan A was simple and straight from a bad "B" movie, but we all agreed it could work.

We were to meet at the truck stop off the interstate north of Pueblo during the lunch rush. Jeff and I were familiar with the place since we used to stop there on trips back from the quarry. I had drawn Jayne a sketch so she, too, could familiarize herself. We planned to drive the back roads and take multiple detours to ensure we were not being tailed. Jayne would be parked among the big rigs when Jeff and I arrived. We would pull into the car wash area west of the restaurant.

Once inside the car wash, Jeff would leave the stall for the change machine. Jayne would wait to see him, then pull into the stall next to us on whichever side was unoccupied. She would leave her car and go around to the side where the trash bins are located. When she did, Jeff would return to her stall and she to his. I would remain on the floorboard while Jayne and Jeff switched places. They planned to dress in similar clothing and wear ball caps to further disguise themselves.

Plan B was even simpler: go straight to the pickup site and make as much noise as possible to keep Alvin from showing his face. We couldn't contact him to let him know what was going on, and we didn't even know for sure if he would still appear, given the circumstances at Jayne's office the last time he saw her. Jayne said he would, though, and I felt sure, as well.

Rain was pouring down when we left our house to start the end of the bad dream we'd all been trapped in. Never in my life had I seen it rain like that in Colorado in February. The temperature was just warm enough to prevent it from freezing but just cool enough to make the drops ice cold. I was on the floorboard covered with a light blanket while Jeff drove with all his senses on alert.

"It's going to be a long ride down here." I was thankful he had a big four-wheel drive, but I already felt cramped. "What do you see?" I asked as we pulled onto the highway.

"Nothing but water. If we're being followed, they're really keeping a distance."

"Where are you going next?" I was disoriented when he made another quick turn.

"Just cruising. Taking the scenic route."

"Still no sign of anything?" I was nervous and chatty.

"Not a soul around."

We drove another thirty-five minutes in relative silence. It took all I had not to keep babbling and distracting him. I remembered Desert Storm, the times I got on the radio in short bursts when I felt a similar need to talk.

"We're approaching the truck stop," Jeff announced a little later. "It's crowded as hell."

"Perfect." I released a long breath. "Do you see her?"

"Nope."

"Good." It seemed to be going as planned.

"Shit," Jeff said suddenly.

"What?" I peeked my head from under the blanket.

"The car wash...why would anyone wash their car in the rain?" He was grimacing.

"Damn. Okay, let's don't ditch just yet. Do you see Jayne anywhere?" I was calm and fully engaged. "Hesitate and die," I said aloud to Jeff.

"Huh?" He looked confused.

"Never mind, just go to the far side of the car wash where the change machines are."

He obeyed.

"Pull up like you need change, your side to the machine."

He followed my instructions.

"Do you see Jayne?" I asked again.

He looked around as the car came to a stop. "There's a car behind a semi-trailer to your side. It could be her...It is her." He sighed in relief.

"What's she doing?" I monitored the scene through Jeff's eyes.

"She's talking to the driver of the semi...He's nodding...He's coming this way...Do you want me to drive off?" Jeff was nervous and ready to flee.

"No. Stay put. Jayne knows what she's doing."

"He's motioning me out of the car, Abby," Jeff informed me.

"Go," I almost yelled. "He'll know there's a person under here if you let him get all the way to the window."

Jeff got out as I remained under the blanket for the longest ten minutes of my life.

The next thing I heard was the car door opening. A familiar smell wafted in. It was Jayne. She said nothing as I heard the click of her seat belt, the thump of the gear lever, and the sound of acceleration out of the parking lot.

"What part of that was fun?" She sounded like she might faint.

"What happened?" I had most of my head sticking out of the blanket.

She looked at me and broke into a chorus of nervous laughter. "I don't know what you look like, but it's funny." She stroked my cheek and stared for a second.

"Are you driving?" It didn't look like it, considering she was busy watching me.

"Yes. Are you breathing?" She was still laughing.

"How did you get that man involved?" I ignored her question.

"I just asked him to go get the guy in the car and tell him I was waiting for him. He didn't question why." She shrugged. "I'm sure he thought it was some interstate rendezvous and was delighted to assist. It doesn't matter because it worked." She beamed.

"Clever. Anyone hanging with us?"

"Not that I see." She looked in all directions. "I was very cautious getting here."

"Us too. No one followed."

"Is this what they teach you in the Army?" She patted my head in an almost patronizing manner.

"What, to hide under blankets in cars during rainstorms?"

"No, silly, to make new plans when the old ones fail."

"Yes. It's called 'stay alert—stay alive.' You pay attention and think fast or you die. I've about had enough practice, though."

"It's almost over, Abby. We're only about an hour from the pickup time. It's all downhill from here." She sounded so confident. I felt nauseated.

"Let's go through the pickup plan." I insisted we rehearse. I needed to consider every angle.

"Okay. We get to the fork in the road just before the Amtrak station in La Junta. We stop at the convenience store by the fork and call to be sure the train is on schedule."

"Sounds reasonable so far."

"Assuming the train is on time, we take the fork in the road toward the station but go past it. When we see the train coming at us, we turn around and head back to the station. We should arrive at the exact same time as the train.

"We pull into the parking lot as close to the boneyard as possible. That's where Alvin will be, hiding among the stationary trains waiting for the distraction of the incoming engine. He is to blend with the passengers when they all come off the train. I get out of the car, find him, bring him to the car, he gets in the back, and we drive. That simple." She had obviously rehearsed this in her mind several times.

"Okay. That simple," I repeated. "Except he might conk me on the head with his feet if he's not careful." I tried for lightness. "What next?"

"…To the police station to meet my friend," she recited. "I know the way."

"If the train is late…"

"…We assess how late it will be and drive into a residential area to wait out of sight."

"Good. And if anything looks suspicious…"

"…We do not risk getting Alvin caught by the FBI."

"And if anything goes wrong while we are in the process of picking up Alvin…"

She wasn't ready for that one.

"We stay alert and stay alive?" She sounded afraid to even consider the possibility.

"Exactly." I rubbed my eyes. "But nothing's going wrong."

We were within minutes of our destination and still there was no sign of tailgaters. I couldn't believe we'd actually made it out of town without them. The rain stopped somewhere along the way, but I scarcely noticed.

"Are you nervous?" Jayne asked as I felt the car slow to a stop. "We're at the convenience store."

"Only a little." I took a big breath. "Is there a phone handy?"

"Yep. Right on the corner of the building." She stopped the car. "Be right back."

The train was right on schedule, and minutes later, we were on the road again.

"Okay." Jayne looked to the left of the car. "We're passing the station now. It looks busy but normal."

Just then I heard the whistle blast of the oncoming train.

"There she is," I said nervously. "I guess it's show time."

Jayne turned the car around and headed toward the station.

"We're pulling to the farthest edge of the asphalt. There are a lot of people here, Abby. I hope he sees us."

"He will." I was hoping, too.

"Okay. The passengers are coming off. There are quite a few. It must have been a full train."

"Are you ready to find him?" My nausea intensified, but I kept it in check. It wasn't surprising given that I had been balled up on a floorboard for hours.

"Wish me luck." She touched me on the head.

"You'll be just fine," I guaranteed.

I suddenly wanted to tell her how much I loved her and how brave she was to be doing this. I wanted to let her know that I would be forever in her debt, but she already knew anyway, so I said no more.

The time that passed while I sat alone on the floorboard of Jeff's car was probably about fifteen minutes, but my mind was so far removed from the scene that I had no concept of time. I heard the shouting the minute it began, but I forced myself to lie still and evaluate the whole scenario before springing from the car into uncertainty. I couldn't make out what the man's voice was saying.

Then it came again—loud and clear and too close to miss.

"Hands over your head and away from the car," the same voice yelled again. "Both of you." My heart dropped into my stomach.

"I'll kill her." I heard my brother's voice and was out of the car before my mind fully processed the danger.

I didn't get far before a plainclothes cop had me on the ground.

"Let me go, you bastard. That's my brother."

"Let her go or I shoot this woman," Alvin instructed. "Let her go now." The gun was to Jayne's head. He was convincing.

I jumped to my feet and ran to him.

"He won't hurt me, Abby," Jayne whispered. "It's our only way out. They set us up."

Alvin stayed focused on the crowd of police surrounding us. He had Jayne around the shoulders, her back to his chest, holding her with one arm—the gun in his other hand.

"Don't come near me or she dies," he warned as he continued to look in all directions for a way out.

"Get away from the car," he screamed and started moving toward it.

I followed his every move and his every thought. I knew his plan was to get into the car and run like hell, but he wasn't thinking clearly. There was no way out.

"Give up, Alvin. Please," I pleaded softly with him. "They aren't going to let us go. It's over. Please give in. Just lie on the ground and let them take you."

He ignored my plea and yelled, "Open the driver door, then get away." He waved the gun in the direction he meant for them to move, repeating, "Open the driver door."

The officer closest to the car obeyed. The others moved away as if they knew what was coming next.

We were almost to the car when I heard the muffled sound of a silencer. A single, rapid burst of air and my brother fell to his knees as Jayne scrambled for safety.

The scene unfolded in slow motion. The world began to march in marked time. I had to fight all the fibers that hold my body together to even move. But I did move, and I moved quickly. I grabbed the gun from his hand as Jayne stumbled to get away. I aimed in the direction of the air burst. They shot my brother. They changed my plans. I snapped.

I didn't feel the bullet pierce my body, but I saw the light of the sun peeking over the trees as I fell next to Alvin. I felt no pain and certainly no remorse. Once again, it was all following the blueprints of a perfect design.

Even Jayne's scream could not dampen the satisfaction I felt knowing all was as it should be. She threw herself onto our bodies, as if to say "no more"; and just as I had done recently, I smiled and closed my eyes.

"Breathe, Abby. Please," she whispered to me as the sirens grew louder.

It's hard to say what happened next as Alvin and I lay side by side in a pool of our mixing blood. It might have been a dream, or it could have been a hallucination, but it is definitely vivid in my memory.

I tried to black out as I had the last time an ambulance crew came for me, but it was a useless attempt. I was destined to know the minute-by-minute details of our fate. A force that gripped my whole being directed me to stay alert and stay alive. I had no option but to listen.

I could feel Alvin leaving as we lay on the asphalt together with the paramedics in a frenzy around us. I tried to talk to him, but the words formed a paste in my throat. I tried to reach out to him, but I didn't have control of my limbs. I could only turn my head. It was then that I saw the bullet hole in his skull.

The second I saw the fluid oozing from his head, I felt his spirit and his body begin to separate. He was really leaving; he had made the decision to go. I'd like to think that if it had felt right to me, I would have simply said goodbye and let him fade. It could have been a suitable ending to our simultaneous beginning except for one small detail: I was not ready to go. I struggled to use all the energy around me to implore him to stay.

No, Alvin. You can't go yet. My words appeared in the air between us like captions in a cartoon. It was as surreal as the rest of the experience.

I have to, Abby. His words appeared to cover mine. *I'm not strong enough to face the consequences. I can't go through any more of this hell.* The words faded from view as fast as I could read them.

No, Alvin. My reply appeared blacker and bolder. *If you go, I go, too.*

You can't do that appeared faintly.

Watch me. The words in the air became dim before our eyes. *See, I told you. You go, I go.*

Why are you so damn stubborn? A flash of words as dark and intense as a desert night appeared.

That's it, Alvin. That's right. I'm stubborn and I'm never going to change.

Give me one reason why I should stay. His words were dwindling again.

Because I need you... The words were the size of the trees.

You better be telling the truth appeared over and over as he interrupted the transfer of his soul from his body.

"I promise."

"Don't talk, Abby." Jayne heard me. My words were all at once audible. Maybe they always had been.

We were loaded into the ambulances and transported without much further intervention. Jayne refused to leave my gurney. As I heard her instructing the paramedics not to forget I was diabetic, I remembered being in their position with nervous loved ones hanging around. I would have laughed openly if I could have.

Chapter Twenty-five

Having had it both ways, I'll say from experience that I prefer unconsciousness to consciousness when extreme pain is involved. The bullet entered through my left shoulder and exited though my back. I was thankful the police sniper was a bad shot. He missed my heart and spinal cord. He also missed all my major organs completely. It was nothing short of a miracle.

Alvin's injuries were more serious and long-term. With a gunshot wound to the head, the doctors said he was lucky to be alive. I knew better; he was alive thanks to no part of luck. He made the choice to live. While his brain remained intact, his mobility was the casualty. Time will determine the full extent of his paralysis.

His wife came at once, but our parents did not. Just as when I returned from Desert Storm, I suppose they figured they'd see us soon enough. I decided then and there that under no circumstances would they ever see me again.

Alvin took their absence even harder, but Janis, his wife, stood by him. We all worried that she would ditch when forced to deal openly with the affair he had with Clara and the fact that he had killed a man, but she did not. She immediately began to make arrangements to move herself and their children to Colorado for as long as Alvin was in the hospital.

I assured him I would keep my promise to need him, as well as to be there for him. I pledged to remain his ally no matter what the trial, the sentencing, or the media revealed. I was surprised by my apathy. While in the thick of the search for Alvin, I had thought that when I finally saw him, I would want answers to my questions—questions such as how he became involved with Charlie Stokes in the first place and why he tried to steal my journals. The reality was, I no longer cared about any of it. It was over.

We were right to assume that Alvin was in for a long ride, but none of us could have known how painful it would become. He would be allowed the necessary time to recover from the wounds he received, but he would also stand trial for murder, among other charges.

I knew Jayne and I were in trouble from the start, but our predicament had a much happier outcome. It scares me a little that the FBI is capable of erasing criminal charges as easily as they levy them, but I was not going to argue the principle of it and hang us both.

I'd say it was more Ted than Pat who orchestrated the dismissal of the charges against us, but she certainly didn't try and interfere. They only came to the hospital once, and that was to tell us we were exonerated. The words between us were brief but effective. The sincerity in Ted's face was apparent, and the stoicism in Pat's was standard operating procedure.

Jeff took the whole incident harder than I expected. Even after they dropped the charges, he had nothing but contempt for Pat, Ted, and the entire FBI. We asked him to leave the room when Pat and Ted arrived because we feared he would make matters worse. His mind recorded only that they could have killed me and saw no other part of the entire drama.

I didn't try to talk him into anything, and Jayne spent a good amount of time trying to help him deal with his anger. Jeff was more than just angry, he was intensely bitter and hugely resentful. She said he was suffering the effects of all we'd endured lately and that we should be patient with him. I had no problem with that, after how he had seen me through the last six years. I could certainly wait while he adjusted to normal life again.

If I wasn't in love with Jayne before this all began, I was unquestionably in love with her now that it was nearing a close. She could have walked away and been free during any phase of our journey through hell, but she never even winced.

Evelyn and Laurel listened to reason and remained in South Carolina while I was recovering. We spoke frequently on the phone, but I did not have the energy to sustain them both for another extended visit. I wanted to see Rachel, and I spoke with her long enough to tell her I was okay. She said she didn't know if she could make it out to see me, and I didn't want to know the reasons, so I let it go.

Shannon was remarkably intact considering the disruption to her life and relationship. She came to the hospital a few times and even accompanied Jayne to see me at home after my release. She was kind, but her presence was difficult for me because Jayne was so different when Shannon was present.

I couldn't put my finger on exactly what changed when Shannon was around, but Jeff thought it was that I knew a different side of Jayne than Shannon did. He said we were connected on a spiritual level, and they were connected on a more physical and real-life plane. He said they fit well together, and I told him to mind his own business. We both got a good laugh. He also said he believed I bonded with Jayne in part out of stress.

Jeff was right about at least some of it. Jayne and Shannon did fit well together, and the more time I spent with them, the more I saw why. Shannon was treading water in this lifetime. She must have had a hard last few rounds because this lifetime was all about rest and relaxation. While part of her wanted to be more in tune with her surroundings and part of her longed to connect with people the way Jayne did, it was not in the cards this time. Happy-go-lucky and a slave to peace, Shannon's path could not to be altered for more than a few hours at a time.

Jayne, on the other hand, was swimming upstream. She had a million things to say and a mile-long list of tasks to complete. It was almost as if she was fulfilling a bargain she made somewhere along the way, a promise to live enough for two this time. I'm sure whoever who got the benefit of her labor was someone very dear to her.

Despite the other obvious connections, I had to agree that Jayne and I did link on an ethereal level. I couldn't explain it any more than she could, but I felt it as strong as the life in my chest. I was desperate to understand our connection before I relinquished my feelings to a box in a room of my heart. I didn't want to believe that my unrequited love for her was just another punishment for all the evil I'd done in my life.

I needed one more opportunity to be alone with Jayne, away from Shannon, her office, my house, a hospital, any place stressful and any place resembling any place we'd ever been together.

Maybe Jeff was right; maybe we were drawn to each other simply because the stress of dealing with all this alone was too great to bear.

That's what happened in Desert Storm. We bonded to each other and to our higher powers because the fear of being scared and alone was too much to handle individually. None of us wanted to die alone. We needed to feel a part of something stronger than ourselves; this need created friendships between people who would otherwise never speak and family out of total strangers.

I needed to see Jayne away from it all, apart from the drama, outside of the stress. If I could make that happen, perhaps the mask and mystery would fall away, just as it did with my comrades from war. Perhaps she would become just another person who played the role she chose in my life. Sure, we'd be bonded forever, as I will be with them, but my question about the role I chose to play in her life would be answered.

The phone rang and interrupted my thoughts. I looked at my watch and was shocked to learn that I had been sitting in the same spot for an entire morning.

"It's for you, Abby. It's Jayne," Jeff called from the kitchen. "Do you need me to bring you the phone?" I was totally ambulatory, but he insisted I was an invalid.

"I got it, thanks," I yelled back. "Hello."

"Hey, what are you watching?"

"How do you know I'm watching television?" I was a little defensive about my newly acquired TV addiction.

"Just a guess." She sounded playful.

"Wrong!" I laughed. "I was sitting quietly on the couch thinking about the last six months of my life."

"And you're okay?" She tried to sound light, but I wasn't fooled.

"Of course I'm okay. I'm just thinking." I knew she worried about me thinking myself into a panic.

"Okay." She sounded hesitant. "Want company?"

"Who?" I teased.

"Me, silly. I want to come over."

"Sure. Come on."

"Are you up for a little trip?"

She surprised me to the point of speechlessness.

"You still there?"

"I'm here. Are you being psychic again?" I couldn't help asking.

"I've never been psychic. You just keep forgetting that." She laughed. "So do you want to go somewhere or not?"

"Where?"

"Why does it matter? Just away. We're going to go away." She sounded a little annoyed that I wasn't cooperating.

"I'd love to." I felt the butterflies take off. They were fluttering wildly.

I didn't ask how long we'd be gone or where Shannon was. I merely got up from the couch, went to my room to pack an overnight bag, and sat back down to wait. Jeff was not exactly overjoyed that I'd be going somewhere without him, but he didn't make a production of it. He was more protective than ever since my release from the hospital.

Jayne arrived within the hour, and Jeff greeted her at the door.

"Ready?" She obviously didn't want to visit.

"All set." I grabbed my bag with my good arm, hugged Jeff the best I could with no arms, and headed out the door before he could question us.

We started out of town going west. I didn't ask again where we were bound because it really didn't matter. We listened to music and talked about nothing for the first hour we were on the road. By the time we neared the middle of the second hour, we were pointed north toward Leadville. The conversation was so smooth and relaxing that I almost hoped we weren't stopping anytime soon.

Jayne finally said, "There's a lodge at the foot of Mount Elbert. That's where we're bound. Ever been there?"

"No. What's there?" I didn't really care.

"Nothing. Some small cabins, a beautiful creek, and a lot of animals." She smiled. "I love it up there."

"I'm sure I will, too." I looked out the window and felt total peace.

When we arrived, she drove straight to the door of the farthest cabin in the group. It was bordered by a stream and surrounded by trees. She bypassed the lodge house entirely, but it looked as though she knew what she was doing, so I remained a spectator.

"This is it." She had a wide grin on her face. "What do you think?"

"It's beautiful." I smiled back. "Do you come here often?" I suddenly imagined her with Shannon and me as the violator.

"Not since I was in college." She knew why I was asking. "Nothing's changed, though. My family used to own it. I called the new owner and asked for a favor."

"Oh, good." I relaxed again.

The cabin was very uncomplicated. While it had plumbing, there was no electricity. There was a fireplace for heat and several lanterns for light. The rough-hewn wood furniture was probably made whenever the place was built, and I marveled at its simple, natural beauty. The one main room housed a table and chairs, a bench, a wood-burning cookstove, a sink, and one bed. There was also a bathroom. We had all the necessities, right down to flannel sheets and a feather comforter that Jayne had packed in her car.

We unpacked and settled in without much exchange. She made a fire in the fireplace while I started a fire in the stove. I think she was surprised that I knew how to use it, but I reminded her where I was from and she nodded in understanding.

Dinner was wonderful but also very silent. Not a tense, awkwardly wordless silence but the peaceful and serene stillness of total tranquility. The place was awe-inspiring. The beauty of both our location and her face in the glow of the fire humbled me.

"I can't describe how I feel," I said softly when she caught me watching her.

"Me neither, but it's not required." She touched my hand. "All we have to do is breathe."

The words had barely left her lips when I closed my eyes, drew a long and deep breath, then opened them again.

"Good." She smiled. "Now let it out slowly."

Just as I had seen my brother's words leave his mouth and hang in the air when we were in a suspended state of reality, so then did I see Jayne's. As she spoke, her words turned to color and the color turned to energy that encircled her. At the very moment I released the breath from my lungs, I saw every particle that was dancing in the room around us as we bathed in its electricity.

The aura extending from her and to her had no real point of origin. It just was, as she just was. It was all part of the same phenomenon. I watched in spellbound amazement. We sat in the shine across the table from each other and beheld the spectacular unfurling of heat and colored light. I didn't search my head for words from then on. It would have been a futile attempt. For the first time in my life, I really had nothing to say. All the words were in the air around us as loud as thunder and as pure as new snow. I let the energy speak while I remained mute. It was somewhere between the time her body became a spirit and my mind was freed that all the questions were answered.

She had the car mostly packed when I woke from my trance. I dressed in silence, made coffee, and sat in the window where the sun was fully up. A tearful, wordless embrace preceded the closing of the door that I knew we'd never reopen. I didn't see Jayne for another three weeks after she dropped me at the sidewalk in front of my house. We didn't discuss seeing each other, but then again we didn't discuss anything at all. There was no need. She left town for vacation with Shannon that afternoon, and I set about the task of healing my body to the same level my mind had been healed.

I was ready to be fully alive again. It was time to forgive myself and move on to my next experience. I had a hole in my heart the size of a person, but I could live with it. It was the hole that had opened when I let her drive away without a struggle, without a plea to stay. And like the scars on my body, it was a rite of passage from one place to another. Unlike the scars on my body, I could feel it with every breath.

About the author

Alex Alexander was born in rural Kentucky in 1960-something. Joining the Army was her ticket to education and an opportunity to get paid to be bossy.

After Desert Storm, Alex was assigned as a team leader to the drug interdiction team in her state National Guard organization, which meant hiking the hills of Tennessee with other misfits looking for marijuana and moonshine stills. When the futility of this endeavor dawned on her, she headed west to Colorado and lucked into her dream job. Creating beauty by building stone walls and lush landscapes, she designed and installed outdoor living areas in a stunning and tranquil space in Colorado Springs, Colorado, as part of a wonderful and supportive family organization.

Alex is currently in her last year of medical school at Bastyr University in the Seattle, Washington, area where she'll graduate in 2006 with a doctorate in naturopathic medicine.

Other Titles Available from Intaglio Publications

Code Blue
KatLyn
1-933113-09-X
$18.50

Gloria's Inn
Robin Alexander
1-933113-01-4
$17.50

I Already Know The Silence Of
The Storms
N. M. Hill
1-933113-07-3
$17.50

Infinite Pleasures
Stacia Seaman & Nann Dunne
(Editors)
1-933113-00-6
$18.99

Storm Surge
KatLyn
1-933113-06-5
$18.50

The Cost Of Commitment
Lynn Ames
1-933113-02-2
$18.99

The Price Of Fame
Lynn Ames
1-933113-04-9
$17.99

The Gift
Verda Foster
1-933113-03-0
$17.50

Misplaced People
CG Devize
1-933113-30-8
$18.50

Crystal's Heart
B. L. Miller & Verda Foster
1-933113-24-3
$18.50

Graceful Waters
B. L. Miller & Verda Foster
1-933113-08-1
$18.50

Incommunicado
N. M. Hill & J. P. Mercer
1-933113-10-3
$17.50

Southern Hearts
Katie P Moore
1-933113-28-6
$16.95

These Dreams
Verda Foster
1-933113-12-X
$17.50

The Last Train Home
Blayne Cooper
1-933113-26-X
$17.99

The War Between The Hearts
Nann Dunne
1-933113-27-8
$17.95

Murky Waters
Robin Alexander
1-933113-33-2
$16.95

Josie & Rebecca: The Western
Chronicles
Vada Foster & BL Miller
1-933113-38-3
$18.99

Forthcoming Titles Available from Intaglio Publications

The Chosen
Verda Foster

Assignment Sunrise
I Christie

The Illusionist
Fran Heckrotte

Journey's End
LJ Maas

Lilith: Book Two in the
Illusionist Series
Fran Heckrotte

None So Blind
LJ Maas

Printed in the United States
85403LV00002B/154/A

9 781933 113395